Thank you for Smiling

by

Soul Singh

ISBN: 979-8-89175-093-7 (sc)
ISBN: 979-8-89175-094-4 (hc)
ISBN: 979-8-89175-092-0 (ebk)

Preface

I have walked a million miles and with each step I learn something new. Life has not been a gracious teacher to me; rather many of my lessons have been taught with brute force, coercion, and heartache. Regardless of my obstinate nature and my foolish, unwarranted pride, life presses its lessons into my soul. So, I have learned. I've learned that without tears, smiles are meaningless. I have learned that without much disappointment, hope is hopeless. The back alleys of life are of full of darkness and uncertainty, but without the darkness the dawning of a new day goes unnoticed.

My mother was a card-carrying member of the streetwalking profession. Yes, she was a paid whore and then when her figure was no longer desirable, she was just a whore. She walked the streets of Denver at the beat of her pimp and dared not take a break unless she wanted her ass whooped. She was a woman that was lost and lonely, having run away from home at fourteen.

She hitched a ride from Corpus Christi, TX to the majestic mountains and plains of Colorado and there she planted her roots and her many seeds. She was shunned by her family, society looked down on her, men abused her, her children longed for her and she blamed everyone. The circumstances of her life were always placed on the shoulders of others and because of this she bore no responsibility. Even when confronted with obvious truths, the filthy vagina from which I emerged never apologized, nor did she admit to any wrongdoing. It was always someone else's fault; thus someone else's problem to fix. So, I grew up with the scarlet letter of my mother's sins engraved on my destiny for the entire world to see and judge. It is a difficult task being the daughter of a prostitute; the standards for individual success are set so low. What is even more difficult is finding one's own path through the turmoil of life, after being stamped a tramp's child and doing so without using anger as the fuel. People see the streetwalker; they rarely see her offspring, standing with watchful eyes in the shadows. They condemn her, but by doing so they also condemn her children. They condemned me.

My journey is not unlike so many others. I am the bastard child of drug addicted prostitute who had little regard for the lives she continuously created to gain the love and attention of some stupid, controlling man. I grew up not knowing a mother's love, father's embrace, or the warmth and comfort of a real family. I grew up in fear, loneliness, anger, confusion, sadness, and a general feeling of despair. Did I mention anger? I had a lot of it. I questioned often the purpose of my existence and my circumstances. I had to grow up fast and have not been allowed to slow down. Like I said, many have walked in my shoes, so I am not that unique. Many have worse stories and experiences. So many children live their entire lives in the gutters of society and are only recognized in some promotional commercial during the holidays or when some fancy celebrity has a cause to promote. For the most part, what differentiates me from others is that at a young age I KNEW there had to be a reason I was permitted to continue to live, despite all the opportunities presented to end my existence prematurely. So, with the millionth and one step I continue to search for the meaning of the experiences in which I have embarked so that I can understand my celestial purpose in this life, at this time in eternity.

This is my story, but it also the story of so many children who, like me, are born into circumstances without their consent and must figure out how to survive in a world that is either repulsed by us, pities us, or simply chooses to ignore us. There are champions, though, that bring light to our humanity.

1

The sky was a soothing clear blue speckled with fluffy white clouds. I watched them float about, constantly changing shape, so I had to change the stories I was making up about the shapes. The clouds morphed from dragons to butterflies to ships sailing the great ocean. I loved looking at the sky and clouds. I imagined that if I could climb to the top of the mountains, I could touch them. They looked peaceful and I needed peace.

As we ascended higher into the mountains, I did my best to count the evergreens. I began to wonder why they were getting sparser the higher we drove, but I did not linger on that thought too long. I loved when we went driving in the mountains. Something about those age-old rock formations that seemed to span into eternity always uplifted my spirit. The air was thinner here, crisper too and I relished the coolness as it trickled into my nostrils and into my lungs. Today, she was in a good mood. She was driving with all the windows down and I enjoyed watching her long black hair dance in the wind. She was singing along with the radio, though I silently wished she would just let the music play. Watching her from my view in the back seat made me feel normal. My mother was a beautiful woman. Her skin was flawless, it was creamy and smooth.

The angles from her cheekbones highlighted her Native American roots, while the olive tint of her skin proudly boasted her Mexican heritage. She was slender, but strong. She stood a little over five feet tall, but her presence made her appear to be a giant to me. Behind her strength, she was fragile. Her beauty was tormented, like the beauty one finds in a storm. I could only see this beauty when she was not looking at me. Her eyes scared me. I never looked at her directly and from this view I could not see her eyes. I never wanted to look like her because under all that beauty I saw her true nature and it was hideous.

My brothers were in the back seat with me. We were all one year apart, me being the oldest. Eddie was one year younger and Lam was two years than me. Eddie was destructive. He torn up any and everything he could and he would throw the most atrocious tantrums. I usually received the ramifications of his behavior, as my main responsibility was to care for both when my mother was not around, which was often. He had her eyes; dark, moody, sad. He was a lovely mocha latte color with brown curly hair. Eddie was covered in scars on his arms and legs. Like I said, he was always destroying something, including himself. He was not potty trained and showed no desire to acquire the skill, so he still wore cloth diapers and depending on my mother's mood, he may or may not get changed. I am sure this is one of the reasons he was always so irritated. If I had to sit in my excrements all day, with an already aggravated rash, I would be less than happy too. I loved Eddie, but he was difficult to feel close to. He was too much like my mother. I took care of him, he was my responsibility and I wanted him to be happy. He hated hugs, so much of my affection was rejected. Truthfully, he hated being touched at all. Only when he was sleeping was I able to tenderly stoke his curls.

My youngest brother Lam was my heart. He also had my mother's eyes; his were kind and inquisitive, but cautious. He regarded everyone with a guarded and suspicious glare. His skin was a buttery olive and his light, straight brown hair made him look more Mexican than either Eddie or me. He had full, thick lips like our mother's. He was more advanced than Eddie. Since I could read, he enjoyed sitting on my lap while I read all sorts of things to him, absorbing every word. He always mimicked me, running his little fingers along the pages saying the words. Lam was a troubled lamb, but gentle. He regarded the world with an old soul and his eyes were piercing as if he knew your darkest transgressions. He was my heart and when in despair, he would run to me before our mother. She hated that and I paid for it, dearly.

Eddie started crying in the seat next to me. He probably was hungry. We were always hungry. I grabbed his hand and started to gently stroke it and whispered in his ear to be quiet. Nothing angered her more than crying children and since she seemed to be in a good mood I did not want anything to spoil the serenity of the drive. Too late, she turned the radio up so loud that it encouraged my brother to cry even louder. I kissed his cheek and tried to divert his attention by tickling his side. A pain shot through my heart as I strummed his ribs. He was way too skinny, but then again, we all were. Lam was sitting on the other side and he sensed the pending danger. We had to keep our brother quiet or she was going to be angry. Nothing good ever happened to us when she was angry. So, we tagged teamed trying to console and keep our Eddie quiet. He must have realized what we were trying to do because he calmed down and started sucking his thumb. Sucking his thumb was his way of tricking his stomach that food was entering and thankfully it also soothed him to sleep. The best way to deal with hunger was to sleep. I was grateful to him for this. She noticed he'd stop crying so she turned the radio back down to a tolerable level. Unfortunately, she was already agitated, I could feel it in the air. Her presence in the front seat became dark. Her singing stopped and it seemed like the nature had taken notice of her mood change too. It appeared that the clouds were forming above us and followed us as we continued driving through the mountains. My heart sank and I became angry with my brother for ruining everything with his stupid crying. Granted he was only three, but he should know that crying makes her have to confront the notion that she is a mother of bastard children she does not want.

In fact, I believed, she hated us and did not want us. We were obstacles in her life, but in some sick way she kept us because we were hers. Her relationship with us was no different than someone owning a dog they keep chained up in the backyard with barely enough food to eat.

Why don't they just let the dog go instead of treating it so poorly? Well because it is their dog. They keep it because of the obligation of ownership, not out of love or care, but simply because they own the dog. That is how I felt she viewed us. We were a part of her; thus she owned us, and because she owned us she could treat us anyway she wanted. And she did. She also gave other people permission to treat us any way they wanted too. They were not kind to us, especially me. So, when my brother started crying, even though he stopped fairly quickly, her mood of indifference changed to hate. She did not speak one word to us. The fact that she had stopped singing, turned the music down, now off, and she was on her fifth cigarette was all I needed to see to know that something bad was about to happen. I tried to thwart her mood by telling her that I thought her hair looked pretty blowing in the wind. She did not respond to me. She merely rolled up the window. Lam leaned forward and looked at me and I saw tears forming in the corners of his eyes. I stared at him hard as if to say, "Don't you dare start crying." He understood and reached out to hold my hand across our sleeping brother in the middle. My heart cried as I held my brother's hand. I did not know what was going to happen and I had to think of a way to make sure whatever this bad thing was would not happen to my brothers. So, we sat there, my baby brother and me holding hands and waiting.

We drove what seemed like hours in silence. We were surrounded by mountains. Usually, this sight soothed my spirit, but I had a feeling of dread in my stomach. I looked around and the cars were few and far between. There were hiking trails, but I did not see anybody on them.

Also, I noticed we were not only deep into the mountains, but we were higher too. There were snow drifts here and I did not see any more Aspen trees, only evergreens. I did not dare ask her where we were because I was secretly hoping that she would forget she was angry. Lam fell asleep holding my hand and I slowly let go of his, as my hand had become numb. Eddie was still asleep, with his thumb in his mouth. I was lost in thoughts of how peaceful the two of them looked and wondered if I ever look that peaceful when I slept when my thoughts were interrupted by the sharpness of her voice.

"What are you doing?" she barked at me, shattering the quietness of the moment. I was caught off guard so I jumped.

"Nothing mommy," I replied.

"Well you are doing something. Why are you just staring at your brothers?"

"I like watching them sleep. They look so sweet when they sleep." As soon as I said the words, I knew I had opened Pandora's Box.

"You little cunt," she said this with the most wicked sweetness, "You think you are their mommy. Well, I am their mommy and only I can look at them when they sleep." I had nothing to say so I muttered that I was sorry and looked out the window to avoid her glare in the rearview mirror. Silence ensued and she started chuckling to herself. I knew she was doing it to unnerve me, so I could not react. Reactions always means further engagement with her, and I did not want that.

We were too far in the mountains to get help if she decided to do something drastic; as we drove in silence for a bit longer I allowed my mind to wander and daydreamed about what was on the other side of the mountains. We had been driving for so long I was sure we were crossing the Rocky Mountain Range. I believed that China was on the other side, or Russia. Obviously, I did not have a good grasp on geography. I also believed that when it rained in Colorado, it rained all over the world at the same time. Little did I know that the rain was exclusively for me and my siblings. We spawned from the Wicked Witch of the Midwest; the only problem is she never melted in the rain. She turned off the freeway onto a two-lane dirt road. My stomach sank and my heart started racing. She had started chuckling to herself again and I had the omniscient doom angel sitting on my shoulder. I glanced at my brothers and I said a little prayer that they would stay asleep. Her chuckling was like knives cutting into my humanity. Something was about to happen and she seemed pleased with whatever decision she was about to make. We drove up the dirt road at quite a steep incline. I searched for road signs, anything that would give me a clue to where we were; nothing was visible. I was surprised her jalopy could make it up the grade, but I guess with evil intentions as the fuel anything is possible. The road came to an end. I could tell that this was a designated hiker's trail, but I did not see any other cars in the makeshift parking lot.

"Get out of the car and smell the fresh air," she hissed at me from the seat. I was paralyzed. I did not want to stay in the car with her, but I needed to stay here so I could try to protect my brothers. I did not want to get out because I knew something bad was waiting for me on the other side of the car door. I did not know what to do. She smiled at me and repeated very quietly and calmly for me to get out of the car. She put her right index finger to her lips to indicate that I should be quiet so my brothers could stay asleep. My heart was pounding so hard, I was sure they'd wake from just hearing it. Reluctantly, I opened the car door. I tried to look at her eyes, but she was getting out of the car too. For a moment, I thought to close my door and quickly jump in the front seat and drive off leaving her there. Then I remembered, I did not know how to drive. I got out of the car. My mother was wobbling around the car. She was very pregnant and looked like she as going to have the baby any minute. Maybe I was just being paranoid, maybe she just needed to get out to pee. Pregnant women pee a lot. I started to feel a little bit better, because this seemed like a viable explanation. After all she had not hit me on the whole ride up the mountains, she had sung to the radio, she did not yell when my brother started crying, and we had been driving for a long time. I was almost giddy when she approached me standing next to the rear passenger door.

"Alma, you think you are so grown. Do you love your brothers?"

"Yes." She looked at me, almost tenderly. She cocked her head to the side and studied me for a minute and then turned on her heels. She walked off into the brush and seconds later I could hear a steady stream of urine hitting the dried leaves. She came back through the brush and asked me if I needed to go to the bathroom. I was so elated that nothing bad was happening that I realized that I indeed had to go too. I walked in the same direction she had gone and prepared to relieve myself. As I started to squat, I heard the car start up. I did my best to rush the urine from my bladder without having it splatter on my legs because I did not want her to become impatient. As I was pulling up my pants, I heard the wheels of the car crushing rocks and leaves. I ran out of the brush and saw my pregnant mother driving off with my two sleeping brothers. She had left me.

I do not know how long I stood there watching the mirage of my mother's car driving off, leaving me alone in the mountains. It was early evening and I knew that night would rapidly approach. I did not run after her because I knew it would be futile. I knew that something bad was going to happen, I had let my guard down, and now I was in the mountains, on a hiker's path, by myself. I turned to survey my surroundings. She was kind enough to leave my coat. When I grabbed my coat from the ground a brown bag fell out. In it there was a sack lunch we packed before the trip: a bologna sandwich, Oreo cookies, a bag of Cheetos, a generic brand of pop and an apple. I put on my coat and found my mittens and a lighter in the pockets. She had left me a survival kit. I guess this was her way of telling me that even though she left me alone in the woods she cared. I did not cry at first. I just took time to understand my surroundings and the situation I was in. I had enough food, so I thought, but in these parts bears and mountain lions were common. My imagination was going wild. It was too cold for snakes and the only other thing that could hurt me, besides some crazy mountain man that eats children, was the cold.

There were snow drifts all around me and I could smell the snow in the air. It may not snow tonight, but from the look of the sky it was going to be super cold. Even though I had my coat and mittens, for which I was thankful, I did not know what to do with the lighter. I thought of my brothers sitting in the back of the car asleep. Panic gripped me because I did not know if she was going to drop them off somewhere else in the mountains by themselves. They were too young and would not know what to do. They needed me to protect them. Surely, she would not be that evil. I started crying, something I rarely did. I could not stop. I felt so alone and scared. I felt stupid because I should know what to do. I was smart, my teachers told me so, yet my mind was frozen. The shadows were growing and all I could think of was that my brothers were probably dropped off too and they were scared and calling out my name to help them. I felt like a failure and I was angry at myself for slipping up and letting her see me watch them sleep. I should have known that any sign of affection is a display of weakness. She always told me only the strong survive and the weak are devoured. Well, she had devoured me.

Since I knew this was a hiker's path, I figured that the best thing for me to do was to stay put. There was an old rotten wooden park bench and a trashcan which meant that the path was used regularly and eventually the park ranger would come to empty the trash. It was Saturday, surely hikers were on the trail. Coloradoans love being outdoors, so it would be a matter of time before someone would cross my path. I needed to find a safe place to wait that would protect me from the wind. I walked around, half expecting her to drive back up the road laughing at me and telling me that leaving me was just a joke—wishful thinking. There was a big boulder just off the path. It looked like it had fallen hundreds of years ago from a cliff that no longer existed. It was frozen in a roll and when I pushed it, I half expected it to roll forward. There was a snow drift that had not melted on one side. This side shielded the snow from the sun and the wind. I would wait here. I remember my teacher telling me that if you bury yourself in snow, the snow could keep you warm. This did not make sense to me, so I sat down on the park bench to wait. As I sat, I ate the crust from my sandwich and ate one cookie. I was hungry but needed to make this food last as long as possible. I did not know how long I would be here. I had to keep my mind off the fate of my brothers because it would paralyze me and if I did not make it through the night, then I could not help them if they survived. Time glided by. The clouds appeared to mock me and the wind started to sing me a lullaby. The sky was turning pink and orange. Daylight was bedding down to sleep as night stood guard. I decided to nestle down besides the boulder and take a nap. The best way to deal with problems was to approach it like my brother; suck my thumb and sleep. Sleep did not come easy.

I was scared out of my mind. Every bird, insect, deer, mountain lion, and rustling tree was out to get me. There was a bright moon on this night, serving as my night light. I prayed and prayed and even tried to light a pile of twigs for warmth. The wind quickly snuffed it out. Just the other week in school, Smokey the Bear, came to my preschool class for the gifted and told us that we should not play with fire because it could cause forest fires. I did not want to set the mountain on fire; therefore, I left the lighter alone. I did not want to get in trouble with Smokey. It was cold. Even with my coat on, I was freezing. I was wearing jeans, a pink turtleneck shirt that was a size too small as was my coat, and tennis shoes with no socks. I did not have on long johns because my mother forgot to tell me to dress for survival. The boulder did shield the wind, for which I was thankful. As I hugged myself and pressed up as close the boulder as I could. My head started hurting. I was four years old. My mother had abandoned me in the mountains, and I was aware enough to know that I needed to stay near this hiker's path so that I could be found.

My only hopes were that my brothers were sleeping soundly at the house, that she had not hurt them, and that whoever found me does not hurt or eat me.

The morning light kissed my eyelids and I woke to a crisp, blue morning, and talking.

The eyelids of the night sky had just opened, so I knew it was early. I slowly sat up and blinked several times. For a minute, I could not remember where I was. Despite the events of previous day, I somehow slept through my nightmares. As my vision focused, I saw a Jeep parked near the trail. There was a man and a woman standing next to it, looking at me. Their dog was sitting quietly by them. I got up quickly so I could assess the situation. My mind temporarily was blank and I struggled recollecting why I was in this strange place. The lady asked me my name and I just stood there looking dumb. I could not conjure up sound from my mouth. The man asked me my name again and if I was OK and where were my parents. I just stared and then like a fool, I started to cry. The lady came close in an apparent attempt to comfort me with a hug. I cowered away and sat back down on the ground. Their dog, a beautiful golden retriever, walked over to me and nestled his cold, wet nose on my neck. I gingerly touched, then hugged him. I felt suddenly safe. These people were going to help me. The man walked back to the Jeep, while the woman sat down next to me. He radioed someone with the CB. The static voice that responded confirmed something and they both looked at me. The woman stood up and the man walked next to me and told me they called the Park Ranger and that everything was going to be fine; he was going to take me to my mother.

Apparently, my loving mother reported me missing as soon as she descended the mountain. She told the police that we had set out to have a picnic in the mountains and that I had wandered off. She claimed she started having labor pains and that she needed immediate medical attention so she drove to the nearest town which so happened to be miles from where she "lost" me. My distraught mother had given birth to my sister that evening. I asked about my brothers and the couple radioed again. Words were exchanged on the CB and they reported they were with her. The ranger came and drove me to the hospital where my mother, brothers, and now sister were. The couple were so kind and followed the ranger to the hospital. They let their dog, Rex, stay with me in the ranger's jeep until I reunited with my family. She put on quite the show. She exclaimed how happy she was that God had brought her sweet daughter safely home. I could not look her in the eyes. She and I both knew the truth, I think everyone knew she was not being completely honest, but they tended to lean on the notion that a mother would never abandon her young child in the mountains, so she got off scot free. My brothers were excited to see me and the ranger completed his report. That was it. I overheard the doctor telling the ranger that the case needed to be reported to Child Protective Services. He was concerned about our weight, my getting "lost," and the track marks on my mother's arms were of "some concern." She was high on something when she gave birth to my sister, Toni. The doctor told her she would need to stay at the hospital for a couple of days. She refused. Having just given birth, no more than ten hours prior, she gathered her offspring, refused additional services, and drove off. The small-town mountain doctor was no match for her, so he and the ranger let us go. I was mad at them, but I kept quiet. They told her to be sure to take the baby and herself to the doctor when she got to Denver. She smiled and placated them. She was a chameleon and a master manipulator. She had everyone there believing that she would do absolutely anything to make sure her precious children are cared for and that she would get herself together. We left the hospital in the raggedy car and headed to the city.

The ride back was subdued. My tumultuous mind was thinking all sort of things, but I mainly thought about how I wished the hiking couple and their dog would have kept me. My mother made me hold my sister, Toni, on the way back home. Toni was tiny. I did not understand why the doctor let her take such a tiny baby home. I also found it odd that she did not cry. All my young, four-year-old mind could think of was that when Toni had been in my mother's tummy, she had learned that crying was not allowed. My mother pulled over a few times to breast feed her, but beyond that we were all quiet. My brothers stared at our sister with curiosity and I can only imagine what was going on in their little minds. I was happy they had not been dropped off on the side of the road. I felt a huge sense of responsibility for them and now my sister.

Toni was white. Maybe they gave our mother the wrong baby, because not only was she white, she had a head full of light brown, almost blond silky curls. She did have our mother's eye shape, yet unlike hers, there was a spark in them. She was comfortable in my arms and I vowed, silently of course, to take care of her. Both Lam and Eddie touched her small, clenched fists and her rosy cheeks. I tried hard not to stare at any of my siblings, lest my mother see me. I did not want a repeat of the previous night. So, my day-old sister, brothers, and I sat quietly in the back seat riding out of the mountains to the hell that awaited us. Our mother did not turn the music on and the dark clouds followed us.

2

She was crazy. Bat shit, certified crazy. She hated life, herself, and children. We were an everyday reminder of the heroin addicted whore she'd become. She wasn't born into this world to become the woman she was. But circumstances and decisions landed her here in this cesspool of her existence. She hated me the most because I reminded her of all her broken dreams. She did not have the capacity to love for she had never truly received love from her own parents. I believe I was the personification of her self-loathing and I felt every bit of it. She had a terrible temper and anything would set her off. A grain of rice left on the counter after she told me to clean up could result in a kick in the leg or slap across the face. She would beat me to release her rage. I have been thrown across the room, kicked, punched, bitten, hair pulled, slapped, whipped with just about any available object, spat on, laughed at, burned, tied up, cut, forced to smoke pot and cigarettes for her amusement, forced to kiss her male friends, or to stand naked in front of them so they could make their snakes spit, all by my mother. Thankfully, my brothers were spared from much of it. I watched her dope up and at times I was made to tie the tourniquet on her arm and insert the heroin-filled needle into her deteriorated veins. I must admit, while I did not quite understand addiction, I understood that she could die from it and I was tempted to give her too much. The fear of what would happen if she did not die, kept me from helping her to overdose. She would make me be a part of her sickness, then beat me for helping.

Her favorite form of torture was tying me up hog styled with a rag stuffed in my mouth covered with duct tape. She would put me in the cold, musty, vermin infested crawl space underneath the house and leave me there. She would leave me for hours, sometimes days, in the dark. If she was in an especially torturous mood, she would hang a glow-in-the-dark skeleton from the string on the cellar door. I could hear the walking above me and my brothers and sister crying, her yelling or there was an eerie silence, and there was nothing I could do. She had me tied up like a discarded carcass. I usually received this punishment when I questioned her or stood up against her violence towards my siblings. She hated me and she let me know every day. I usually figured out how to get out of my bondage, because I was freaked out by the mice and roaches that crawled about and on me. I would sit in the dark for hours wondering what I had done wrong and if my siblings were okay. The darkness was comforting and horrifying at the same time. While I was in engulfed in it I was safe from her clutches, yet it was my tormentor. I would wonder how I was going to sneak back upstairs to check on my brothers and sister without getting noticed. It was a gamble, but one I was willing to take because I had to know how they were doing. Sometimes, she would find out I snuck out of the cellar and whip me and put me back with tighter knots and throw me down the stairs. Other times, it was as if she simply did not remember she put me there and she was nice. I never betted on the second response, but I always tried. My tenacity infuriated her. My devotion to my siblings and their devotion to me made her rage with envy. Imagine that, a mother jealous of her preschool aged daughter. We lived in the rabbit hole and there was no escape.

We moved frequently. There were times we would sleep outside behind buildings, in abandoned buildings, with her friends, or in motels. Regardless of where we were, men were around. When we had to leave one place and find another we had to walk the city.

She would tell us to put our thumbs up to help her hitch a ride. Men always stopped. We would sit in the back seat or in the bed of the truck. She never had money to pay for the ride. Her currency was between her legs. She paid for the ride in front of her children. She would tell us to close our eyes and plug our ears. After my sister was born, I would nestle her deep into my chest to protect her eyes and ears, but I saw and I heard—everything. I hated her. When the driver would drop us off, before he left she told us to tell the "nice man thank you." I hated her more. Many times, I would hear the man or men ask if they "could have the girl." She would say no, I was not ready yet, but maybe next time. Later in life, I was told that she wanted to turn me out onto the streets to make her money and that she was happy she had another daughter, because maybe Toni would be more cooperative. Toni, because she looked white-looking, would have made her a fortune.

Before I was remanded into the custody of the State of Colorado permanently, we lived in a yellow Section 8 house. To be honest, I think she broke in and squatted there. The neighborhood was full of such houses and poverty permeated the air. Everyone used food stamps and on every corner was a druggie, gangbanger, or bum. There were churches and liquor stores across the street from each other. Public transportation was the mode of travel for most, though most of the people never appeared to go anywhere. We were taught how to shoplift and with a simple note, the liquor store owner would sell me cigarettes to take to my mother. He was smart, he kept the cigarettes behind the counter, or I would have stolen those too. Depending on how much pussy credit my mother had with the owner, he would also give me some beer to take to her. Most people went to church on Sunday, because the churches usually provided meals after service. God was a silent bystander to the degradation of the people who lived in my neighborhood. Graffiti covered buildings, broken glass glistened the streets, used heroin needles lined the gutters. The whole place smelled of urine, Afro sheen, fried food, collard greens, cigarette smoke, and cheap cologne. Birds did not seem to fly in the area. Stray dogs and cats wandered the streets as aimlessly as the dope heads and prostitutes. There were only blacks, a few trailer park whites, and fewer Mexicans in our hood. Kids played outside, jammed music on boom boxes, and the pimps would roll through handing out candy. The Black Panthers passed out coats in the winter and turkeys during the holidays. We lived near Martin Luther King Boulevard. Everyone knows that in any city in the nation, a MLK street meant you were living in the most desolate place in the city. Police sirens, crime scene tap, and chalk lines were a part of the landscape. We were poor, but so was everyone around us. Chaos was normal.

We did not consistently have electricity or water. The house we lived in had a one-car garage with a rotted-off-the-hinge door, two bedrooms, a bathroom, small kitchen and a living- dining room combination. It was an old, smelly house, with wood floors and a crawl space, a space I grew to fear. We did not have much in furniture. Anything we had we stole off the Goodwill donation trucks at night or picked up from the dumpsters. If someone was evicted and the landlord put their things on the street, everyone would take what they wanted. There was a Dutch door in the kitchen that lead to the back yard, a term I used very loosely. It proved to be convenient for selling drugs. The heroin addicts and weed buyers would knock on the back door and depending on the knock I knew what they were buying. My mother taught me the signals, because I had to sell the drugs when she was not home, which was often. The money flow had to keep flowing no matter what. It was an efficient method, almost like a drive through for addicts. I was taught at the age of five how to roll joints, use a scale, and cook heroin for my mother's needle. One of my chores was to rotate the marijuana plants that were growing in the garage. I was in kindergarten and I proved to very business savvy. My mother would have all kinds of men in the house helping her with distributing and selling the drugs. She made me roll and sell ten joints a day. I had to sell them before I could come home from school with my siblings. If I did not sell all that she gave me in the morning, she would make us sleep outside. I was good at selling. The trick was to find a consistent buyer and in our neighborhood, there was always someone willing and ready to buy drugs. I guess staying doped up helped them face the dire reality of their shitty lives. I did not care, I sold because I was told to and I wanted to make sure my brothers and sister slept in the house at night. My mother used to smoke her own supply, which anyone who know about the drug game knows that is a faux pas. The drugs were not really hers, rather the men that came in and out, so if she used she had to pay in more ways than one.

She never had money and always paid in other ways. As a five-year-old I did not understand what exactly my mother was doing. I understood that she had sex, but I did not really understand what that meant. I knew I was uncomfortable if she made me stand naked in front of men, especially if she let them touch me. She would let them touch my vagina or butt, just touch. It sickened me and made me hate her more. I learned, at such an early age, how to emotionally disengage from my physical self. I did whatever I could to be out of the house when her male friends were there. Most of the time she was so doped up she did not notice that my siblings and I were gone. There were times, I would hide us in the crawl space until she and her suitors left or fell asleep. I did not want them touching my brothers or sister. If I found out they had, I had decided that I would kill them and her. I knew where she kept her gun. My job was to protect them and if that meant murder, then so be it.

Men touching her made her sad, though she laughed when then touched me. When they left, she would become angry. On one such occasion, I was told to watch my brothers and sister in the living room. She was going to have a private talk and pay her male friend for the gift of heroin he had given her. It was nothing new so we barely acknowledged her and she gave me a stern warning to stay away from her room. I was told to stay in the living room and to keep my siblings occupied. I replied I understood and off she went with her friend. I played with my siblings for a while, however, she had been in the room for a long time. My sister started crying. Crying meant trouble. I tried to calm her down and thought of taking her outside because I did not want my mother to get annoyed and then angry. Unfortunately, my mother had not given me permission to go outside and I had just spent two days in the cellar for disobeying her. I knew better than to interrupt her and ask. I picked my sister up and walked her around the kitchen. She was not calming down. I checked her diaper and it was a mess. I went to get a clean one, but then froze. I could not change the diaper because the diapers were in my mother's room and I would be put in the cellar if I bothered her. My sister was inconsolable and I was scared to decide because I felt it was a lose-lose situation. I weighed which decision carried the more severe consequence. Did I interrupt my mother and make her anger or will it make her angrier if my sister did not stop crying? I struggled but finally decided on trying to sneak into my mother's room to get a diaper. I secretly hoped the door would be locked because I was losing courage. I gingerly tried turning the doorknob and found that it was unlocked. Slower than frozen molasses, I turned the handle. It moved without a sound and I said a silent prayer of gratitude. I deliberately eased the door open. I planned on making a small crack and then crawling on the floor undetected. The logic of a five-year-old. As I was sliding the door open I saw the man lying on top of her, naked, and she was making a noise like she was being hurt. The need to protect her clouded my judgement so I stood upright. She saw me. Initially, I did not hear what she said because I was confused and had an overwhelming feeling of disgust. Things started to clique in my mind and I realized at that moment my mother was nasty. She watched me see her for the first time. She yelled for me to close the door and get my ass back in the living room. I did I was demanded and numbly walked towards my siblings. The three of them were sitting on the floor in front of the couch as we were not allowed to sit on it. My sister was still wailing. I was angry at her and went and slapped her. I immediately felt horrible. I had never been aggressive towards my brothers or sister, so this caused her to stop crying. I know it does not make sense, but she did. Lam picked up Toni and held and rocked her. He looked at me in disbelief. Tears started forming in the corners of his eyes. He was a strong boy and he held them back. They saw my face and all three became silent. I must have looked like my mother in that instance, full of rage and anger, but how was I supposed to look after becoming consciously aware that I was the daughter of a whore. My father was one of her many "friends." I existed because she either had to pay for drugs or he paid her for a good time. She was a cheap whore, so it most likely cost him ten dollars to spit me out of his snake. I felt like a horrible human being. I had become her and I wanted to die. I took my sister's filthy diaper off and threw it on the floor. I kissed her red cheek, where my imprint still lingered. I hated myself. I wanted to run out the door, but knew better. So, the four of us sat in silence, me holding my sister trying to make amends, my brothers staring at me with weary caution, until our mother finished her vile act.

When she had completed her session, I did not have to look at her to feel the pending attack. She walked the man to the door. He was a big black man, which larger than life hands. He had a Jheri curl and his collar was dirty and greasy from the afro sheen. One of his front teeth was cad in gold, and a thick gold necklace adorned his greasy, sweaty neck. He was angry about something. She pleaded with him not to go yet and that he still had to pay her. He slapped and pushed her against the wall then grabbed her by her neck. She was struggling to breathe and I was secretly hoping she stopped. He called her a 'trifling bitch' and walked out, slamming the door behind him. The air became still in the room and a coolness crept up my spine. I sincerely prayed that I would survive what was about to happen, because I knew something was about to happen. She was pissed. I just hoped that she would leave my siblings out of this. This was between her and me. Before I could finish my thought, my whore-mother grabbed my hair from the top and told me to stand up. I did as I was told—it was not like I had a choice. She told me to look at her and I became afraid. Her eyes were evil and a part of me believed she was about to turn into a demon. I was scared to death to look at her. I remember in school reading a comic book about Medusa and I, at that moment, knew I was about to be turned into stone and die. It would have been a merciful death.

I looked up but stared at the center of her forehead to avoid her eyes. She slowly, too slowly, repeated for me to look in her eyes. I could not. As I was trying to settle my fear so I could decide to look or not, she became impatient and made the decision for me. She poked me in the eye. I cried out in pain and covered my eye with my hand. I looked at her with my uninjured eye and she punched me in the face. I heard my siblings cry out. I could feel blood leaving my body. I could sense that a portion of my body hit the couch, because the fall was not too hard. I would feel myself being dragged on the floor by my hair and I vaguely remember thinking she was taking me to the cellar. I woke up what could have been hours later. My last thought before I blacked out was correct. I was in the cellar, but I was tied up differently. I struggled getting my thoughts together and orienting myself. I was in the cellar, tied up, but something was different. This crazy bitch had me naked, hung by my ankles from the rafter, my hands tied and I was gagged. I used my tongue to push the rag out of my mouth. I took in a deep breath and flinched because my side hurt. It did not take me too long to undo the hand binds with my teeth, so I folded my body upwards to undo my feet. My head was throbbing, I felt like vomiting, and I was scared because I did not remember getting here and I did not hear noises upstairs. Where were my brothers and sister? The distance from the ceiling of the cellar to the floor was not too great so the fall after I untied my feet was not too bad. I lied on the floor for a minute trying access the damage.

My head, side, and back hurt. Every time I took in a breath, I had a piercing pain in my side. I gingerly sat up and patted around to see if I could locate something to wear. I found a dirty sheet and wrapped it around myself. I laboriously walked to the trap door and pulled the string to bring down the folding stairs. As I exerted energy to pull down the string, I became dizzy.

I do not know how long I was in the cellar, but it felt like years. The demon returned to retrieve me from the depths of hell to perhaps torture me some more. I retreated to the farthest, darkest corner and hugged my knees. I hoped she would just leave me there. For a split second, I hoped she would just kill us all. She called me to come to her, but I remained in the corner, like a cornered feral cat. She came and grabbed me by hair and pulled me towards the stairs. I was lifeless. She pushed me from behind up the folding ladder to the world. She somberly escorted me to the bathroom and pointed to the tub of water. I could see steam dancing about the water, but I did not protest and went to the tub and got in. I remember thinking, "When did we get water?" The water was boiling hot, but I refused to make a protesting sound. I quietly stepped into the lava and sat down. I was convinced she was trying to boil me alive, because witches eat boiled children. She pointed to the soap and I grappled for it because my left eye was swollen shut and I tried not to wince due to the stabbing pain in my side. I washed my body. I closed my good eye and started really smelling the soap's scent and really feeling the soothing warmth of the hot water. I imagined I was being cleansed from the inside out. I was broken, that was for sure. My mother was a demon and wanted to destroy me, but at this moment, all was well with the world. I was peacefully seeping when I was yanked from my peace by a cry. My heart was racing and I worked quickly to rinse the soap off me and to dry off. I had to go check on my siblings. I thought maybe she was being nice to me because she felt guilty for whatever she had done to me in retaliation for opening the door and discovering her truth. Now I was thinking she was really trying to boil me and was perhaps butchering one of my siblings at this moment. I did not have any clothes in the bathroom, so I just put the towel around me and ran out the bathroom. She was sitting in the living room with my sister on her lap rocking her side to side. My brothers were not in the there. She could see my eyes racing around the room and darting into the kitchen. I then looked into the bedrooms and my heart sank when I realized they were in the cellar. She looked at me and very coyly smiled and told me to go put on some clothes. I was numb, empty. She had won, so I walked to the second bedroom to put on some clothes.

My mother walked in behind me. The hairs on my neck rose. I was not going to resist whatever was about to happen. I wanted her to just end my miserable life right then. I had failed to keep my brothers and sister safe, so living on was optional. She told me to sit down. I did. She proceeded to ask me how I felt and if I wanted some water. I politely said I was doing fine and that I did not need any water, I thanked her for asking. She sat in silence for a while and told me that I needed to learn to mind my own business. She told me that when I go to school the next day that I needed to keep my mouth shut, and if anyone asks me about my bruises that I better tell them I was not listening to my mother and fell down the stairs. She reconsidered that story and told me to tell them I had been jumped by some older kids in the neighborhood. That was a more plausible explanation. She left the room and I sat there contemplating, yet again, what to do. I decided to keep my mouth shut. My brothers and sister lives were at stake. I remembered hearing someone say that silence was golden. Well I was about to become a millionaire. My mother returned to the room, while I was deep in thought. She handed me a bag and told me to open it. Inside was a pretty shirt and a pair of pants. It was probably stolen from a thrift store. I expressed my gratitude.

It was as if she could read my mind because she smiled and said meekly, "Don't worry, I'm taking your brothers to school and your sister to daycare. I got things to do."

I looked up and again the mind reader spoke my thoughts. She assured my brothers were fine, they were simply playing in the cellar. I felt betrayed. How could they play in my torture chamber? I am sure it was some sadistic way of her getting into my head, making them play there. I was then told to go get them. I obeyed and was relieved to find them unharmed. I dared to let hope enter my mind. After I called my brothers out of hell's belly, my mother called me to the room all the children shared. She had the top dresser drawer open. My hope died.

I was a thinker as a child. I really listened at school. So, any time there was a program at school, I absorbed the information. If Smokey the Bear said not to start forest fires, I complied. When McGruff the Crime Dog came to school and said to stay drug free, I believed the message fiercely. There was an anti-pollution campaign going on at school and the presenter talked about how cigarette butts were not biodegradable and aided in the death of innocent birds who mistook the butts as insects. I thought that was the reason we did not have many birds in our neighborhood. I wanted to save the world and save the birds, I mean I was only in kindergarten, so my resources to save the world were limited. Therefore, I devised a plan to save the birds by collecting all the cigarette butts I could find. I do not understand my own logic, but at the time it sounded like a great idea. So, I collected cigarette butts. I picked them up everywhere and put them in my dresser drawer. I did not throw them in the trash; I wanted to keep them to see how many I could collect. I counted them daily. It was a weird thing I did as a five years old girl, and I admit it was strange. Well, my mother found my collection of cigarette butts this day, the day of my release from the dungeon. Standing at the entrance to the bedroom, looking with my one un-swollen eye I held my head in shame and I truly did not have a logical excuse for the drawer full of cigarette butts. Even as I tried to explain to her my rationale for collecting them, I sounded stupid. She, of course, concluded that I had stolen and smoked all the cigarettes. Really?

When did I have time to smoke three hundred cigarettes amidst trying to survive? So, she very calmly told me since I like smoking, she was going to watch me smoke. Well, at least she was not going to beat me, I did not think my body could handle any more and I also thought, hell, all the shit I have endured, I could use a smoke. She told me to go sit in the living room. I remorsefully complied. She pulled out a new pack of Kool 100s in a box. She tenderly pulled out a square, lit it, and then gave it to me. I mimicked how I saw her holding her cigarettes and took a short draw. I held the smoke in my mouth and then blew it out. The smoke triggered a coughing attack and I felt like my lungs were going to explode and the pain in my side was unbearable. She laughed.

She told me to finish the cigarette, but that I had to swallow the smoke. I did not understand, that's not how I saw people smoke. She told me in the sweetest voice that if I did not swallow the smoke she would burn me with the cigarette lighter. We've played that game before and I was not in the mood to be burned. I took another short draw and swallowed the smoke. This triggered not only coughing, but vomiting. My side, swollen eye, head, and chest hurt. I felt faint and dizzy. She laughed and told me that I had to finish the cigarette and then clean up the vomit or she was going to make me eat it. I cried and begged her to forgive me for collecting the butts. I swore I had not smoked them and that I would never touch a cigarette again. She slapped me on the side of my face with the swollen eye, picked up the discarded cigarette that fell out of my hand as I was convulsing with coughing and put the cigarette out on my shoulder. I did not feel the pain of the burn as my head was hurting so bad I thought I was going to explode. I sat and waited for either more abuse or to be excused to clean up my mess. She excused me. She had shown me mercy. Lam, Eddie, and Toni sat in a corner, watching me. My vision was blurred so I could not read their expressions. Once again, I had failed them.

3

School started and I was so happy. I loved school. I did not love being around the people, but it was a daily escape from my hell and I got to learn. I liked learning and I asked a lot of questions. So, I suppose it is more appropriate to say I loved going to school to learn. I walked my brothers and sister to school every day. We would leave the house early so we had time to eat breakfast at school. We got our best, sometimes only, meals at school. I did not interact with my peers much. To be honest, I thought they were all babies. I would look at the other kindergartners and wonder if their mothers hated them too. I was leery of the teachers. My mother considered school "authority" and we were taught to be careful around authority. The less I interacted with others, the less chance they had to get into our business. They were nice enough, but they were adults and in my world adults hurt little kids or they do not do anything to help like the park ranger and the doctor who delivered my sister. I was more advanced than the other students so I found the kindergarten curriculum to be meaningless, more disrespectful and insulting than anything. Everything my teacher gave me, I finished quickly. I mean, a deaf-blind-mute monkey could color. So, she would send me to the library and I would pick out encyclopedias or books meant for older children. I read a lot of magazines too.

I did not get along with any of the other students, so I did not have friends or acquaintances for that matter. I was withdrawn, watchful and temperamental. I did not like getting in trouble, but if someone touched me, I would go into a rage because touching did not feel good to me. I did not want to be hugged by any-one. Elementary teachers tend to be huggers and after a few of my tantrums they stopped trying. I did not play with the other students. If they got in my space, I would simply bite them. They learned to leave me alone. My teacher gave up trying to make me work cooperatively; it was easier for her. She simply did not have enough strategies in her teacher toolbox to get me to engage. I would refuse to get out of my chair if she told me to go to a group, simply because there was nothing I felt I could learn from them. She would try having the group come to me, but I would simply sit stoic and refuse to talk. She finally gave up and let me work all assignments independently. When I finished the assigned task, I read. I challenged myself to learn big words and I stole a dictionary from the library so that I could find the words I did not know. I do not know why I stole it; I guess I had not been taught how to ask for things.

New words fueled my passion for learning. A part of me knew that the smarter I became the better equipped I would be to escape my mother.

The pre-K was at the same school I went to, so I got to check up on my brothers. The daycare was near the school. When school was out, I would walk to get my brothers from their class and then walk down the street and pick up my sister. Sometimes, we would put her in a grocery cart we had taken from a store parking lot. It made traveling a lot easier and faster. I often put my brothers in the cart too and would run with them. They laughed and it made me feel good.

Laughter in our lives was so scarce that I learned to capture it when opportunities arose. When we got home, I always went in first so I could do a mood assessment and determine how we needed to approach my mother. I also had to give her the money from the drugs she would make me sell before we could come in.

On this particular day she seemed more agitated than usual, if that was possible. I could see her through the screen door, which I thought was odd. She rarely left the door open. She was sitting at the table, her head in her hands and mumbling something incomprehensible. I peered around the room from my perch on the stoop to see if someone was in the room with her. I did not see anyone. I took the twenty dollars out of my pocket, put my finger to my lips to signal for my siblings to be quiet. Eddie was holding Toni and Lam was making circles in the dirt with his tattered shoes. They looked at me and in our sibling sense agreed to be quiet. I slowly opened the screen door and walked even slower towards my mother. I extended my hand with the money, something like a peace offering, though I did not know what was wrong with her. She looked at me and I tensed in preparation for the unwarranted hit I thought she was going to deliver. She looked at me, more accurately, she looked through me. I figured she was high, so laid the money on the table in front of her and went to get the others. She did not say anything as I ushered them into the house. They felt her mood too. We walked in with reverence for the storm that was about to hit. Our mother looked at us with such distain that I am surprised we did not instantly combust. We sat dutifully, without word, on the floor in front of the couch. We all sat in silence for several minutes. She finally stood up and grabbed the money. She simply told us that she was going to the grocery store and would be right back. My mother turned to me and said that I was to watch the younger ones and I better go to school. I was not, under any circumstance, to open the door for anyone. If I did she would kick my ass and put me in the cellar until I died. The fear was instilled. She said there was food in the house, left a book of food stamps, and vanished through the back door.

Time crept away. It seemed like we sat in silence, the four of us, for an eternity. Our wretched, broken mother just left. Why the speech just to go to the grocery store? Where was she going? Is she coming back for us? What am I supposed to do? I was only five years old, but I felt like I was going on fifty. My sister started crying and interrupted my string of unanswered questions. I realized that eternity was only thirty seconds and I had responsibilities. I turned to her and felt sorry. She was a beautiful child. Her white skin had turned in to a sweet toasted coconut brown complexion. Her light, curly hair was sweetly wild. She was thin, too thin, I thought to be barely a year old. Her laugh was both soul crushing and uplifting. She was too beautiful for this shit. I got up and went to her. She needed a diaper change; I decided at that moment she needed to be potty trained. I felt I could earn some grace from my mother if she did not have to worry about buying or stealing diapers anymore. She did not leave money or enough of anything. There was not enough food. There were no lights. Luckily, we had running water, but who knew how long that was going to last. Why did she tell me not to let anyone in and did that mean she will be close enough to watch the house? My mind started racing. I picked my sister up, hugged her and wet a towel and wiped her down. I found a pair of Lam's underwear and put on her. In the kitchen, there was a pot of rice on the stove. That was nice of her to make dinner before she left. I took the pot off the stove and served my siblings. I did not eat because I did not want to take from them. It filled me with joy to see them happy. Good. She is gone and for now I am responsible for them. My mother did not return from the store. That night or any night.

For over two weeks, maybe longer, I took care of my siblings. I did not have a sense of how much time had passed, but my mother had left us. I cracked the window in our room so I knew when the sun rose; that was my clock. I got up, dressed in one of three outfits, woke my siblings, got them ready and walked them to and from school every day. I felt like her eyes were watching me, so I was careful to keep up the routine, not miss school and did not say anything to anyone. I stole food from the cafeteria, so

I could feed the younger ones. I was losing weight and smelling, since I had to wear the same clothes, unwashed. I could hear my classmates make comments, but I did not care. I kept to myself, read my books, cared for my family. I focused on making sure the boys and my sister were taken care of. I was glad she was gone, but I did not relax. She had warned me for a reason, so I knew it was a matter of time before she returned. In caring for my siblings, I forgot about myself. Something I did or said or didn't say triggered someone to call Child Protective Services.

One evening, I was sitting in the house, on the floor in the dark. My siblings were down for the night, but I could not sleep. I feared the dark and the threat of the cellar loomed over and under me. I could not turn off the thoughts of where my mother went and if or when she would be back. As I sat on the floor, listening to Lam's gentle snore, a bright light shown through the front window. I ducked so as not to be spotted. There was a hard knock on the door. I was terrified. There was another, harder knock and the man shouted 'Police!' Aww, shit! I did not know what to do and I prayed the pounding on the door would not wake the baby. They would know for sure we were in the house. He banged on the door one more time and shouted that he knew we were in the house. How? I wondered. I thought I was doing a good job at being quiet. He yelled if I did not open the door, he would break it down. Panic set in. If I opened it or he bust it down, I would be punished and I resolved either way, the cellar won. I opened the door.

The officer looked me over with his flashlight. I felt so exposed and little. He asked me where my mother was. I told him I did not know, because it was the truth. He told me not to lie and I promised I did not know where she was. I told him she left to go to the grocery store. He asked me how long ago and I said I did not remember, because I did not. He looked me over with the flashlight again, sliced the darkness of the tiny living room with it, and talked into the mic on his shoulder. Within minutes the house was full of people. My brothers and sister were awakened and we stood in a line looking like suspects in a line up. Wide-eyed, disheveled, dirty and tragically skinny, I am sure we looked like we were survivors of some horrendous camp. We were told to sit on the couch, we all sat on the floor while the adults talked amongst themselves outside. I was scared because I had disobeyed my mother, but I had not seen her in weeks.

Maybe she was found dead somewhere and that is why the police were here.

If she was dead, she was resurrected that night. My mother slipped in to the house through the back of the house and I could feel her fury. She had been watching the house as I suspected. Surely, she knew why the police were there then and heard him threaten to break the door down. I was trying to process everything at once so I did not have enough time to brace myself for her slap. I yelled out, Toni screamed, and the police officer ran in. He grabbed her so quickly I thought he must be a ninja wearing a police uniform. Within seconds, my mother was handcuffed and forcibly sat down at the table. Another officer came in to the house and asked her where she had been. My mother tried to play it off as if she had just gone to the store for some groceries. She became belligerent and demanded to know why they were in her house. Did they have a warrant? She exclaimed several times she knew her rights. I just stared at her. Lam and Toni were both crying now. Eddie was sucking thumb. She looked at me with such toxicity that I feared her gaze would kill me. I felt weak. Funny thing, all I could think about was I hoped all this would end soon so I could get some sleep before school in the morning.

A lady officer and another lady, introduced to me as a caseworker, came and gathered my brothers, sister, and me up and ushered us outside. Our mother was screaming at the top of her lungs not to take her babies. She started yelling at me that everything was my fault. One of the ladies put her arm around my shoulder and I cringed and shrank away from her touch. I wanted to run away. I felt like a bad person, because I did not understand the ramifications of forgetting to take care of myself. I had brought an unknown and scary future onto my siblings and I sadly accepted defeat. We were taken in the back of a police car to the hospital for health examinations. We watched our mother be put into another police car, alone. I did not know where they were taking her. All I knew is that if she got out of wherever she was going and got us back, she would kill me. I knew that for sure. I was so stressed and all I wanted was sleep.

Maybe when I woke up in the morning things would be better or I would realize all of this was just a horrible, horrible dream. They were not and it was not. We were admitted to the hospital for malnutrition and physical abuse. I was the only one examined for evidence of sexual abuse. I remember hearing the doctor say that this was the worst case of neglect he had ever seen. I was sure that was an exaggeration. Again, I was only a kindergartner, so what did I know. That night we entered the foster care system permanently. My fate was sealed.

4

After we were treated and released from the hospital, we were taken to our first foster home.

I was told by the young caseworker that it was a temporary home until our mother could get some help. Ms. Pearl was a big, strong, hearty black woman. Her frame took up the entire doorway as she stood there to greet us. We slowly piled out of the caseworker's car and stood by it until Ms. Pearl motioned us to come near. I gathered my brothers and sister behind me. They were my responsibility and I had yet to decide if this large, black old lady was safe. She looked nice enough, but so did my mother. Evil comes in all shapes and sizes.

She reminded me of the black lady I had seen on the syrup bottle in the corner store. Her hair was white, sprinkled with black, but she kept it hidden under a turbine. She had a deep voice, almost like a man, but I was sure it was because she smoked a lot of cigarettes. Her brand was Newport 100s in a soft pack that she kept in a black cigarette pouch with her lighter. Her hands were as big as a catcher's mitt and I immediately thought that if she hit me, she'd break my butt. Ms. Pearl smelled like bleach, cigarettes and mints. She carried mints in the pockets of her housecoat and readily chewed them after every smoke. Her beady, nearly black eyes were kind, yet somehow, they betrayed her. Her eyes told a story of a life of hardship and taking in unwanted and abused children was her way of making right the wrongs committed against her.

Or perhaps it was her way of righting the wrongs she had committed. Either way, she was welcoming. She was religious too. On every wall of her tiny house, which was only a little bigger than the one we just left, were pictures of Jesus and his disciplines, crosses, and photos of her family in church clothes. She was missing all her teeth except her molars. Ms. Pearl always appeared to be chewing something, like a cow chewing cud. My brothers took to her immediately and complied, without hesitation when she told them to give her a hug. She did not ask me. I think she knew that touching was not my thing and she sensed me sizing her up. Toni seemed to like her too and allowed her to pick her up. The air in her house was thick with cigarette smoke, old grease, and bleach.

She was kind, but she did not like the fact we were mixed. When the case worker left, she told us so. She made several comments while sucking her gums that the races should not mix. It made the babies retarded. I did not understand why she felt the need to comment on our mixed heritage. Her comments confused me. I did not understand race-mixing; hell, I did not really understand race, but she made it a point to talk about it. I was a bit upset that my brothers and sister took to her so quickly. Eddie was the least loyal of them. He clung to the hem of her skirt as she showed us around and laid out her rules. Lam and Toni, while they hugged her, held my hands tightly.

She required silence when spoken to and said that children should never look an adult in the eyes. That rule was easy for us to follow because our mother had already trained us to submit to adults. Ms. Pearl also did not like noise, especially crying. She said if we ever felt like crying to just pray to the Lord. I rolled my eyes and looked at Lam and Toni. I did not know where the Lord was, but he had not been listening to me all these years, so why would he start now. Ms. Pearl showed us our rooms. There were small and stark. Each room had a set of bunkbeds and one dresser. The bedding was flowered sheets with a thin knit blanket. That was it. They were not happy rooms, but they were clean. The girls were in one room, the boys in the other. Since we did not have any belongings beyond what we were wearing, Ms. Pearl told us that our caseworker was going to come the following day to take us to the donation center to pick out some clothes. She asked us to come to the living room to go over the rules, before she started dinner. I could not remember the last time someone made us dinner. We had gotten so used to eating rice and school food, that someone making us dinner was a foreign concept.

Ms. Pearl told us to follow her into the living room. The furniture was covered in plastic and there were plastic runners in front of the couch and in the hallway. Trained that we were, we sat on the floor in front of the couch. She looked at us quizzically.

"Lawd hep me sweet Jesus. Whys yous sittn on da flo? Gets on up on sits on da couch like civil people. Yous ain't no animals." Her speech was difficult to understand since she was talking without front teeth.

"Mama told us that we are not allowed to sit on couches, only adults can." I took the opportunity to school Ms. Pearl.

"Wells yo mama don't lives here. Dis mys house and we sits on the couch. Now gets up." We were scared to move. Our experience taught us that sitting on the couch resulted in getting hit or humiliated. She repeated for us to get off the floor and sit on the couch. My siblings looked to me for direction, so I slowly got up and sat on the couch. I was preparing myself to get hit, but it did not happen. I was slightly confused and irritated. Just get it over with, I do not like being surprised. Nothing. We sat quietly on the couch. The boys were fidgety and the plastic on the couch made it difficult to stay put. I think they were moving on purpose to make noises with the plastic. My irritation was growing. Sitting on the couch was a new experience, so it was challenging to pay attention to Ms. Pearl's laundry list of what-not-to-dos in her humble abode.

We stayed at our first foster home for a few months. We had to change schools. Toni did not go to daycare, since Ms. Pearl did not work she stayed home with her. My brothers went to preschool and I was transferred to a school for the gifted and talented across town. Ms. Pearl would walk me to the city bus stop in the morning and greet me each evening. I liked riding the bus to school, it made me feel important. The bus driver always let me read the newspaper to him on our morning route to my school. He said that since he worked all day, he did not have time to read, so me reading to him helped us both. He got the news and I learned new words. He also let me pull the stop string at each of his stops. It was one of the very few joys I had in my life. I also liked my new school. The work was a little harder, but I was always finished before the other students. My teacher started letting me go to a first-grade class.

All things considered, we were recovering. Our foster mother was strict, but she did not hit, which was a relief. We went to school and I was encouraged to read every day after I finished my chores. I had a lot of chores, but I did not mind. I wanted to show her I appreciated her kindness and the only way I could was to clean. I remember my first night sleeping at her house. I could not. Every time I closed my eyes, I saw my mother. I feared she would find us and hurt me. My brothers came into my room and got into my bed. Toni slept on the bottom bunk with me so we arranged ourselves so we could all fit. It felt safe. Our foster mother came into the room without saying a word turned on a lamp, put an extra blanket on us, and left. It was the kindest act I had experienced in a while. I cried silently. I could not stop crying, so I sobbed the entire night. It was not a cleansing cry; it was just unshed tears that finally had a chance to come out. I was upset with myself for crying, because I did not want to be heard and get Ms. Pearl upset. She already said she did not tolerate crying. However, I could not stop. The floodgates had opened and there was no stopping. So, I cried for my brothers, my sister, our future, our pain, our mother. I literally cried myself to sleep.

I knew our time with Ms. Pearl was going to be short. She was a temporary foster home and we were told that once our mother got help, whatever that meant, or another home became available we would leave. I had grown to like Ms. Pearl well enough, but I did not get attached to her. Toni did. Probably because she spent so much time with her. It was clear that Ms. Pearl had a special affection for her too. It was hard not to. Toni was angelic and even though we came from the same mother, she was not marred with abuse like I was. She was still innocent, wise for her young years, but innocent nonetheless. I was always comforted in her presence.

As I've already explained my siblings and I are all the shades of a brown rainbow. We are all mixed with Mexican, Native American, and whatever john that impregnated her. Eddie, who was one year younger than me, was starting to act out in all sorts of way. He liked starting fires. Ms. Pearl said that the devil had gotten ahold of him. I wasn't sure about that, but he definitely was not loving. I loved him and was protective over him, but kept a watchful eye on him. He was not to be trusted. In many ways, he embodied our mother's temperament and it was best to love him at arm's length. At school, he got into trouble for hitting and refusing to do his work. I overheard Ms. Pearl on the phone one day asking the person on the other end when someone was going to come pick him up. She could not deal with him anymore.

His father was supposedly our mother's pimp. So, one bright and sunny afternoon Ms. Pearl called us into the living room. It appeared that she had been crying, her eyes were glossy and red. I knew she was about to tell us something important because the living room was where business was discussed. We sat on the couch. I was glad I was wearing pants because I did not like when I suck to the plastic. Ms. Pearl told us that she bought each of us a new outfit. That was exciting, but I wondered why? Something did not feel right. She handed me the bag of clothes and told me to get my siblings dressed because we were going to our forever home. I did not know what that meant, but I was excited. I enthusiastically dressed my siblings and combed their hair. We were told that Eddie's dad was coming to get us. I had no clue that any of us had a dad, so I was super stoked about meeting one. So, the four of us: Eddie, Lam, Toni and I sat on the couch cleaned and anxious about meeting a dad. When Eddie Sr. arrived, my heart fell.

Eddie Sr. was an imposing figure. He was a big man, with smooth, dark chocolate skin. He towered over Ms. Pearl, which meant he was a giant. His gold tooth in the front and the long dark scar that crossed over his left eye, down his cheek gave me the impression he may have been a pirate in a previous life. His booming, yet surprisingly gentle voice commanded attention. He was nice enough, but I felt a negative energy from him that tugged at my consciousness. I had seen this man before and he made me uneasy. I just could not remember where I had seen him, but whenever and wherever it was, he had not left a good impression on me. I tried to push the feeling aside and chided myself to grow up. He walked into the room, we all stood. I picked up my sister and held her on my hip. He walked over to us and patted each of us on our head. Do I look like a dog? I looked past him. I did not want to go live with him. My gut instincts screamed for me to gather my siblings and run. I could see him in Eddie, so I was sure he was his father.

He could take Eddie, but not the rest of us.

He looked at my sister and turned to Ms. Pearl.

"That one," he said pointing at my sweet baby sister, "that one is staying. I'm not taking no white child. The lady only told me to take the them."

Ms. Pearl said, "Wells dats not wuts she done told me. Hold on a sec, yous can't break up dez hur chil'ren. They alls each others got. Besides, lil mama here," she pointed at me, "she's ain't bout to leave wit out her baby sista. Lemme call that worker."

He told her to call who ever she needed to, but he was not taking the baby. We all looked at each other. I must have misunderstood him. He repeated that he was not taking Toni, that CPS only told him to take my brothers and me. I held my sister for dear life. If she was not going, I was not going. I held her so tight, she squirmed and told me to put her down. I could not. I could not let this man take me away from my sister. I started crying. I did not care if I got in trouble for crying, I was not going to leave my sister. I would fight anyone who tried to make me. Eddie Sr. took ahold of both of my brothers' hands and told them to come to the car with him. Eddie eagerly walked with him; traitor. Lam grabbed my hand and said in a quiet voice that he was staying with me and Toni. Eddie Sr. picked Lam up, he did not fight back, and walked out the house with my brothers.

Ms. Pearl could not get in touch with our caseworker. So, she looked at me with pity and said there was nothing she could do, I belonged to the state, and she had to follow what the caseworker told her. She also told me there was nothing I could do and that I was upsetting my sister. She promised me she would call me later when we got to our new house and let me talk to Toni, but I needed to go take care of my brothers. What horrible position for a six-year-old to make. I was made to choose between my brothers and my sister. I cried because I did not know what to do. Eddie Sr. returned to get me. He told me to put my sister down and come with him. He first tried saying in a nice voice, then I could tell he was getting impatient. I did not care. He went to grab her out of my arms. She held on to my neck for dear life. Ms. Pearl helped pry her arms from around me. I hated her so much. Eddie Sr. grabbed my hand and I bit him, hard. I then kicked his shin and tried grabbing my sister from the other traitor. Toni and I were making quite a scene; grabbling for each other, screaming, crying, kicking and trying to bite. Eddie Sr., though visibly irritated, was patient considering I was behaving like a rabid hyena. He shouted to Ms. Pearl to take the baby outside and put her in the car. I ran after them, thinking that he had decided to take her. They tricked me. It was their way of getting me out of the house. As soon as I ran outside, Eddie Sr. snatched me up from behind, held me in a bear hug. I was no match for him. Ms. Pearl hurriedly returned to the house with my screaming sister, who was reaching for me over her shoulders, and closed the door. I resigned and went limp in his arms. He tried to reassure me that he would do whatever he could to come back for my sister. He told me he could not take her because there was not enough room in the car. I knew he was lying. He became impatient and forcibly placed me in the back seat of the station wagon. My brothers looked at me, I stuck my tongue at them. I hated the world, I hated them for being so damn weak. Eddie Sr. got into the front seat and peeled off as fast as he could, to make sure I did not have time to get out and start the whole fiasco again. I looked out the back window until I could no longer see the house where my sweet, loving sister was imprisoned by Ms. Pearl, the conspirator in tearing my family apart.

In the car was Eddie Sr.'s wife, Carla. A tall, slender woman with a gold tooth and visible track marks on her neck and arms. Great, CPS put us in the hands of a junkie. She looked like life had been unkind to her. Mocha brown skin, a short greasy Jheri curl, and dark, almost black lipstick made her look like a Soul Train reject. I'm sure at one point in her life she was beautiful, but the drugs she had done had withered that beauty away. I could tell that she was faking her happiness in acquiring three children. Her smile was a lie and she knew I knew it was. We avoided eye contact. Like my mother, her eyes scared me. They were dead eyes that were windows to a black soul. I could not stop crying, but when she reached out to comfort me, I shrank away and hissed at her. Lam climbed into my lap and wrapped his little arms around my neck, I cried harder because just a while ago my sister's arms had been there. I accepted his comfort though. At least he was there, until I could figure a way to get our sister back. My heart turned ever so slightly hard towards Eddie. This was his family now. Lam and I were merely commodities.

Carla handed my brothers and me Smarties, like that was supposed to make me feel better about abandoning my sister. I refused the candy and secretly loathed my brothers for falling for her bullshit. This stranger was telling me to call her mom. She was trying to be nice, but I sensed mal intent from her and I wanted nothing to do with her or Eddie Sr. She apparently knew our mother, which meant she was a trick too. I asked when could I call my sister and Carla told me later that evening. I did not believe her. I tried to memorize the route to their house so I could find my sister later. I was not sure where we were but I knew that the hell I left was only preparation for another hell. We drove to Five Points.

We drove up to a row of duplexes. The front of the house had a shared porch; we entered the door on the left. I remember this house in detail because the moment I walked through the door, I knew my life here was going to be challenging. There was an electricity in the air that shocked me to my core; it felt evil. I think my youngest brother felt it too, because he stopped at the entrance and refused to cross the threshold. Carla, tried to gently guide him from behind; he dug his heels in and looked at me with wide eyes filled with fear. Eddie walked into the house, but stood to the left, near a corner. There was an ominous presence that grabbed our attention. Carla tried again to get Lam to step into the house. He braced himself, holding the door frame. Anger flashed across her face. Eddie Sr. picked Lam up, carried him into the house, smiled and told us there is nothing to be afraid of. He carried my brother to the kitchen. I looked at Eddie and we agreed with our eyes to follow his dad into the kitchen. The kitchen was at the back of the house. It was small, old, and we could see the roaches scattering on the walls and the in the sink.

Roaches really did not bother us; we were quite familiar with them. What caught our attention was the big wooden paddle and the long leather whip that hung on the wall, near the back door. The three of us looked at these items at the same time, we then looked at each other, and telepathically agreed that the goal in this house was to avoid whatever those were used for. This was going to be a long, long stay because I sensed that Carla enjoyed her toys.

Still carrying Lam, Eddie walked to the cupboard and grabbed a box of powder milk. He took out three glasses, put in two spoons full of powder in the glasses and filled them with tap water. He told Eddie and me to sit down and he gingerly put Lam down. He immediately scooted towards me and was basically sitting on my lap. Both of my brothers were looking at me to see what to do. Eddie Sr. grabbed a container that had cookies and took out two for each of us. I saw the roach escape when he opened the lid, needless to say, I was not all that eager to indulge in the cookies. When he placed the treat in front of me, I scooted them towards Eddie. He was greedy; he never turned food down. I was acutely aware of my surroundings and I looked again at the looming torture devices that hung on the wall in front of me. I looked at my brothers and thanked Eddie Sr. for the milk and cookies. I picked up my glass and was disappointed to see that the powder had clumped. It was going to be hard to swallow, but all the crying and screaming had made me parched. I knew it would not be wise to complain, so I took a big gulp. My brothers did the same. Eddie Sr. and Carla stood near the sink and watched us, in silence, as we quietly consumed the snack prepared for us. When we were done, I felt like throwing up, but somehow managed to control the urge. I picked up the glasses and went to the sink to wash them. I had to stand on my tiptoes to reach the facet, but I dared not ask for help. Eddie and Carla just stood there watching me. My nerves were unraveling and I really did not know what to do. Why are they staring at me? I wished myself invisible; no such luck. Eddie Sr. finally spoke and told me not to worry about cleaning the glasses, he would take care of it. Carla on the other hand told him I needed to clean up our mess because we are not living there for free. Confusion and fear settled in and once again, I found myself in a dilemma. Who do I obey? I decided I would wash the glasses, because Carla seemed to have a malicious spirit and I did not want to unleash whatever beast she was trying to contain.

The glass washing ordeal felt like an eternity. Lam started crying and when I looked at him I noticed he had wet himself. I quickly went to him to comfort him. I had a bad feeling that this was going to anger Carla. She did not seem to be all that excited we were there. Trust me, we were not excited either, at least not Lam and I. Eddie on the other hand had taken on a certain air of ownership. After all, Eddie Sr. was his father, so this was his house. I asked where the bathroom was so I could clean him up. Eddie Sr. pointed upstairs and said he would go get our things out of the car, not that we had much. Our few clothes and toys were in one trash bag. He quickly left the kitchen and we stood there looking at Carla. I dared not move and I was frustrated that Lam was still crying. Crying never ended well. When would he learn this? Eddie looked at Lam. I saw his anger too, but I warned him with my look to keep his mouth shut. He complied. Eddie Sr. came back into the house and told us to follow him upstairs. We followed him up the stairs. They were worn, wooden and creaky. I paid close attention to the stairs that creaked the loudest so that if I ever had to plan an escape in the middle of the night, I would know which ones to avoid. The bathroom was at the top of the stairs. Eddie Sr. told me that I did not need to worry about cleaning Lam up, he would. Lam looked at me and shook his head no. He did not like people touching him and I feared that if Eddie Sr. persisted, Lam was going to throw a tantrum; which I was sure would piss off Carla. We were all emotionally and physically drained, so I insisted I help my brother, until he gets more comfortable. Eddie Sr. did not protest and I took my brother into the bathroom and helped him wash up and changed his clothes. Eddie Sr. stood at the door, like a centurion, until we were done. When I started dressing Lam, Eddie Sr. went back downstairs. I did not know what to do with the soiled clothes, so I stuffed them into the bag he had brought from the car. That proved later to be a grave error.

Carla came upstairs and showed us our room. The hall was shaped like an L. Along the longest part of the hall were two rooms.

The adults stayed in the third room that was at the end of the short hallway. We were ushered into one of the rooms. There were three twin sized mattresses on the floor. Each had a pillow and a folded blanket. There was a closet to the right of the room and two windows. The windows faced the front of the house. The awning that covered the porch was easily accessible under the windows. I made a mental note of that as it could possibly be another form of escape when the need arose. I resolved that I would run away from here with my brothers, well Lam, and find our sister. I doubted Eddie would come with us. He was home. I was prepared to find an abandoned house and raise them so we could live happily ever after. I had taken care of them when I mother left for the store and never returned, I was sure I could do it again. Besides, I was a little older and wiser, so I would be sure not to get caught. If only if was that simple. Carla, told us which beds we were assigned to. She put me near the closet. I was afraid of closets, because the entry to the cellar was in a closet. I was logical enough to know that a cellar did not lie beneath this closet since we had to come up stairs, but nonetheless, closets freaked me out. Funny how afraid I was of closets at that time, because that closet would later become my safe place. Yet, that day, looking at the mattress next to the closet I was afraid, but knew not to complain. Carla told me to unpack the trash bag that contained our clothes. Eddie Sr. had brought it from the bathroom. She asked that I fold the undergarments and to hang everything else up. I picked up the bag, but then she snatched it out of my hand and dumped the contents on the floor. She first smelled, then saw the urine soaked underwear and pants I had just taken off my brother. She looked at me, then at my brothers, then at Eddie Sr. She turned and stomped out of the room and I could hear her walking down the stairs. She was hitting all the high notes on the squeaky stairs. We stood, mute and unknowing.

My heart was beating fast and my brothers crowded around me. I had now become the centurion and I knew that something was about to happen. Eddie Sr. knelt next to us and asked me why

I had put the dirty clothes in the bag with clean clothes. I shrugged my shoulder. He asked again and I replied I did not know where to put them. He kindly touched my shoulder and told me that if ever I do not know something, to ask. He looked at the three of us, I could see sadness in his eyes. His eyes did not scare me, but they were hiding something and I frantically wanted to understand. Carla appeared, as if an apparition, in the doorway and she was holding a trashcan in one hand and the whip in another. Damn! I had made her mad and know she was going to beat me. I did not understand why she had a trashcan, but I knew I was about to find out. She looked at me, I lowered my eyes, and my brothers stood behind me. She threw the trashcan at my feet. "What the hell are you doing?" he grunted at her.

"I am not going to deal with that whore's pissy ass children! I told you I didn't want these bastards," she, through clinched teeth, hissed at him. She looked past Eddie Sr., at me, and told me to throw all of our clothes in the trashcan. I stood frozen; what she was asking me to do did not make any sense to me. Why would I throw away our only possessions in the world? I was grasping for reasoning in my mind, when I heard Eddie Sr. in his booming voice tell Carla to take our clothes to the laundromat and just wash all of them.

"Goddamit woman, these are children! It's been a hard day, so stop being a bitch! Don't piss me off or you know what will happen."

"I'm not touching these filthy brats' shit. You wanted them, you do it!" She said yelled.

They faced off in the doorway for what seemed like a lunar cycle. My brothers and I just stood there; watching. We were going to do whatever the winner of this duel told us. I vehemently prayed that Eddie Sr. would win. Between gritted teeth, he looked at Carla and told her to wash our clothes. She looked at him, then at us, and back at him. She lowered her eyes, pierced her lips and scooted past him in the doorway. He reached out, grabbed the whip in her hand, snatched her by the hair and threw her towards the trash bag, causing her to be sprawled at my feet. We scooted back. I am amazed how she swiftly gained her composure. She got up, smoothed out her clothes and walked towards us; we instinctively took a few steps back and looked at Eddie Sr. for guidance. The air of violence hung stifling in the room. I braced myself to be hit by her, thankfully Eddie Sr. had taken the whip. Relieving myself of guard duty, I knelt down and began gathering the clothes. I thought I was being helpful, since clearly, she had lost the stand-off. I heard the whip before I felt it. The sting from the whip felt like I was sliced in two. I was sure I was bleeding and that my spine was severed by the lash. My brain had trouble processing the pain because I momentarily believed I was paralyzed. I anticipated another lash, so I fell to the ground and went into fetal position. I heard Carla yell something, but the second whip did not come. Eddie Sr. had meant to hit her, instead he hit me. My brothers had started screaming, which quickly brought me out of victim mode. I jump up to rush and quiet them because I did not want my brothers to get hit with the whip. They would die if they did. I rushed over to them and braced myself again to be hit. I heard Carla's earth piercing curdling scream. I slowly turned my head to face her. I expected to get slapped. Instead, I saw Carla cowered on the floor and Eddie Sr. was whipping her with her weapon of choice. I was glad, but angry that he had hit me, though mistakenly, he had hurt me. She howled fiercely and screamed as if she had never been hit before. It was a little dramatic in my opinion. I had been hit with the whip and didn't scream like that. From what I counted, she received five lashes from Eddie Sr. After he dealt the last blow, he repeated his command of washing our clothes. Carla, gingerly got up. Blood was seeping through her shirt and I noticed an open wound on her left forearm. Eddie Sr. beat her like the slaves I had read about in school. She half crawled, half dragged herself to the pile of clothes and picked them up one by one and placed them back in the trash bag. After she had gathered all the clothing, she looked at me and smiled. It was an evil, all-knowing smile that said, "Your ass is mine when he leaves." She thought that so loud, both of my brothers looked at me at the same time. I looked pleadingly at Eddie Sr. and I panicked because I remembered something from the car ride over here. He had told my brothers and me that he was a truck driver. Therefore, he worked a lot and Carla was going to be our guardian in his absence. He was going to leave us alone with her, she knew it, now I knew it and she was going to make me pay for the whipping she just received. Moving slowing as to not irritate her wounds, Carla gathered our clothes and left.

Eddie Sr. read my concern the moment she walked out of the room. He had to know what I was thinking because he reassured me that in his absence, Carla will take care of us and if she did not she would pay the price.

He said, "You are my responsibility now, it's the least I could do for your mother, she was one of my best girls and this here boy," pointing at Eddie, "is my son. I take care of blood."

That explained her attitude towards us. Carla had a grudge against my mother because of her perceived position in the hoe game. She hated my mother because her man was showing compassion for another bitch's kids and now she had to take care of them. She resented this and since I reminded her of my mother, I was going to pay for her transgressions. All I could do was sigh. I knew in my gut that anytime Eddie Sr. was away, Carla was going to make me suffer and deny it to him. I felt doomed and defeated. For a moment, I felt sorry for myself and my brothers. I mourned my sister not being with us, but glad she would not be subjected to the torture I was sure we would experience. I felt so weak and small. I was frustrated because I felt vulnerable. I tried with all my power not to cry; not to feel the throbbing on my back; not to think about my impending doom. I just stood there trying to understand why I was born into this life. Eddie knelt before me and took me by my face. He looked deep in my eyes and kindly, but remorsefully assured me everything would alright. I felt suddenly exhausted and the only thing I wanted to do was go to sleep. I needed to escape into my dreams and find some peace. I looked at Eddie Sr. and asked him if I could go to bed. I did not have any more fight in me today. He told me I could, so I turned to my brothers and told them to go to bed too. We clambered into the same bed; they understood. The sun still shimmered through the windows. It did not matter. We needed sleep so we could regain our strength to face whatever tomorrow was bringing. The new battle for survival had begun. Eddie Sr. tucked us in and with his large, heavy hands gently touched our heads. I don't know why he showed affection this way, but I did not have the energy to protest. This was a kind gesture; but it was hard to find comfort in it. He repeated that everything was going to be fine; he promised. He lied.

5

A few days later Eddie Sr. left for the road. He told us he was taking a load from Colorado to Mississippi. He was going to be gone for two weeks. My brothers and I stood silently by the front door as he was gathering his things for the journey. I had not heard anything about Toni, nor had I talked to her. I asked him about her again, before he left. He told me Carla would be sure to get me in contact with her. Another lie. I purposefully refused to give Carla eye contact, I felt her presence and that was disturbing enough without looking at her too. My brothers crowded around me. They stood so close that I felt they were going to absorb into my flesh.

Watching Eddie Sr. put the last of his clothes into the duffle bag made me frustrated and angry. He damn well knew we were going to suffer when he left. Why did he not just leave us where we were? I asked him for the name and phone number of our case-worker, just in case I needed to call her. Again, he told me Carla would get me that information. Lying came easy to him.

I needed to figure out an escape plan. I just did not have a good bearing on the area yet.

Since the first day we came, we were not allowed to go out-side. Monday, Carla was directed to enroll us in school. I would have to pay attention to the route to school so I could figure how to leave. I was sad I had to change schools. Hopefully the new school would let me be bussed to my old school. Eddie Sr. called my name, which pulled me out of thoughts. He asked me to give him a hug; I did not move. I did not want to hug him or anyone else for that matter. Touch was not comforting to me, rather quite abrasive and unwanted. He called my name again and again I stood there with downcast eyes, hoping he would change his mind about leaving or at least offer to take us with him. Carla's voiced sliced through the air and she screeched for me to stop looking stupid and give "my dad" a hug so he can leave.

"No. He is not my dad. If he was, he wouldn't leave me here with you." I knew I was going to pay for my defiance, I did not care.

"Do not talk back to her. You don't have to hug me if you don't want to. I have to work.

Carla is going to take good care of you and I'll bring you a surprise when I get back."

He was abandoning me and my brothers and leaving us at the mercy of this demon-woman and he wanted a hug for it. Too bad and I did not want a surprise. I wanted to leave this place and go back to Ms. Pearl's. I planted my feet, kept my eyes steady on the floor.

Eddie Sr. knelt in front of me, placed his heavy and calloused hand on my shoulder and whispered, "I will see you soon. Listen to your new mother. Everything will be OK, I promise." All I could think, "She is not my mother, you are not my dad. My only family are my brothers and my sister, who you took away from me. Do not touch me!" I maintained my position, he got up and patted the three of us on our heads. "We are not dogs!" I screamed in my head, even though people keep trying to reduce us down to such. He said something to Carla, she responded. My ears had gone deaf because all I could hear was the sound of my pounding heart. My brothers and I were motionless in the corner by the door as Eddie Sr. said he last goodbyes and left. Carla followed behind him. As she passed us, I could feel her darkness graze my skin. My brothers must have felt her negative energy too, because they both grabbed my hands at the same time. I gently squeezed their tiny hands as a means of reassuring them that I was going to protect them, by any means necessary.

It seemed like forever that we stood in the corner by the door. Eddie Sr. had left and Carla was outside talking to a neighbor. We did not know what to do or where to go, so we remained fixated by the door. I was tense with anticipation. It felt like we stood by the door for years. The muscles in my neck were tight and my brothers had not let go of my hands, so my hands were hot and clammy. We probably stood by the door for a few minutes, but when you are waiting for your destruction, time plays funny tricks on the mind. Carla stayed outside talking to the neighbor, I assumed it was a neighbor, for some time. When she finally came back into the house, she simply walked past us, as if we were an unsightly cluster of statues that was awkwardly placed by the front entrance. We stood still, but our eyes followed her to the kitchen. After her beating with the whip, the whip disappeared from the wall. I tried to think of what she was up to, but all the sounds that came from the kitchen sounded innocent enough. I dared not move to investigate though. I could hear the drawers and cupboards opening. The silverware clanked as she shoved the drawer closed. I, in my statuesque state, started to panic. Maybe she went to the kitchen to get a knife and now she is planning on killing us. I planned our escape in my head and thought if we ran into the streets, screaming, then maybe the neighbors would be able to stop her. For a fleeting moment, I discarded that plan, because I thought maybe they were on her side. After all, my brothers and I were new to this neighborhood and we had not been allowed out of the house in the week we had been there, so the neighbors likely did not know we existed. My young mind scrambled for a solution. My highly tuned in ears analyzed every sound she made in the kitchen. Lam tugged my arm and looked at me. His doe like eyes shown of desperation. He, too, did not know what to do, but it was obvious he was getting restless. He was holding his knees tightly together, which indicated he needed to go to the bathroom.

That meant that we had to unfreeze from our position and venture to the bathroom, undetected. Carla was still in the kitchen. To get to the bathroom, we had to pass by the kitchen's entrance and walk up the very creaky stairs. I looked back him, pleading for him to will his urge away, he started bouncing and then grabbed himself in an effort to stop the impending flow. It was now or never, so I grabbed my brother's hand and started towards the stairs. Eddie refused to go and sat on the floor. I did not have time for his obstinate behavior, so we left him. Lam and I walked quickly towards the stairs. I glanced in the entrance of the kitchen to see if I could see what Carla was doing. From my viewpoint, I could not see her. It was as if she had become a ghost and the noises we heard in the kitchen were just her spirit causing a raucous. My nerves were taunt. We started up the stairs without any incidents. I took Lam to the bathroom.

As he was washing his hands, he peered at me and asked, "What are we going to do now, sis?"

"I am going to figure something out. Just be super good so Carla does not get mad." In my mind though I was thinking, "Hell, I did not know, I'm just a kid too." I was just happy that we made it to the bathroom in time before he had an accident, for I was sure had he wet himself there would have been consequences to pay.

"I am scared. Are you, sis?" He whispered. I simply shrugged my shoulders and started towards the stairs since Eddie was still down there. Lam followed.

At the bottom of the stairs, Carla stood glaring up. She had Eddie's curly hair entangled in her claws. He was trying hard not to cry, but I could tell she was hurting him. She looked at me and in a quick gesture, slammed my brother's face into the banister. He yelped in pain. My motherly-sisterly instincts took control and I ran, rather, slid down the stairs. I should not have left him alone, now this witch was making him pay for my mistake. I yelled out for her to stop. Carla let go of his hair and Eddie crumbled to the floor; screaming. I saw a glint of blood on his face. I was enraged and wanted to hurt this woman. No, I wanted to do more than hurt her, I wanted her dead. Eddie Sr. had barely left and she was already hurting us. Eddie was his son! Hurt me, not him. I was stronger. When I got to the bottom of the stairs, Carla laughed. I lost all rational thought and I kicked her in the shin. She yelped out and I kicked her again. I wanted her to move so I could check on my brother. I looked up the stairs briefly and saw that Lam was not there. Hopefully, he ran to one of the rooms and was hiding. It was about to get ugly down here and I did not want him to witness it, he was too young for this shit. Carla reached out to grab me. I was quick enough to move out of her grasp. I yelled at Eddie to get up and run outside. He seemed to understand the impending doom. Instead, of running outside like I demanded, he got up and ran upstairs; undoubtedly to be with Lam. As he ran past Carla and me, I saw that blood was coming from a cut above his eye. This bitch was going to pay for what she had done to my brother. She reached out for him, but I rammed my head into her stomach. I knew I was going to die after this battle, but she was going to die too. Carla swung at my head and landed a hard-right punch on my left ear. She then put her hands on my throat. I kicked and scratched her with all the might my little body could muster. I could feel my throat being crushed. My head was hurting, yet I told myself that I had to survive for the sake of my brothers. She picked me off the floor, hands crushing my throat. She was trying to choke me to death. When she lifted me into the air, she lifted me too high, because I was able to knee her under her chin. She must have bitten her tongue, because she winced in pain and dropped me. I laid on the floor for a second grasping for air. Then I had a brilliant idea. I was already on the floor, so I lunged at her legs and sunk my teeth into her calf. I bit so hard, I could feel my teeth sink into her skin and I tasted her blood.

She was screaming and punching me on the back of head and back. The more she hit me, the more determined I was to destroy her leg. If she was going to treat me like a dog; I would show her what a mad dog could do. I locked my jaw and she tried to pull me off her leg. Not happening. I was so focused on removing her calf from her leg, that I did not notice her dragging me, attached at the leg, to the kitchen. I was temporarily insane. Carla managed to open one of the drawers. I suddenly felt a hard hit on the back of my head. I saw a flash of light, then nothing.

I awoke in the dark. My head was killing me and my entire body felt like it had been tied into a knot. I lay still for a second, trying to remember. The more I tried to remember, the worse my head throbbed. Darkness swallowed me again.

Someone was putting something wet on my face. I slowly opened my eyes and I saw Eddie kneeling next to me. His features were fuzzy, but I sensed that he was not doing well. I tried to sit up and was overcome with a wave of a nausea. I still could not remember what had happened that landed me in this condition. Maybe I was dead and I was waking up in hell. Eddie pulled my arm and assisted me in sitting up. I surveyed the darkness, but could not connect my thoughts.

He placed a cup in my hand and gently guided it to my mouth. I immediately felt parched and was eager to drink. There was a problem. I could not open my mouth, well, I could but only slightly. My face hurt so intensely, and I realized my lips were swollen. I tried to remember and felt afraid that whatever had been done to me had caused brain damage. Eddie, still silent, pushed the cup to my mouth again. I tried to drink the water, but the pain was unbearable. The pain in my head was intensifying and again darkness claimed me.

I woke to a gentle push on my shoulder. Both of my brothers were sitting next to me. With my blurry vision, I could see the concern on their faces. They were dirty and the remnants of tears stained their faces. There was light in the area and I felt better. When I convinced my body to sit up, I realized I was in the room we shared. I was sore all over and my mouth and throat still hurt. My brothers looked desperately into my eyes. I could see that

Eddie had a bandage over his eye. Lam had bruises on his wrists. My mind still was not connecting. We sat, quietly, accessing each other's wounds. Lam had a look of concern on his face and I asked what had happened to his wrist. He started crying.

"I thought you were dead," he said.

"Why, what happened?" I managed to croak.

"She hit you with a gun to get you off her leg. Then she kicked you forever with her good leg. You really bite hard; a piece of her leg is missing," he slowly explained. There was an air of pride in his voice.

Eddie looked at me with such intensity, that I was sure my face was disfigured. "You looked dead. She called us downstairs and made us drag you up here. Don't you remember?"

"No."

"She tied us up at night, because she thought we would run away. Sis, we thought you were dead." He, too, started crying and I moved to hug him. The pain, one I've experienced before in

my side, crippled me, momentarily. I searched around the room to see if Carla was lurking in one of the corners. Both of my brothers said, simultaneously, that she was not there.

"Where is she?" I inquired. They did not know. I felt an urge to go to the bathroom and with great consternation got up from the bed. They asked if I needed help, I assured them I did not. At the pace of a frozen snail, I shuffled to the bathroom. It seemed like the bathroom was a half a world away. I prepared myself to look in the mirror. Based on how my brothers were looking at me, I expected to resemble some hideous creature. As I entered the bathroom and switched on the light, the pain shot through my head again. I felt sick. I decided to prolong the discovery of my countenance until I relived myself. When I went to pull down my pants to pee, I realized I was wearing a diaper. What the hell? I was a big girl. Why was I wearing a diaper and who put it on me? None of this was making sense and any explanation that sounded reasonable eluded me. Where was Carla at this very moment? How many days have passed since Eddie Sr. left? Why were my brothers tied up at night? Above all, why in the hell was I wearing a diaper? I urinated, it hurt. I re-pinned the diaper, it was cloth, since I did not have anything else nearby to change into. I felt tears welling up in the depths of my being, but I refused to allow them to flow. At that moment in time, I vowed to never cry again. Nobody cared about my tears and maybe I had cried when Carla was kicking the shit out of me and that is why I was wearing a diaper. I flushed and went to the sink to wash my hands. They were bruised, as were my wrists. She must have tied me up too. The mirror above the sink was small and I had to stand on my tippy toes in order to see my face. It was shocking. I am sure this is going to come off as an exaggeration, but I remember thinking I looked like the Elephant Man. I had read about him at my last school in an Encyclopedia. I had huge knots on my forehead and my mouth was so swollen and bruised that it did not close completely; my lips were cracked and dried blood had settled into the groves.

When I opened my mouth, I saw that the sides of my tongue were raw; it looked like I had bit my tongue repeatedly. Yeah, I looked hideous and no wonder my brothers thought I was dead; I looked like a swollen, bruised, decaying corpse. I was wearing the same clothes I had worn the day Eddie Sr. left to Mississippi. They were torn and dirty.

I finished up in the bathroom and shuffled back to our room. My brothers had not moved. We were good at staying still. When we moved, trouble was surely to follow. I was scared to go searching for Carla around the house, I just did not have the energy to deal with her. I got back into the bed and laid down. My brothers both snuggled up next to me. I did not fall asleep, rather did my best to enjoy the peace of the moment and the warmth of my brothers' closeness. My ears were highly tuned to the sounds of the house, but a sharp pain in my head accompanied every noise. I waited patiently to hear Carla's footsteps. I did not know if she was still angry about me biting her and I did not know how I would react to her, knowing that I looked like I belonged in a circus exhibit. I was hungry and thirsty, but I dared not move as not to spoil the peace my brothers, who both fell asleep, were enjoying. They deserved some peace. Though forsaken, only God only knew what trauma they experienced while I recovered from my beating and believing I was dead. If I was incapacitated, I am sure they received all of Carla's fury. I should have controlled myself better when I saw her slam Eddie's face into the banister. I should have checked on him, but not try to fight her. I damn well should not have bit her on the leg. A piece of her leg was missing? I should have been more mature and less reactive, but no one taught me how to respond to my brother being attacked. I had brought misery on myself and my brothers because I did not control my anger. I knew Eddie lied when he said everything was going to be alright when he left, yet I did not know how much of the blame would be placed on me.

The dreaded footsteps finally came up the stairs. I remained as still as possible so that Carla would think I was sleeping. I heard a second pair of footsteps, so I immediately thought Eddie Sr. had returned. Had I been out for two weeks? That was insane. There were whispered voices that accompanied the footsteps. The voices belonged to women, one was Carla's. I did not recognize the other voice. They walked into the room and stood in the doorway for a second. I tried to pose as if I was sleeping, but kept my eyes slit enough to see what was going on. Carla and the other woman walked into the room quietly; but then she barked for me to stop faking and get up. I complied immediately, but slowly. Sitting up hurt my head and made me feel sick. I sat up, warily, as not to disturb my brothers. The other woman gasped.

"Damn Bootsie! Daddy is going to kick your ass. You know if you mess with these kids, you are messing with his money," she said. "What the fuck is wrong with you!! She's a baby for God's sake!! Damn, damn! If the police or CPS sees this your ass is going to jail!"

She was a tall, slender woman. Her complexion was mahogany and smooth. She had the prettiest eyes I had ever seen. They were shaped like almonds and the color of hazelnuts. Her hair was a nicely picked out afro. She wore a red mini skirt, a white tank top that allowed her breasts to balloon from the top. Her high heels matched her skirt, as did her long nails. She looked nice. I did not know who daddy was and why he was going to kick Carla's ass, I figured he might be too old to really do anything, but I was curious. She sauntered over to the bed where I was sitting. She bent down, reached out to touch my face. I was startled and moved out of her reach. I thought she was going to hit me. She looked at me, tenderly and shook her head.

"Bootsie, you did a number on this precious baby. Were you on that shit? We need to come up with a good lie, 'cause Daddy just might kill you for this shit! She looks like she needs to go to the hospital. We can tell them she got jumped in the street."

"The little bitch bit me," Carla protested. "Big Daddy should never have taken them in. I ain't no mother to my own damn kids and don't want to be one to Nay's. Watching them is messing with my money."

"Bootsie, you know the state pays him to keep these kids. If their caseworker finds out what you did to them, especially her, they will take them away and Daddy will lose the money. That means he will beat your ass until you look like her," the other woman explained.

"Well, what the fuck was I supposed to do? She bit me!" she protested, "She nearly chewed my damn calf off!"

"Why do the boys have injuries?" She asked as she softly touched the bruises on Lam's porcelain wrists.

"They might have attacked me too! I had to tie them up when I left at night. These kids here are savages, just like their cunt mother."

I sat quietly, listening to their banter. I kept my eyes on the lady in red. I knew, as well did Carla, that she was lying, yet I was not going to contradict her. I figured out that "Daddy" was Eddie

Sr., so this woman must have been one of his working girls, just like Carla and my mother. She truly seemed concerned about us, though I think it was more about how Eddie Sr. was going to react towards Carla than a genuine concern for our wellbeing.

She looked at me and smiled. "Suga, you doing alright?"

I just sat there staring at her, not really knowing what to say.

"Can you talk? I'm not going to hurt you, promise. My name is Star." Star put her hand out for me to shake it. I just sat there.

"See, she's a fucking retard. That's all she does, sits and looks, then attacks! Shake her hand you stupid bitch before I come over there!" Carla hissed at me. The sound of her voice made me sick to my stomach and I believed she would come over to me, so I reached out and took Star's hand.

Star could barely look at me. I knew I looked horrible and I, in that moment, appreciated her kind touch. She got up and walked over to Carla and out of nowhere backslapped her. "What is wrong with you? You better not touch these children again. Daddy will be back next week and I know he will be pissed. You need to let her heal, feed her, and calm down. They are kids for God's sake. You probably deserved getting bit, by the looks of them."

Carla stormed out of the room. Star came back towards me. She opened up her purse and lit a cigarette. She looked at me, then at my brothers, around the room as if she was trying to absorb the situation and devise a plan. She slowly and deliberately drew on her cigarette. Thankfully, she blew the smoke away from my face. She told me to get my brothers up and then to meet her in the bathroom. She was going to give me a bath and put me in clean clothes. She wanted to get us out of the house and take us to a park. She told me she had to go get me some medicine to help the pain she was sure I was feeling. She said she would get us something to eat, too. I obeyed. I was eager to clean up and get out of the diaper. Based on the conversation between the two women, I understood that I had been in and out of consciousness for about three days. Eddie was coming home next week. I prayed that he would kill Carla and then take us to school. I desperately wanted to go to school. Maybe the school people were looking for us since we had not shown up yet. I would tell them everything.

Star ran a warm bath for me and was very gentle when washing me. The soap stung some of my wounds, especially when she was washing my face and hair. I held my breath when she washed over my sides. More than once she whispered, "poor baby." Once she was done bathing me, she dried me off and walked me to the room to put on clean clothes. Using the same bathwater, she bathed both of my brothers. It was a privilege to be the first to bathe. After they were cleaned up and dressed, Star came into the room with a comb, brush, and a jar of blue stuff.

My hair had not been combed in a while. She took a glob of the Blue Magic hairdressing and put in all over my hair. She gently untangled my curls and was mindful of the bruises that were hidden on my scalp. She brushed my hair into a ponytail, braided it, then put a plastic barrette on the end that she had taken out of her purse. Maybe she had kids of her own, so she knew how to take care of us. I didn't ask any questions, just let her care for me. I felt good and was excited about going to the park. I forgot how I looked and that my body was still racked in pain; I just wanted to play outside in the sunshine. I also made a small mental note to survey my surroundings, so when the time for me and my brothers to escape Carla's grip came, I knew where to go.

I did not know where Carla was, but I felt safe with Star. Star herded my brothers and me out of the house. The four of us stood on the stoop. The sun was blinding and the piercing light stung my eyes. I winced and immediately a flood of pain engulfed my head. I tried not to show it, I did not want Star to change her mind about taking us to the park. Carla was sitting on the porch steps in front of us, smoking a joint. I grabbed my brothers' hands and Star told her to move. She acted like she did not hear us and took another deep drag on the reefer. She held the smoke in her mouth, which immediately made me think of when my mother made me do the same, but with cigarettes. I shuddered. Star grabbed Lam's free hand and guided us down the steps, around Carla. Once we were on the sidewalk, Star turned to Carla and told her we would be back before dark. Carla mumbled something. My head was throbbing so I could not make out her words. Star called her a dumb bitch and started walking down the street holding Lam's hand. He held on to me, I held on to Eddie. We walked, the four of us in a line, holding hands. Star was talking to herself; I was busy looking around. The neighborhood was comprised of duplexes and small houses, like Ms. Pearl's. Some of the residents were sitting on their porches, there were teens blasting music on radios, and kids our age playing in the small front yards. Each person looked at us. Some made comment to each other. I heard a few, "Oh, Lords" and "Whose babies are those?" Star ignored them, so did I. I mean, we were new to the neighborhood and my swollen and bruised face was cause for conversation. On top of all that, we were being led down the street by a woman who was dressed in red, talking to herself. We were misfits. When we got to the intersection, Star turned left. There were men hanging outside a corner store who knew her. The called her name, she responded that she would get with them later. One of the men asked who we were and she said, "None of your damn business." The men started chattering amongst themselves; she ignored them. When we got to another intersection there was a phone booth. Star told us to wait, she stepped in and closed the door. We stood there, silently, observing our surroundings. I wondered if she was calling Eddie Sr. to tell on Carla. Maybe he would come back earlier, kill her, feed us, then take us to school. It was wishful thinking, but comforting. I suddenly realized I was famished. I dare not ask Star for any food, she was being so nice to us that I did not want her to think I was ungrateful, plus I knew not to interrupt an adult on a phone call. After she finished her call, she stepped out of the phone booth and as if she had read my mind asked us if we were hungry.

We were. She walked back towards the corner store, past the men. One asked what happened to my face.

"She saw yo momma! Mind yo damn business!"

He put his hands up in surrender. "No need to be salty sistah. Just showing some concern." "Concern yourself with your damn self."

We went inside and she gathered some bread, bologna, chips, and Pepsi. She also grabbed some Twinkies and Snowballs. At the counter, she asked for cigarettes and rolling papers. She pulled a food stamp book out of her purse. She paid for the food with food stamps and the cigarettes and rolling papers with cash that she pulled out of her bra. The clerk asked us our names. I looked at Star to see if was OK to answer.

She replied, "Hell, what are your names? I forgot to ask you." I told them. The clerk looked at me hard and long. He leaned across the counter and said in a low voice that it was nice to meet us and then he handed each of us a Jolly Rancher stick. Again, I looked at Star for permission.

She did not look happy, but nodded and we each took the candy. When we walked out and back towards the phone booth she told us to give her the candy. Star told us to never to eat candy from him or to go to the store alone. I did not know why she warned us, but if she did not trust him, I would not either.

We walked a few more blocks and came to a school. The playground was full of children playing. It was a little intimidating to me because I was not comfortable around other children. I really did not know how to play with them and I found most kids my age to be big babies. Star told us that before we played we had to eat, so we walked to the far end of the playground and sat under a tree. She pulled the groceries out of the bag and made us sandwiches. My brothers and I devoured our food. Star told us to slow down or we would choke. We probably looked like ravaged dogs eating our food. After we gorged on the food and consumed the pop, we sat under the tree and watched the other children play. Eddie and Lam asked if they could go play. I told them they could, but to stay close by. Star told me to go play too. I told her I my head hurt too much, plus I enjoyed watching my brothers. She told me that she was going to leave in a few minutes to make another call, but that she would be right back. I just looked at her. I mean, she was not obligated to stay with us and if she did not come back, I was good staying at the playground. The school would eventually open and I would just walk in with my brothers and go to class. School was safe, so she could leave if she wanted to. I was just thankful that she had been kind up to this point. My brothers looked so little on the playground. My heart started aching worse than my head. I needed to figure out a way to never go back to Carla. I did not even want to see Eddie Sr. again. Not only had he taken us from our sister, he left us with a demon.

Star got up and told me she was going to the pay phone and would be back. I watched as she walked off. She looked out of place on a school playground wearing a short skirt and high heels. It was almost comical. She crossed the street and I stopped watching her and turned my attention back to my brothers. They played together on the monkey bars. The other children did not seem to notice them, which was good. No one approached me, which was also good. Star returned a while later and sat next to me. She told me that she talked to Eddie Sr. and he told her to make sure I get better and come Monday to enroll us in school. That made me happy, though I did not show it or say anything. I just sat there, watching my brothers. I knew they would be excited about going to school if for no other reason than we would not be with Carla and we would get at least two meals and a snack.

A black car pulled up alongside the sidewalk by the playground and honked twice, then once. Star waved and then reached into her purse and took out a small package. I knew what was in the package, my mother had had several of these in the house before she disappeared. It was heroine. Star gave me the package and told me to take it to the car. She said to make sure I got the money first. I did as I was told. The man on the passenger side looked at me and asked about my face.

"I bit a bitch who hurt my brother, she was not happy about it."

"I hope she looks worse than you. Way to look after blood little one." He offered his sympathies and handed me the money, I handed him the package. He asked was I going to be around, which meant was I going to be the one passing packages now in the area. I shrugged and walked away. I gave the money to Star. She pulled out her rolling papers and another package.

There, on the school playground, I was being interviewed for my skills. I had been taught well by my mother, so I took the reefer out of the package, broke it up, and rolled a tight and even joint. I could roll a joint better than most adults. I could count money, make change, weigh grams, and I knew the difference from heroine, reefer, and cocaine, and crack, though crack was sort of new. I even knew how to roll loose tobacco cigarettes from the leftover tobacco from used cigarettes.

These skills made me useful to grownups; but isolated me from childhood.

Later into the evening, we returned with Star to the house. Carla was still sitting on the porch smoking a cigarette and drinking a beer. She barely looked at us, but mumbled for us to get in the house and take baths. We barely looked at her as we passed, nor did we acknowledge her.

This was a big thing with adults, acknowledging them when they spoke. Being with Star made me feel bold. I did not grow up saying "Sir and Ma'am," that would have been considered sassing them, but I definitely had to let them know that I heard what they were saying. I said, "OK," but looked at Star. We proceeded into the house, up the stairs. Star stayed outside on the porch with Carla. We walked dutifully upstairs and I went straight to the bathroom. There were roaches crawling in the tub, so I cleaned it out before I filled it with water. I hated roaches, they were filthy creatures and I always felt like one was crawling on me. The boys bathed first, then using the same water, I bathed. Night had fallen, Carla was still outside and an eerie silence cloaked the house. I figured that the next thing she would tell us was to go to bed, so I directed the boys to go to sleep. They had worn themselves out playing at the playground, so they did not hesitate and were soon sleeping. I lied awake listening to the silence in the house. I prayed that I could get a good night's rest, that Carla would stay outside all night, and that Eddie Sr. would be home in the morning. I had prayed many prayers before and they went unanswered so I do not know what propelled me to offer up this petition, I figured it was worth a try. I drifted off into a state of awaken sleep; I was sleeping, but I was still aware of sounds. I guess fear always keeps a watchful eye. I heard laughter and loud talking. In my semi dream state, I imagined that the women on the porch had started smoking reefer and were drinking beer. All the advice and concern of earlier regarding "Daddy" and my face were forgotten in their haze. I heard the front door close and footsteps that hit the high notes on the stairs. I was fully awake now and lay in anticipation. Who I assumed was Carla walked to the entrance of the door and stood there for a minute. She walked away and I heard another, presumably either the bathroom or her bedroom door close. My heart was beating rather quickly and I realized I was holding my breath. I slowly exhaled and felt a little giddy, crisis averted and I turned onto my side, facing the door, and slept.

Eddie Sr. finally came home that Sunday, a week earlier than planned. Star's report forced him to return to check on his investments. My face had started to heal, but the damage was still very evident. Eddie Sr. was not happy and when he looked at me and told me to take my brothers and go to the park for a couple of hours, I was sure that Carla was going to get a beating. I hoped he would beat her to death, but that was wishful thinking; karma was not that generous. I took my brothers to the park. The last couple of days, Carla had really ignored us, which was good.

We spent most of our time exploring the neighborhood and playing at the park. I felt happy because I knew he would make sure to enroll us in school. Technically we were foster kids, and the state required us to be in school or they would remove us from the home. If we were removed, that would mess with Eddie's money. I wondered what lie he would tell the school in regards to the bruising on my face, because that would be a red flag if they enrolled me looking like a swamp creature. Our caseworker, whoever she or he was, would be notified and we would be removed. We played at the park for several hours. I had learned the names of the guys that hung out in front of the corner store. They were Crackhead, Alcoholic, Errand Boy and Crazy.

They had heard from the guy Candy had me give the dope to that I was cool and to watch out for us, so I in a way I had some street protection. They called me Lil Bit. I did not trust them, but I knew that it was a good idea to be friendly, in case I needed help one day.

We stayed at the park until the street lights came on. That was the universal signal that kids needed to head home. We had not eaten lunch, but we were used to being hungry. I gingerly turned the knob on the front door. The door was pulled out of my hand and swung open. Eddie Sr. was standing there, shirtless and sweaty. Carla was in the kitchen. I could smell food aromas so I assumed we were going to eat dinner soon. Eddie Sr. told me to take the boys upstairs and clean up and get ready for dinner. I did not get a good look at Carla, but I saw what appeared to be blood splatter on the wall near the staircase. I felt a tinge of fear, since I knew that Eddie Sr. had given her a beating because of what she had done to me. He still had to leave for his job, so she would find a way to retaliate. Such was my life.

We washed up and then Eddie Sr. called us down to eat. We obediently filed into the kitchen and stood by the table. We were not permitted to sit before the adults. So, we stood watching Carla's back. She was at the stove putting food onto plates. She put Eddie's plate in front of him.

She then went to the cabinet and took out newspapers and walked into the living room. She placed the newspapers on the floor. A roach scattered from its paper haven and scampered under the couch. This house had so many roaches. She then went to the kitchen and one by one placed our plates on the newspapers. She ordered us to sit. We did. This was where we had our meals until the day we left; on the floor in the living room. She did not look at me, but I could see she had a black eye and a swollen and busted lip. I did not feel sorry for her; I assumed the consolation for her beating was that we no longer were permitted to eat at a table like humans.

So be it, at least we were given food.

Carla avoided me like the plague. She would bark orders meant for me to my brothers. I was good with the silent treatment and I actively stayed out of her way. Eddie Sr. would try to mend our relationship by having me do extra chores in the house, to prove my usefulness. The one weird thing that Eddie Sr. told me I had to do every night was to give her a kiss on the check and tell her good night. I was tempted to fight this command, it was like kissing my enemy and I was lying. I had no affection for this woman and I did not want her to have a good night, but I did what I needed to do to survive. My brothers followed suit and it seemed like my brother Eddie was becoming more and more fond of Carla. He had even started calling her mom. I started to dislike him even more because I felt betrayed.

Carla was "motherly" with the boys and she would do for them and not me. I had a lot of resentment towards them for accepting her kindness, but I could not blame them. They were little and did not have the strength to resist her. I think being nice to the boys was also her way of staying in Eddie Sr.'s good graces; after all, Eddie was his biological son. I felt more and more isolated. I still cared for my brothers, but I was excluded from any affection, activities, and human connection. Carla would buy them ice cream have them eat it in front of me. Everyone was served before me. My brothers would get new clothes; I was taken to the city closet…sometimes. I was given all the chores and denied privileges. Carla hit me less, but I would still get an occasional slap or hit upside the head with a shoe, brush, once a lamp for moving too slowly or being too loud. My punishments morphed into low level torture such as being forced to kneel on dried rice in the corner or standing in the corner on one foot, or standing with my hands held above my head for hours. I had to be careful when I put my arms or leg down for rest, because if Carla saw me out of position, she'd up the discomfort level by adding time and weights. I spent a lot of time in the corner, while other children, including my brothers played around me and outside. I got good occupying my corner time by developing stories out of the shapes created from the texture on the wall. Similar to how people cloud gazed and find shapes; I'd wall gaze and see shapes and make up stories. I got very used to being isolated and lonely, so much so that it was very difficult for me to relate to most people.

We were enrolled in school. I found such solace in going to school. I loved learning. Since I was academically more advanced than my first-grade class; I was given an IQ test. Based on my life circumstances, it was difficult for the school to believe I was so smart. The results of the test proved that I had an above average, way above average intelligence. So, did Lam. Eddie hated school and was becoming more and more disruptive each day, so he was put into special classes. Lam was also put in special classes, not because he wasn't smart, but because he refused to talk. When I asked him why he only talked to me and Eddie, he said that he had nothing to say to anyone else. Made sense to me.

I did not get to go the school for the gifted and talented, rather a specialized teacher pulled me often from class. Some dumb school person thought if I learned to be "normal" I would adjust better to society. I kept to myself and I did not respond well to my teachers. I felt like a science experiment when the special teacher came. She gave me all sorts of tests. Sometimes I was defiant and would tear them up. This prompted her to refer me to the school psychiatrist. He took a special interest in me and wanted to do art therapy. I would purposely draw or paint disturbing pictures, just to see how he would react. I found it funny watching him mull over my red scribbles trying to find their meaning. He would ask me what they meant, but I would say, "You're the shrink, you tell me." This usually caused him to end our sessions.

In the classroom, I would do what was asked of me, without comment or emotion. I did not smile, play, engage or ask a lot of questions. If I did not understand something, I would read more and figure it out. My teacher felt my lack of engagement was problematic and called my caseworker several times. My CPS caseworker visited me at school to see what my issue was. I refused to talk to her. I would have another one in a few weeks; caseworkers did not stick around. She left our meeting frustrated. She must have shared her concerns with Carla, because when I got home from school that day, I was greeted with a slap and told to stop making trouble for everyone. She was told to start taking me to see a psychiatrist outside the school; which angered her because now more people were going to "be in our business." The message here for me was to keep my mouth shut in therapy; which I did. I refused to talk to the psychiatrist and I stopped talking even more so at school. I would still do runs in the neighborhood for Star, but beyond that I limited my interactions with most people. I did not say anything or ask questions. I did not learn names and anytime someone slipped me a tip, which was often, I would take it and hide it in my snow boot lining so I would have money the day I decided to run away.

We were evicted from the townhouse and moved to another house in Montebello. We had to change schools, again. The house was a one-story with a full basement. I was put in the basement. I did not mind, since I had found comfort in isolation. Carla did her best to isolate me and my brothers were eating up her kindness. We were left home by ourselves quite a bit. When Eddie Sr. and Carla were gone, I was responsible for caring for the house and the boys. If anything went wrong, I was whipped with a belt. She stopped using the rice method, because it did not have an effect on me. I was whipped for anything; the purpose behind a whipping was unpredictable. The roaches from the previous house packed and moved with us and invited their cousins too. The house was infested with roaches. I was whipped because I was told I am not keeping the house clean enough; hence the roach problem. We received food stamps and once a month we picked up a government food box. The box contained powdered milk, rice puff cereal, wheat puff cereal, peanut butter, rice, blocked cheese, powdered potatoes, a loaf of bread, and occasionally there would be Kool-Aid packets.

One day, I went to eat wheat puff cereal with the nasty powdered milk. When I went to take a spoonful of the cereal, I noticed it was moving. It was full of roaches. I was not going to eat it, so I got up from my newspaper on the floor. Carla asked me what I was doing, I told her I was throwing the cereal away. She called me ungrateful and told me it was my fault there were roaches in the cereal. She went to retrieve her belt, hit me in the face with it, and then forced fed me (grabbed my hair, took a spoonful of the wiggly cereal and shoved the spoon in my mouth). I was made to sit on the floor and eat the entire bag of wheat puffs with roaches. I did: through tears, the pain of the abrasion the forced spoon created on the back of my mouth; and the throbbing welt on my face. Eddie Sr. was gone, of course. I went to school the next day and no one asked about the welt. I was invisible.

Carla and Eddie Sr. would have parties in the basement. I was the bartender, waitress, custodian, and sometimes entertainment. When their friends would come over it was a night full of food, booze, reefer, and for some heroine. They played music, talked shit to each other, danced, told stories, laughed, argued, fought. I learned how to play dominoes, Spades, and shoot dice at these parties. Carla liked to try and humiliate me in front of their guests. Thankfully, most of the adults would correct her. Some of the men they invited would offer money to Carla to spend time with me alone. Eddie Sr. told them, in front of me, that if any of them touched me, he would kill them. Had Eddie Sr. not stepped in on my behalf, I am sure I would have been prostituted out. Carla would do other things like make me walk naked in front of them. Most would look away, some did not.

One evening, after hours of partying, Carla told me to take a bath. I complied. After I got out of the tub, she called me to her. I wrapped the towel tightly around me and hastened to her. She told me she was going to lotion me down. There were four men in the room, Eddie Sr. was not amongst them. I stood scared and confused. She pumped the lotion into her cold, skeletal hands and demanded I come to her and drop the towel. I went numb and did what she told me. I searched the eyes of the men there and silently pleaded with them to save me. With a cigarette lingering on the corner of her mouth, Carla lathered the lotion on my emaciated, scarred body, in front of the men. I was tense and this apparently angered her because without warning, she picked up a brush that was laying on the end table next to her. She yanked my arm and commanded I bend down and rub the excessive lotion into my legs. Stiffly, I complied and when I bent over she took the handle of a brush and jammed it into my vagina. I screamed, she laughed and then slapped me, one of the men yelled at her to cover me up. He became enraged, I slumped to the floor in pain, the brush protruding from my body. I did not understand what had just happened. He picked up a throw off the couch, covered me and began beating Carla. She and I both were screaming, just for different reasons. Another man swooped me up and rushed me to the neighbor's house. He hastily told her what had happened and told her to care for me before Eddie Sr. returned. We lived in an area that the rule is to never call the police and trips to the hospital meant trouble. She removed the brush and gave me a warm Epson salt bath, a sip of whiskey and aspirin. Thankfully, the damage was not as extensive as the pain I felt. Besides Carla getting a beating and me being treated with home remedies, nothing else happened. Eddie Sr. whooped up on her some more when he came home and the men told him what she had done. He pulled a gun on them and told them that they should have stopped her. He then told me to keep family business in the house.

The last time I was with the Eddie Sr. clan was when Carla hit me with a belt buckle. They had left me in charge of my brothers while they ran errands. I was given a laundry list of chores to do, so I focused my attention in getting them done. While I was cleaning, my brothers had gotten into some black shoe polish and smeared it all over the bathroom. I was busy cleaning out the oven, so I was not paying attention to them, so of course it was my fault. When they returned, I had not yet had an opportunity to clean up their mess. Carla was furious. Eddie Sr. yell at me to clean up the mess, which worsened and smeared with every attempt. Carla was livid, as Eddie Sr. left the house to get a better cleaning product. No more than one minute after he closed the front door, she called me stupid and told me to go to her room and lay on the bed for a whooping. I told her no. She went to grab me and I moved out of her reach and ran to the other side of the room. Anyone who has ever put up resistance against an ass whooping knows I was making things worse for myself, but that day I was just feeling bold. If she wanted to whoop my ass for something I did not do, she was going to have to catch me. She threw a shoe at me, I dodged and then crawled under the bed. I grabbed the corner of the bedspread and pulled it under the bed with me. For a minute, we played tug-o-war with blanket. I started rolling myself up in the blanket. I admit, this was not well thought out, but hey, it was my best solution at the time.

She grabbed the blanket, of which I was now wrapped up in, and pulled me from under the bed. She started swinging the belt. I kept moving and tried to wrap my face in the blanket. I did not feel the hits of the belt due to the blanket's padding. I refused to cry when the belt landed on my exposed foot. This infuriated

Carla. She sat on me and started punching me through the blanket. She took a pillow off the bed and covered my face. I turned my head in time, so I could keep breathing. I wiggled and bucked violently trying to get her off me. At some point, she managed to pull the blanket off me. She grabbed the belt and went to swing, buckle first. I caught the belt in mid-swing. Stalemate. She held her end, I held mine. This was not the brightest idea of mine, and honestly, I did not try to catch the belt, it just happened. However, I was now in a dilemma; do I let go or not. Either way I was going to get beat, probably as severely as I had the day I bit her. She yanked hard on the belt, pulling it out of my hand and cutting me in the process. I had no choice but to let go. She commenced to hit me with the buckle anywhere it would land. My brothers stood in the doorway and watched.

She finally stopped beating me with the belt when she had expended all her energy. Blood covered the bed. The blood was from my hand, welts, and my nose. I had only received three hits in the face, one on my ear, and a plethora on my legs and back. She told me to get up and clean up. I got up and walked to the kitchen. I walked out the back door of the kitchen, tattered and torn and ran down the street. I had made up my mind that day that I was not going to return. A neighbor intercepted me and dragged me back to the house of torture. I hated everybody at that moment, my brothers included. Eddie Sr. was pulling up to the house as I was being forced to return to my doom. He grabbed me and asked what happened. I refused to talk to him. He brought me in the house, told me to go to the basement to my room. I obeyed. I was determined to slip out in the night through the window well. There was arguing upstairs. I heard my brothers crying, I did not care. They had turned on me. Eddie came downstairs and gave me a beer and an aspirin that his dad told him to give tome. He asked me to come upstairs to eat. I refused to move from where I sat on the floor. He threw a towel at me and told me to clean up and go to bed if I was going to be a brat. When he left, I got up and went to the bathroom. I cleaned up and noted the welts on my body. My brother had become one of them.

The next day I got up and got ready for school. I refused to talk or eat breakfast. Carla reminded me that family business stays in the house. I ignored her. I walked my brothers to school. The welts on my face were faint, but there was several slashes and welts on my back where the buckle had removed skin. My brothers and I walked in silence. They tried to make small talk with me, they had joined the enemy so I refused to speak. Lam cried. I did not care, I was not going to return to that house again, this I was sure of. If I was made to go back, I had decided to set the house on fire. At school, I went straight to class and sat at my table.

My first-grade teacher, Mrs. Adams, always started class with vocabulary. I thought it ironic that her name was Mrs. Adams and she worked at Adams Elementary. That morning, she asked the class to come sit on the talking circle in front of the chalkboard. I followed her instructions.

The vocabulary word for the day was "fear." Each student was to go around and say, in a complete sentence, what they feared. I usually did not participate, but I saw this as an opportunity to escape Carla. Each student said their fears: spiders, darkness, dogs, snakes, and the such. When it was my turn, the teacher skipped me, as was custom, and asked the student next to me. I raised my hand.

"I want to share what I'm afraid of." My teacher was surprised and delighted that I was participating, voluntarily.

"Oh, yes! Soul, please share."

I stood up, walked towards the chalkboard, turned and faced the waiting faces on the talking circle. "I am afraid of the woman who makes me call her mom, Carla."

"Soul, why are you afraid of her?" The concern in my teacher's voice was sincere and full of anticipation.

"I am afraid of her because of this," I turned around and pulled my shirt up over my back so the whole class could see my welts, bruises and cuts. There was a collective gasp from the students and teacher. I slowly lowered my shirt and walked back to my position on the floor.

Everyone sat in silence for what seemed like eternity. A girl started crying, I thought that was a bit extreme, but it jolted my teacher into action. She picked up the classroom phone and called someone to come to the classroom. Shortly afterwards, a counselor came to the room. My teacher and she chatted outside the classroom. The kids were coming up to me asking me if I was OK, I said I was not. I did not like the attention. The counselor asked me to come with her to the nurse's office. The nurse looked over my body and called the police and my CPS caseworker. I stayed late at the school that day while the adults figured out what to do. I had no clue why it took so many people to help me leave the clutches of Carla, I was becoming impatient. My brothers were sitting in another room, unbeknownst to me. The officer came to me and told me he was taking me to an emergency shelter. He escorted me to his car, where my brothers were already waiting in the back seat. No one told me much, except that my caseworker would follow us. As he drove, I realized we were being taken to Carla's house. I started screaming not to take me. My brothers started crying. The officer assured me I would not stay, he and my caseworker wanted to pick up some of my things. When we arrived at the house, I refused to get out of the car. Gratefully, the officer did not insist. My caseworker went into the house with the officer and my brothers. After some time, the caseworker and the officer came out with a black trash bag and without my brothers. The bag had my clothes. I was leaving; my brothers were staying for now. I left in the back of the police car, my clothes in a trash bag, alone. I was taken to an assessment center for children. In the counselor's office, I spilled the beans on everything I had experienced in the home. I was examined by a doctor because of the violent insertion of the brush into my vagina. Damage had been done, but it was not detrimental. My wounds and bruises were treated. I was given a McDonald's happy meal, which I thought was funny because even though I was not with Carla, I was not happy. Actually, I was angry at myself because my big mouth caused me to be separated from my brothers. I battled myself and lost. I had failed my siblings; first my sister, now my brothers.

After I was assessed and given the not so happy meal, I was taken to an emergency shelter for children. I was given a bed in a room with other unwanted, unloved, discarded and broken children. The facility was sterile, but there was an attempt to make the place kid friendly.

However, I did care how bright a room was painted, or how vibrant and cheerful the murals of happy kids doing happy things were, nothing can make a facility for societies' juvenile remnants feel like home. The playground was nice; the people were nice enough. They had sad eyes, but spoke sweetly and softly. It was as if I was in a purgatory meant for children who should have been aborted, but were brought into the world to remind everyone else that their lives did not suck as bad as they thought. Hey, everyone has a purpose in life so I was told.

5

I stayed at the center for a week. It was a short-term placement. I sat in a corner most of the time and read books. They
had a lot of kiddy books like the entire <u>Dick and Jane</u> series,
<u>Curious</u> <u>George</u> and the <u>Bernstein Bears</u>. Reading these books
insulted my intelligence. I found some National Geographic magazines and read all of them cover to cover. I also found a dictionary,
which I started reading. I met with a counselor and a therapist, but
since I refused to talk and sat in their offices and just read, there
was not much they could do for me. I did not trust adults because
it seemed like anytime that I talked to them, something negative
happened. I was not an expert in deductive reasoning, but I figured the best thing for me was to keep my mouth shut. I did ask
when I was going to see my brothers, but I was just told it would
be soon. Soon never happened.

I was placed in a temporary foster home. My caseworker called
it an emergency placement; which meant that I could be there one
day, but not more than one month. I did not even bother to learn
the foster parents' names. They were a nice white family. They took
in foster children because God called them too. I was convinced he
dialed the wrong number because I did not fit in at all. They did not
really know how to relate to me and I did not make it easy either.
They had children of their own. They made fun of my hair and told
me I was the color of dirt. One of the sons had the other kids in the

house try to hold me down and pee in my mouth. They thought it was funny watching me squirm and try to fight them off. The foster mother heard the commotion and found them holding me down. They immediately backed off and let me go. She inquired as to what was going on and they told them we were playing. I said nothing, got up, and ran out the house. I refused to come back in. My case-worker was called and I was sent to another emergency foster home, then another, and then another.

I was heading into second grade and since I was in an honors program, I was placed back at a school for gifted and talented students. So, despite my many placements, I found some stability in school. Towards the end of my second-grade year I was sent to stay at a group home for girls. The home was run by an older black woman who had up to six girls at a time. I was the youngest. We lived off Martin Luther King Boulevard, I was familiar with this area. I had walked these streets many of nights with my mother and brothers. I did not go to the same school as the other girls, as I was bussed to the school for gifted and talented. This became a sore spot for some of the girls in the house. They said I acted "bougie and stuck up." The other kids in the neighborhood called us the Adam's family and they were always mindful to perform the song from the show "The Adam's Family." I got into my share of fights in the neighborhood because that theme song infuriated me. I was taunted quite a bit. Here I was a biracial child, with a Hispanic last name, in a predominantly Black community, and I went to a "white" school. I identified as black, but I was not accepted by the blacks in the area. I also spoke formal English; which made me a target. I had street smarts, but I was a book-worm, so my vocabulary superseded the colloquial language of the hood. I was called whitewashed, which were fighting words. I did not develop a sisterhood with the other girls in the group home and since I found solace in solitude, I did not engage with them much. For some reason, this pissed them off and they would call me names and do hateful shit to me. I was the youngest, thinnest in frame, and I did not have anyone to advocate for me. Many of the girls had been at the home for several years, so they had a close relationship with the foster parent, who they called "momma." I formally addressed her, when and if I addressed her at all. She was not my mother, I did not want affection from her, and it was not my choice to be in the home. It was an expectation that the girls would give her a kiss on the cheek every night before going to bed. (This must be a black thing because it was the same expectation from Carla and Ms. Pearl) I did not participate. I was indifferent towards her, for I knew, based on my experiences up to this point that I would leave, so there was no need to invest emotion into her. She also did dumb shit that annoyed me like giving me three sheets of toilet paper to use for the entire day. If I needed more, which I always did, she'd make me kiss her on the cheek. I started stealing toilet paper at school because I was not going to beg to wipe my ass. The one thing that I enjoyed doing was tending to her garden, which was impressive. In the garden, I found peace.

In that area, many of the houses had gardens. The houses had alleys behind them. The yards were enclosed with chain-link fences so you could see into everyone's backyard. My foster parent, Ms. Baker had the best garden filled with snap peas, watermelon, collard and mustard greens, tomatoes, strawberries, assorted peppers, squash and two corn stalks. I had most of the chores in the house, but my favorite was the garden. I enjoyed snapping peas during harvest too. Many of the neighbors envied her garden, so I would be commissioned out to work their gardens. I was paid with candy, piano lessons, great stories, and time away from the other girls. This angered the girls. They would do things and blame them on me like walking on the greens or leaving the water hose on to flood the yard. I would get punished by being made to stay in the bed on the weekends. I did not mind, because Ms. Baker would let me read. She would make me get up on Sundays to go to church. I hated going to church. These were not good people, but they sure did put on a show on Sunday.

The girls wanted me removed from the home. I did not fit in, nor did I attempt to fit in, and they expressed disgust over the fact that I was smarter than them. Our foster mother would attend Wednesday evening bible study every week, so we were left at the house alone. They took one such evening to exact revenge on me for being different. I shared a room with four other girls and, on one evening, after I did my chores, I sat on my bed with a book. They were outside in front of the house. I could hear their voices, but I did not, nor did I care what they were talking about. I was engrossed in my book when I heard them come into the house. There seemed to be some debating and I heard one girl said, "Leave me out of this." They whispered amongst themselves for a bit and I heard the front door close again. I continued reading, but I had an eerie feeling something bad was about to happen. I had learned to trust that feeling. My ears were tuned into high intensity mode, as I was trying to hear what they were plotting, because that is how I felt, they were up to something. Three of the girls came into the room. They ranged in age from fourteen to sixteen, I was eight. I remained on my bed, looking at the book; no longer reading. One of the girls came up to me and stood directly in front of me. I kept my head down. Another girl walked around my bed, positioning herself behind me. I braced myself. The one behind me pulled my hair, the one in front punched me in the face. A pillow case was put over my head and I fought with all my might, grabbing, scratching, kicking, hitting blindly. The girls dragged me to the floor and I could hear them telling each other to hurry up. Someone grabbed my legs, punched me in the stomach and started trying to remove my pants. My screams were muffled by the pillowcase. The more I struggled the harder the hits, but I was determined not to have my pants pulled off; visions of Carla and the brush bombarded my mind. I fought for my life that day. The girls could not get my pants off, so someone took the pillowcase off my face and above me was an exposed vagina. I was panicking and struggling. The oldest grabbed me by the neck and I felt a sharp point on my throat. She had a knife. She told me to lick the vagina or she was going to cut my throat. I spat in her face and told her to cut my throat. She pressed the knife firmer, I did not budge. The other girl, who apparently was left outside to be the lookout, ran into the room and said, "What the fuck are you all doing?!? Momma's coming down the block!" The girl that was standing over me moved quickly and put on her clothes. My legs were let go and the one with the knife held it in front of my face and told me that if I said anything, she would kill me. She got up, showed the knife to me again as if that was her proof she would be good on her word. I wished that the knife had slit my throat.

I got up and sat back on my bed. I hurt physically, but I was emotionally destroyed. I refused to cry and I had decided I was just going to lay down and pretend to be asleep so I did not have to engage with Ms. Baker. When she came into the house, I heard the girls tell her I was sleeping. They also tried to cover their actions and said I had left the house without permission and was jumped, so if she saw bruises in the morning that was why. I laid there, listened to their lies, heard her call me a trouble maker, and prayed that God take me in my sleep. I was done.

Ms. Baker came into the room later that evening. I was instructed to get up and eat some dinner. I told her that I was not hungry. She sternly told me she was not asking me, rather telling me. I did not want to sit at a dinner table and pretend to be okay with what had occurred earlier. I knew I had a bruise on my face where I was punched. My head hurt from where my hair was pulled and I could still feel, not only the hand on my throat, but the point of the knife. I could not understand what I had done to these girls that was so atrocious that I warranted the violence and the possible sexual assault from them. This was a sign that my time at this group home had come to an end, because if I stayed any longer I vowed to kill all the girls in their sleep. When I sat up, Ms. Baker commented on the bruise on my face to the effect of if I go looking for trouble, trouble will find me. Whatever. I got up and saw that she was holding the roll of toilet paper I had stashed in my moonboots. She called me a thief, I was, and she took the roll. It was dumb, but I was in no mood to plead my case for more toilet paper that I stole from school out of necessity, due to her stupid three sheets a day rule. I went to the kitchen where the other girls were already seated at the table. The knife welder looked at me meaningfully, as if to remind me to be quiet. The others avoided eye contact. Cowards. I sat down to a dinner of fried pork chops, collard greens, rice with brown gravy and hot water cornbread. I sat down and fixated my eyes on my plate. Ms. Baker had one of the girls say grace, this sickened me more. In that moment, God was a joke, non-existent and sinners' permission slips to be hateful because he always forgives. I sat there, looked through my food, refused to eat. My foster mother told me to eat about ten times. The girls chimed in that I should eat. The more they insisted I eat, the angrier and more defiant I became. I sat, fuming in silence. I longed for a dark closet, that I could crawl into and forget this world existed.

"You will not get from this table until you eat your food. Ungrateful, unbelievable!" Ms. Baker admonished.

"Then I will be sitting her until I die or you can just call my caseworker and have her come get me," I mumbled.

"I ain't calling nobody and you better stop sassing me before I wash your mouth out." She said this as the others continued to converse as if nothing had happened.

"You will not touch me!" I hissed.

"Lord, the devil has taken over this child. I pray the blood of Jesus on you."

"Keep your Lord and his blood Ms. Baker. You should cast the devil out of these girls." I stared intensely in my plate, so I did not see their reaction. Silence blanketed the room.

Everyone finished their food and cleaned up around me. Ms. Baker was getting frustrated and told me if I did not start eating she would force feed me.

"You will not touch me," I warned her.

After the girls had finished cleaning the kitchen around me, they must have started to feel guilty because they asked Ms. Baker to just let me go to bed, I was obviously not feeling well. I snapped. I yelled that I was not feeling well because of what they had done. I told everything, took my plate of food and threw it across the kitchen. I stood up with such fury, they were stunned to silence. I turned to Ms. Baker and told her I was not going to sleep in that room tonight with these dogs and if she wanted to call my caseworker do it now. I also screamed that if she even thought about touching me I would be the last person she touched. Without waiting for her response, I stormed out. She turned and looked at the girls and their truth was unveiled by the look on their faces. She followed me and in a more compassionate tone told me to go to the extra bedroom in the basement and she would call my caseworker in the morning. I went to the linen closet, took out a trash bag, went to the room where I was accosted and put all my belongings in the bag. This was familiar and my possessions still fit in my makeshift suitcase. I stomped through the house, down the stairs to my mausoleum. There was a sparsely furnished guest room in the basement. I placed my belongings on the floor, sat on the macramé blanket and sobbed. I could hear footsteps and voices above. The basement was well insulted and the sounds were muted, so I had no idea what was being said or going on upstairs and I really did not care. As long as everyone left me alone, I was good. Ms. Baker came down the stairs about an hour later with another plate of food. She placed it on the nightstand and left without a word. I ate in peace.

Ms. Baker did not call my caseworker the next day. She would most likely lose her license if the state found out what happened in her group home and that meant her income would be in jeopardy. She tried to appease me by allowing me to only have the chores of working the garden and keeping the basement clean. She let me use as much toilet paper as I wanted and I ate all my meals in my room. I did not have to interact with the other girls and she allowed me to stop going to church. Instead, I worked in other people's gardens or cleaned some elderly peoples' homes. This went on for about two months.

As summer approached, I met my new caseworker. She was nice and naïve. She set up visitation with my brothers and informed me that my mother's parental rights were going to be terminated. She asked me if I wanted to go to court. I told her no, I had not seen my mother in years, why start now. I was happy to see my brothers, who had been removed from Eddie Sr.'s home and placed together at a children's home called Myron Stratton Home for Children. I was glad for this. Our visit together was awkward. I still felt like I had failed them. I knew they had some behavior problems and were doing poorly in school. I felt like it was my fault, but at this point what was I to do? I loved them, but did not know them anymore. We were all surviving the best way we knew how. My new caseworker came to Ms. Baker's house to do a site visit.

She asked me why I slept in the basement. I told her in a rather nonchalant way and was removed the next day. I went back to the emergency shelter, had another examination, and asked to talk to a therapist, again. This started to look like a movie on repeat. I was even given the same bed I had occupied before. The magazines were the same, with a few new additions. I read them. I was placed in a few temporary foster homes throughout the summer and into my third-grade year.

I turned nine and no one celebrated. My caseworker came to the foster home I was staying at and told me she had found a permanent home for me. She was really excited and told me I would love the family. She told me I would move to Colorado Springs and there was a good chance that I could be adopted. I had mixed emotions. My brothers were already in The Springs, so visitation would be easier. I did not want to be adopted. Truthfully, I did not really understand what that meant, but it sounded horrible. I did not have a choice regardless, so I packed my trash bag and left for my next foster home.

6

We pulled up to the suburban house on the corner of a tidy street in a tidy neighborhood. This was by far the nicest house I had seen and I was curious why rich people would want a foster child. I knew time would reveal to me the truth behind the kindness, because in my world kindness always has an alternative motive. My caseworker, was beaming with youthfulness and accomplishment. I believe she thought she had finally found my forever home. I was a stray and now I could stop wandering around with no place to go. We walked past the beautifully manicured lawn towards the eerily inviting stairs. I had a very uneasy feeling in my stomach and I just knew that looks were deceiving, but my caseworker's jubilation was a bit influential. If she trusted these people, I had to keep an open mind. Closed heart always, open mind for sanity's sake. She rang the doorbell and I heard a very pleasant chime. The door opened and I stood, holding my trash bag, wide-eyed and waiting. I was shocked. The person that opened the door was a black woman. Her husband, I presumed, was standing next to her as were their children, as son and a daughter. I could not believe that black people lived in this house. I was prepared for a white family. All the black foster homes I had been in were in poor, inner city, and usually older black women. Here was the Cosby family and I was going to stay here. My brain was stuck and I could not move. My caseworker nudged me and grabbed my bag. I did not want to stay here. I wanted to go back to Denver. They were perfect, too perfect, and I did not fit in here. She nudged me again and gave an apologetic grin to the waiting family.

I walked into house and stood by the door. The woman reached out to hug me. I put out my hand for a shake. They were gawking at me like I was an exotic zoo animal and I was trying to look sophisticated. I had never seen a house this nice and I did not know the etiquette around rich people. I was introduced to each member of the family; Mr. and Mrs. Bane, their daughter Kay, and their son Virgil. Kay shook my hand and took me to the room she and I were going to share.

The room was decorated girly, with matching comforters on the twin beds. It looked like a room from a magazine and Kay pointed to my half of the closet and told me to start putting my clothes away. I did as I was told, and I was surprised she helped. While I was putting my meager belongings away, my caseworker, Mary, was talking to Mr. and Mrs. Bane. Mrs. Bane called me downstairs to say goodbye to Mary. We hugged and I had a fleeting moment when I wanted to run after here. Something about these people made me uneasy, but determined to make a good impression, for Mary's sake. I liked her and knew she really cared for me. It must be an exhausting job keeping up with me and finding me nice places to live. After Mary drove off, I returned to the room to finish the task I had started.

Mrs. Bane came into the room to talk to me.

"You may call me Mrs. Bane or mom. I prefer mom."

"OK, I call everyone mom." This was a lie and I do not know why I said that, however, from that day forward I called them mom and dad.

Mr. Bane was in the Army, so he was gone quite a bit. He was kind, very kind to me. I learned from him that they decided to become foster parents after a presentation at their church. Great, here we go with the church business. I did not believe in church, but I knew how to fake it, so I did. Kay was older than me; Virgil was younger. Both were adopted and their relationships with Mrs. Bane were different. She seemed to favor Virgil. Mr. Bane was the glue that held the family together and Kay was obviously his heart.

Kay was tall and slender. Her beautiful roasted chestnut skin was flawless. She looked like a black Barbie doll to me. The only anomaly to her beauty were her big eyes that were amplified by her coke-bottle glasses. She was articulate and moved gracefully. She told me she had asked for a sister, that was why I was chosen. I struggled relating to her because she seemed to have everything, while I had nothing. One thing that was for sure, she loved her dad more than anything. Their relationship was foreign to me, so I was fascinated to watch them interact. She was a daddy's girl and I could tell that Mrs. Bane had issues with that. Virgil, on the other hand, was a momma's boy. In Mrs. Bane's eyes, he could do nothing wrong, so he was very mischievous. He was a mean-spirited boy. His small, beady eyes were mirrors into a dark, little soul. I did not connect with him. I had my own brothers and did not want another. I did my best to keep a respectful distance from him. While I was pleasant to him, I treated him with a coolness. I became his primary care taker when Mr. and Mrs. Bane were not home. Kay was somewhat of a wild child. She broke rules all the time and I just kept my mouth shut. I, again, did most of the chores in the house, took care of the youngest, and played the role of the grateful, unwanted foster child.

Mr. Bane was a handsome man. When he smiled, which was not often, he could light up a room. He appeared strong and solid and he carried himself with an air of authority. His wife on the other hand did not match him. She was tall, plump, and had the worst foot odor. She had a Jheri curl which left her always looking greasy and slimy. Mrs. Bane, too, had a darkness about her, I guess that is where Virgil got it from. I did not trust her niceness.

Mrs. Bane was hateful. I do not know what it is about me that makes women hate me, but they do. She was not as physically abusive as my birth mother or Carla, but she did hit me, twice she drew blood. She was more emotionally, psychologically, and spiritually abusive. She made me feel like I did not belong. The best thing about her is that she supported education and encouraged me to read. Other than that, she treated me like a servant. She hated being a mother and did not have a nurturing bone in her body. Her only agreed to adopt children, because her husband wanted children and threatened to end the marriage if they did not.

Kay and my room was across from Mr. Bane's and hers. When she would come home from work, she would go straight to her room and get in bed to watch television. If I happened to walk by and glance into her room, she would say it was because I was trying to see if she was having sex. She was crazy and I wondered why she agreed to foster me, besides having a live-in servant and someone to whom she could spew her hateful rhetoric.

The first Christmas I spent with them came only a month after I moved in. She came into my room very early in the morning. She and I were the only ones awake. She told me she expected the house to be spotless before everyone else got up. Here I am, nine-years-old, up at four in the morning, cleaning. I did not expect any presents and while everyone else opened theirs, she had me cleaning the bathrooms. This is just one example of how she made me feel less than the others. Kay and Vigil ran away a few times, I was blamed. She would threaten to have me removed from the home nearly weekly, if not daily. I had learned to become numb and emotionless. She talked about my skin color, my body, my hair. I was a straight A student, but she called me retarded because I did not socialize with the other kids at school.

I was made to be responsible for getting Virgil to school in the morning. He had issues and would fight me every day. Mr. Bane was not much help, because he escaped her dictatorial rule by engulfing himself into military duty. I believe that many of the times he told us he was "down field" he really was just using that as an excuse to leave for extended periods of time. Being in the military was his happy place. She was a miserable person and made everyone around her miserable. She treated me like shit in the name of Jesus.

Beside the emotional, verbal, and occasional physical abuse, what I hated the most about this façade of a happy family was the spiritual abuse. We went to a Missionary Baptist Church. All. The. Fucking. Time. Often, I was made to stand in front of the congregation and told to testify on how good God had been to me. I was to testify how God delivered me and how blessed I was to have my new family. I did not feel that God was good and that he delivered me from one evil only to drop me off on another evil doorstep. I loathed church, because everyone was a hypocrite and Mrs. Bane would act humbly and sanctified at church and then pull her horns out at home.

Church was a farce to me and I learned so much about human behavior and interactions watching and listening to the lies people, in the cloak of religion, told. I was made fun of because I was not black enough, since I did not have rhythm and would be off when the choir rocked side to side during a selection. I cannot sing; not black enough. My mother was a prostitute; I needed deliverance. I forgot a bible verse; Satan had conquered my mind. Seriously, it was all full of shit. I did not have peace of heart, mind or soul. Religion and God were used to vindicate my foster mother's vindictive behavior towards me. I was good at playing the game, though, which I think made Kay resent me. She was always true to herself. I was jealous.

Mrs. Bane insisted we be involved in every aspect of the church. We went to church four days a week. Sundays were an all-day event: we went to 8:00 service, devotion, 11:00 service, after service fellowship, and evening service. Often when we got home from evening service, we sat in front of the television and watched Charles Stanley. We were required to take notes and then we would discuss the Word. Monday was choir rehearsal and Tuesday was youth choir rehearsal of which I was forced to join. I cannot sing, but the squeal I made sounded alto, so that's the section I was placed in. There were usher board meetings, Wednesday night

Bible study, Saturday programs and planning committee meetings. We stayed in church and the devil was always a welcome guest. Church and God was the focus of my foster parents, but neither lived the teachings. They were unhappy people. At the young age of nine, I equated God with misery.

Being involved in the church gave them clout. He was one of the ministers. I still do not get how all that works, but in the Baptist community the louder you whoop and holler and if you can shame and convict people, you are ordained a minister. She was the wife, which gave her a certain power that only she knew about. Really, I think being a Missionary Baptist preacher's wife was just justification for wearing ridiculous big hates that block the view of the pulpit.

Having a foster child also made her look like she was a God-fearing, angelic Christian woman. Lies. She had me involved in everything because it was her proof that she was saving the soul of a feral child. I testified when told to, shook hands with well-meaning people, I even "gave my life to God" three times and was baptized twice. Anything to make her leave me alone. I did not smile though, at home, school, or church. I did not find life to be joyful and even though I would get in trouble for not smiling, I refused to lie on that aspect.

I hated being in the choir. I did not fit in and I did not believe what I was being made to sing. Singing songs about Jesus fixing stuff and God's eye being on sparrows were meaningless to me. If this elusive God care so much about a little bird, how had he forgotten about me and allowed my life to be full of such desolation. Believing in a deity that was born of a virgin, only to die so mankind can have salvation and grace sounded stupid to me. Why not just create goodness? I played the charade of church, because it was the path of least resistance. I was good at playing church and the more church I played the firmer my conviction became that it was all design to keep stupid people obedient.

My foster mother insisted I sing a solo in the choir. I was mortified, as was the other choir members. My inability to sing was not a secret. In the mass of the choir I would mouth the words; lip singing gospel music was my specialty. The choir director tried to persuade her that my strength was in the chorus, not as a soloist. She insisted and since she got to wear the big hats, I was forced to learn a solo. I learned the words, but just like you cannot make a fish live outside of water, no matter how much I practiced I simply could not carry a tune. Really, if it was a life and death situation, I would have been executed. For three weeks, I practiced the solo with the youth choir. I felt bad for everyone who had to endure my voice. I think my foster mother wanted me to sing in front of the congregation to humiliate me. That or she wanted to gain brownie points for trying to get the savage child words of praise. Either way, I needed out of this situation.

It was Youth Sunday and everyone loved supporting the youth. The church was packed. I stressed all morning. On the other selections, I mouthed the words. During the prayers, I prayed that the church would catch on fire or that if God was really returning, this would be a really good time to show up and end the world. My song was scheduled to be sung right before the pastor was to preach. My mind raced and I had to think of a way to get out of it; nothing. The pianist started playing the chords introducing the song. The choir director motioned for the choir to stand. I stood in unison with them and she motioned for me to go to the microphone that was near the piano. Walking with laden legs I made my way to the front. The selection began with the choir singing. I could hear their doubt in my abilities by how loudly they sang, like they were trying to drown me out before I began. The moment had arrived for my solo. I HAD to get out of this, so I did the first thing that came to mind: I faked the holy ghost. I started jumping, then shouted "Hallelujah" and "Thank you Jesus." I spread my arms wide and walked the fine line of looking like I was dancing at a rock concert or was having a seizure. Either way the whole damn congregation was "touched" by the spirit and erupted into praise and shouting. I was incredulous. I knew I had faked the holy ghost, so I looked around and wondered how many others were putting on a show too. Some people gathered around me and started fanning me and praising God for using me. I took some time to calm down. It all was really stupid to me. My suspicions that all this was a mockery was confirmed, but hey, I got out of singing and I received a lot of affirmations for letting the Lord use me. Mrs. Bane was proud and she received the pats on the back she needed to confirm she was a super Christian for bringing this poor lost sheep into the fold. That was the first time I was taken to a sit-down restaurant. We went to Olive Garden. The jubilation of the sham quickly subsided when she made fun of me because I did not know I was supposed to place napkin in my lap.

I stayed in this foster home the longest. I learned how to deal and keep my mouth shut. I never told my caseworker, who I would see maybe three times a year, how dejected I was or about any of the abuse I experienced. My foster mother was good about making sure I was dressed in a pretty dress, hair nicely combed and sitting properly when my case worker arrived. She was an expert con artist. Others saw her as a kind woman. The kids in the household and her husband knew the truth; but, sometimes it was just easier to play along with the madness. I learned to relish any kindness Mr. Bane showed me and to expect her to try to sabotage anything positive in my little world. The day my mother's parental rights were terminated, my foster mother went to court. When she came to the house, she told me that my mother arrived late, had an attitude with the judge and said she did not want my brothers, only me. My foster mother told me that the only reason my mother wanted me was so she could prostitute me out, after all, I had a whore's body. I accepted the news that legally my mother no longer was attached to me, even though I had not seen her. There were times in that time frame from when she abandoned us to her rights being terminated that visitations were scheduled. She never showed up. The one time I remember that she met us in a parking lot of a Pizza Hut, she was with her pimp, so I was not allowed to go with her. She had a big pink teddy bear that she was carrying. My foster mother took it from her, I was made to stay in the car. I was given the bear, but as soon as we got home, my foster mother cut it up and threw it away. She made a comment that the devil was dwelling within.

My days at this foster home were limited, I could feel it. I wished often to die in my sleep. I was tired of being treated less than human or when treated with kindness it was only for the benefit of someone else. My breaking point began with watermelon. My room had been moved to the basement, after Kay had run-away and returned yet again. I was fine with the basement, it was comforting to be alone and I could read uninterrupted. One day, I was in the kitchen cleaning. I had just been scolded because the vacuum lines on the carpet in the family room were not even, so I had to re-vacuum the room. My foster mother left with Kay to go shopping. I was not allowed to go; I was not really a part of the family. Mr. Bane and I were home alone. After I had finished cleaning the house, he made me lunch. I sat at the table and saw him cutting watermelon. I was not allowed to ask for anything, but since my foster mother was gone, I felt bold and asked for a slice of the melon. Initially he told me no because I should not ask for anything. Then, as if our little secret, he sliced me a huge piece. I was elated and full of gratitude. I took a bite of the fruit and was greeted with a sour, mushy taste. I made a face and he asked me what was wrong. I told him that the watermelon was sour. He told me I was being ungrateful and I had a choice: either eat what I had asked for or he was going to tell his wife I wasted food. I weighed my choices and decided to eat the rotten melon. I put salt on it to make it more palatable and held my nose to swallow it. I gagged a few times, and through almost shed tears I finished the enormous slice. I asked to be excused. As I was getting up from the table, he took a slice for himself. He bit into in and said, "You were right, this is spoiled." Really? He made me eat it with threats of getting into trouble with my foster mother. I felt nauseous and asked if I could go lay down, since I was finished with my chores. He must have felt sorry for me, since he messed up, and granted me permission. I went to my room in the basement and got under my covers. I really felt like throwing up, the sour watermelon was churning in my stomach. I started sweating cramping. I still had chores to do, so I figured I would resume as soon as the nausea subsided.

This is what I got for asking for something. Lesson learned. I curled up into a fetal position and dozed off.

I was jolted out of my sleep by being slapped. I woke with a startle and for a minute I did not know where I was. Mrs. Bane was standing over me, looking furious. I sat up, but was overcome with a feeling of nausea. My mind was searching for what I had done to her to cause her to hit me in my sleep. I felt sick.

"Why in the hell are in you in bed in the middle of the day? You lazy, ungrateful little bitch!" She hissed.

"I do not feel well," I weakly uttered, while keeping my eyes downcast. I feebly told her that Mr. Bane gave me permission to lay down. She yanked me by my shirt out of the bed and drug me to the next room. I was so confused and I was doing all I could not to vomit. She told me to stand up. I felt weak. I knew if I stood I would vomit and that would enrage her. She kicked me and told me that I had no right to sleep in the middle of day because my chores were not done. I did not understand what she was talking about. I frantically looked around the room to find my omission. The vacuum lines were straight and even; I dusted everything; the well window was clean and streak free. I did not discover my error. She pointed to the planetarium that I had placed on the wicker chair so I could vacuum underneath it. I had not put it back. I did not understand why this caused so much fury. I started to walk to get the planetarium off the chair, but she stopped me with a slap. That slap ensued a wave of nausea, as if it had brought the spoiled watermelon from the depths of my stomach. I turned, ran around her to the bathroom just in time to expel the rancid red fruit from my stomach. She followed behind me. I reeked and heaved mercilessly. I was sweaty and clammy. The cramps forced all the contents of my stomach and bile from the core of my being. Mrs. Bane went to my room, got my bible, and started hitting me with it. She began yelling that she was rebuking the devil in the name of Jesus. She acted as if I was undergoing an exorcism. There was no demon leaving my soul, just rotten watermelon, but she turned it into something else. Once the contents of my body were flushed down the toilet, feebly I stood and went to the sink to rinse my mouth. I was so weak and mentally drained. My foster mother told me that I vomited red because Satan possessed my soul and through her grace and prayer that he left my body. I did not respond; I could not find the words to respond to her insanity. She then told me to strip naked. Hesitantly, I complied, though I had no idea what she was about to do. A part of me did not care and hoped that whatever it was would end my life. I was just shamed for throwing up spoiled watermelon. Life was hopeless.

I stripped down, as directed. I was twelve, in the sixth-grade and was budding. I was physically more developed than most of the girls my age; somehow, I did not feel that it was under my control. My foster mother told me to look at my naked body in the mirror. I did not want to. She grabbed my face and forcibly held it so I could get a good view of myself in the mirror. I looked.

She said, "You see your body? It is a body of a Jezebel, a filthy whore. That is why God purged you today." She grabbed my left nipple and twisted it hard. I cried out in pain, she told me to get on my knees so we could pray. I was defeated. I submitted to my knees she prayed and asked God to forgive me. I prayed that God would strike the bitch down with boils that oozed flesh-eating acid. I knelt in the claustrophobic basement bathroom on the cold tile; pains and threats of more violent vomiting tickling my stomach, naked and asking for forgiveness for being born. After the prayer session, I was told to clean the bathroom, take a shower, then go to bed. I was to go without dinner that night, apparently, I did not deserve it, since I wasted food by vomiting out the watermelon. I was glad when she left. I was sure she would find something else to mess with me about, but for the meantime I was granted the peace of solitude.

I started cleaning the bathroom and a typhoon of nausea swept over me. I had nothing left in my stomach to contribute to the toilet bowl, but I reeked and hacked uncontrollably. I tried hard to keep it as quiet as possible, so Mrs. Bane would not need to find a reason to punish me with prayer again. I laid on the floor, naked, smelling of a weird combination of bleach and vomit. The floor felt good, it was cool. I relished the cool touch on my feverish body. I drifted off to sleep in front of the toilet. I woke when I heard the creaky floorboard on the second floor. I jumped with a start, but my head hurt so bad, the pounding made me feel dizzy and I felt the room spin. Nausea surfaced and I prayed to the porcelain god again. I turned the shower on and crawled, literally, into the stale and laid on the floor, feeling the warm water massage my body. I imagined for a moment, that I was laying in waterfall on a remote island. I fell asleep in the shower. Having been poisoned by a watermelon and then being subjected to verbal and emotional abuse was quite draining. I woke when I was being pulled out of the shower, by my hair, by the beast. She was anger that I used too much water. My showers were only allowed to last three minutes. According to her, I had the water running for ten minutes, which is a crime punishable by beating and bible reading. So, I was dragged to my room, choked, given the book of Proverbs to read, and sentenced to remain in bed until she gave me permission to get up. I was told she would quiz me on my readings, so I best read and commit to memory. After I dressed in my nightgown, I was well received by my bed. I opened the bible, feeling sick not from the watermelon, but from the hypocrisy of my foster mother, my life, religion. I read the first chapter of Proverbs from the New King James Version. Chapter 1, verses 8 and 9 reads:

"My son, hear the instruction of your father, and do not forsake the law of your mother; for they will be a graceful ornament on your head, and chains about your neck."

Well, she chose the bible passage wisely, because she definitely was a chain about my neck and I was sinking to the bottom of life's ocean. Feeling hopeless is like walking in a desert without protection from the sun and only one cup of water to last a hundred-day journey.

Needless to say, to this day I do not consume watermelon. I do not like the smell of watermelon regardless of the form. Watermelon candy, drinks, candles, scented markers, scratch-n-sniff stickers, alcohol infused, flavored tobacco, I don't care. That fretful slice of watermelon was the last watermelon I will eat in my lifetime. I have been told that I need to move on; I have, does not mean that I need to march on the behalf of the plight of watermelons around the world. Silly as it may seem, that day in the bathroom, vomiting watermelon, being forced to face my nakedness, and then forced to read the bible, sealed my fate and molded my perception on religion, womanhood, my place on this earth. Fuck watermelon and fuck being told I was less than because of my lineage. When I woke from sleeping off the effects of the whole ordeal; I sat in bed and read the entire book of Proverbs. I committed most of it to memory and I understood that in order to win this war I was in was to use the weapon of wisdom and understanding to take down my enemies. I guess I could use watermelons as cannons and hit the bitch in the head, but then I would have to smell it as it splattered. Not worth it. I started planning, at twelve, my exit plan from the foster care system, from abuse, from feeling like I do not matter, from hating myself, from caring what others thought or said to me. Watermelon turned me into a scholar and a mason. I would read everything, learn everything, and I would build a wall of protection around me that was impenetrable.

From that day forward, I went to school with only one intention in mind; learn it all. The more I knew, the more I could fight back the ignorance that surrounded me. My sixth-grade year changed my life and watermelon started the change.

6

My sixth-grade teacher was Mrs. Cottman. She was the first black teacher I had had, so I was a little fascinated by her, though I never let her know. She had tiny moles all over her face and freckles. She also wore a short natural afro. On her desk was a picture of her family. Her husband was white, which really sparked my inquisitive mind. I was the only black student in the class, this is something I was used to, but I had never seen a black woman married to a white man. I was used to seeing black men with other women, so Mrs. Cottman was an anomaly. She appeared articulate and smart, so I vowed to watch and learn as much as I could from her, without her knowing it of course.

I took my normal place in the classroom; in the back. She had a seating chart on the first day of school. Based on my last name, I was supposed to sit somewhere in the middle of the rows.

That was not going to happen. There was no way I was going to sit with people in front, to the sides, and behind me. So, I sat in the back, in the last seat in the last row. I kept my hands in my lap, head bowed, and sealed my lips. My quiet defiance did not go unnoticed and Mrs. Cottman came and stood next to me. She asked me to get up and move to the desk she had assigned to me. I ignored her and staged a sit in like I had read in the encyclopedia. Since she didn't have any dogs to sic on me or a baton to beat me, I figured she would leave me alone. She didn't. She repeated her expectation for me to move to the desk she had assigned me. I anchored myself to the chair, pulled out a pencil that I started chewing on. I do not know why I chose to chew on the pencil, I guess I figured it made me look tough, hell I don't know, but it made her walk away. I could feel the entire class looking at me and in my mind's eye I was flipping them all the middle finger. Mind your fucking business is what I wanted to yell, but if I looked up, it would mean I loss.

Mrs. Cottman moved the seating chart around in a such a way that it left me with no one in front or to the sides of me. I think she thought she was punishing me by isolating me even more, all she did was play into my plot to be left alone. Our sixth-grade class was self-contained. Only GT and students were supposed to be in the class, that's what she told us anyways. Mrs. Cottman taught us all our subjects; except for the ancillary courses like music, art, and PE. After the class was settled into their seats, she went to the front of the classroom and formally introduced herself to us. She was a Colorado native, met her husband in college, had one daughter who was in college. She loved dogs and had a been teaching for ages. She stated she has rules and expectations and promised that we would be smarter, better read, more advanced writers and problem solvers. She then asked us to stand and introduce ourselves to the class. She asked that we project our voices, introduce ourselves with authority, and make eye contact with the class.

She wanted us to tell the class our name, talk about our family, and say one fun thing we had done in the summer. As she was giving her directions, I decided I was not going to participate. I don't care about these people, they don't care about me, and I did not come here to get to know people, only to learn. Besides, who knew how long I would be here. I seriously doubted I would last with the Banes another year, so with an exit plan in mind, I decided that when it was my turn to talk, I would remain in my statuesque state.

I thought we were going to introduce ourselves in order. Instead, Mrs. Cottman had a can with popsicle sticks in it. Our names were already on the sticks and she pulled them randomly. As students' names were called, they were docile and introduced themselves and gave their little monologue about themselves. She called my name and the entire class turned to look at me. I refused to succumb to the pressure of the eye gazers, so I sat with my head down, staring into my lap. Mrs. Cottman called my name again. I ignored her. She walked towards my desk. I kept my head down, and as she stood next to me, I focused on her ashy ankles. Surely, she could afford lotion, so maybe if she paid more attention to her ashy-ness and less on me, she would not be walking around looking like her feet lost a battle with a powdered donut.

She knelt close to me and whispered in my ear, "I will leave when you introduce yourself, otherwise, I will stand here all day." Dammit! She won, because I did not want her standing next to me.

I stood up, walked to the front of the room, looked at the cabinet in the back and said, "My name is Soul and I don't have a family. The funniest thing I did this summer was get beat."

I did not wait for a reaction and walked briskly back to my desk and scowled at Mrs.

Cottman. She was now the one looking down. That's what she gets. The room sat in silence for a minute, then she pulled another popsicle stick. After everyone had introduced themselves, she passed out a reading list of 100 books that we were encouraged to read for the year. She explained that we would get points for each book we read and we would get points if, while reading, we come across a vocabulary or spelling words. The points could be used to purchase different reinforcers. I was inspired to read all 100 books and to get the most points, not because I wanted any of the prizes, but because I wanted to be better than everyone else. Our first assignment of sixth-grade was to get a public library card. This annoyed me because I knew my foster parents were not going to take me to get a library card, let alone, actually take me to a library to use. I did not know how tell Mrs. Cottman this. The other issue was that I did not know of a public library nearby. I needed the address and directions, because I did not mind walking to one or taking the bus, I just needed to know where to go. I was determined to figure it out, without getting too many adults involved.

At morning recess, I stood along the wall. We had a morning and afternoon recess and I looked forward to both. I did not play with the other kids, even though I was good at tetherball and four-square. I was not vested in making friends. I loved recess because I could read, uninterrupted. So, as I stood on the wall, reading a paperback I took off of the bookshelf in the classroom, Mrs. Cottman approached me. Why can't she just leave me alone? She asked me what I was reading, I turned the cover of the book towards her to read. She then asked me to look at her, I did. She asked me what I meant when I introduced myself about being beat. I just looked at her. Surely, she is not stupid and knew exactly what I meant. I was used to teachers not taking notice of me and now here this woman would not leave me alone. I just stared past her and thankfully she got the hint and meandered across the playground to supervise the other students. I had won another battle.

I went home a bit defeated that day because I did not know how to ask for someone to take me to get a library card. I followed my usual routine of picking up my foster brother from school, cleaning the house, and watching him until my foster mother came home from work. We were not allowed to watch TV during the school week, so I read the book I had taken from Mrs.

Cottman's class. When my foster mother came home, I was required to go to my room in the basement and wait until called for dinner, if they remembered to call me. It was a Monday, so we were going to go to church for adult choir rehearsal. I was only allowed to read the bible in church, which I did not mind as it kept people from talking to me and it made the adults feel good about themselves. On the ride to church, my foster mother asked me how school was. I told her it was good. She did not ask any more questions. I sat in the back seat of the car, a bit nervous, because I had to tell her I had a homework assignment of getting my public library card. I did not want to hear whatever was going to be the verbal lashing I was sure I would get for asking for something. I played a mind trick with myself and told myself that I would ask my foster mother about the library card if and only if I counted ten yellow cars on the way to the church. As silly as it sounds, I fooled myself into believing that if I did not count that many yellow cars, then God did not want me to ask. Crazy, I know, but fear was very much a part of my existence and I would do almost anything to avoid my foster mother's wrath, which came at some of the most unexpected times for some of the most unexpected and unwarranted reasons.

Dammit all to hell if I did not count ten yellow cars on the way to the church. I waited until we got into the church, figuring I needed some divine intervention and guidance. I was not allowed to look her directly in the eyes, she felt it was not in a child's place to look adults in the eyes, some old backwoods logic. She looked at me and asked what did I want. I waited until another church member was standing next to her and I told her that I was being required to get a library card. I could tell I annoyed her because I put her on the spot. She simply shrugged her shoulders and told me that the school has a library and I need to use that one. If the teacher had a problem with that she could go get me a library card herself. I acknowledged that I understood and scurried to the pews and grabbed a bible.

The next day, I timidly entered class, sat in my self-assigned seat and opened up my book.

Mrs. Cottman was at the door greeting the other students. She did not speak to me when I entered and I was fine with that. As I was sitting there, I took out a piece of paper and wrote what my foster mother said and placed in on her chair, so she would not miss the note. Class commenced and I watched her as she walked to her desk, briefly read the note, and folded it and gingerly placed it back on her chair. I thought that was odd, but at least she now knows why I will not have a public library card. Morning recess rolled around, I went to my spot along the wall with my book. No one bothered me. When we returned to class there was an envelope on my desk. I looked around to see who put it there and based on the eloquent way my name was in cursive on the front, I assumed it was Mrs. Cottman. I opened the envelope and inside was a public library card with my name on it and written directions to the one nearest to the school. I felt myself getting emotional and I wanted to cry. However, crying is a sign of weakness. Mrs. Cottman watched me from across the room. We made eye contact, I mouthed thank you and then walked out of the classroom to the bathroom. I have no clue why I was so emotional, I felt like she had given me a gift and it confused me. What did she want from me? Why was she being nice? I did not feel worthy of the library card because I had refused to sit where she told me. There had to be an alternative motive. So I sat in the bathroom stall and pondered a little library card.

Mrs. Cottman sent a student to come get me. I had to put my game face back on, but I also needed to tell her thank you for it was the right thing to do. So, during the afternoon recess, I walked uneasily towards my teacher and in a low, nearly inaudible whisper I told her thank you. She did not bat an eye, look at me or overreact. She stood there, like a statue of an ancient African queen, and told me to read everything I can. She said that when you feel like you've learned all you can, learn some more. She then walked away from me, leaving me to marinate in her wisdom. I softened, a little bit, that moment. I felt a tinge of humanity. I was going to learn from this woman; I wanted to be her—regal, intelligent, strong. I had found a role model.

She carried herself with such authority and grace that I was mesmerized watching her move about the classroom. I had not really warmed up to the class. I didn't take the time to learn any of their names. I was warming up to Mrs. Cottman though. She challenged me to be a better, smarter, more humanized every day. I did not have many things to be happy about in life. Here I was a sixth-grade student, with no real family, my brothers displaced in other foster homes, my sister long gone, lonely, to some—worthless, and this teacher inspired me to learn more; to become and not simply overcome. I secretly wanted to make her proud of me, so I read. I read every book I could get ahold of. I read dictionaries, encyclopedia's, microfiche film, newspapers, magazines, books of every genre. I tried to use newly acquired words into my everyday speech. I wanted to sound smart. Mrs. Cottman had this ruler that she would hold against our backs when we were sitting in our desks. Her expectation was that you sit straight. She told us that slumping prohibited the blood from properly flowing to our brains, thus we would not be able to think, so we would be dumb. The entire class sat straight. If you slumped she would walk by with the ruler as a reminder to sit with your spine in a straight line. She inspired me to walk and sit straight. It looked smart.

She made learning easy. We were expected to memorize a lot. If you were asked to recite the factors of thirteen up to twenty, you better do so in less than one minute. You were penalized for not memorizing everything. However, Mrs. Cottman made memorizing fun and rewarding. She taught us tricks and simplified concepts to the point it almost made you feel stupid that you struggled learning the concept in the first place. I didn't talk a lot in class, but she always made sure that when I did speak I was listened to. She allowed me to choose if I wanted to work by myself or in groups. I always chose by myself and enjoyed being able to produce a product better by myself than a group of idiots.

One of my favorite things about Mrs. Cottman's class was that she rewarded us for being smart. Learning was celebrated and it was contagious. The point system created a friendly class competition. Our points for learning were our bragging rights. I would pout if I looked at the board and saw that I was in any position but number one, which was rarely, but it did happen. It was the other kids in the class mission to take me down. That made me work harder and read more. Whomever had the most points at the end of the week, Mrs. Cottman would let them choose a king sized candy bar. Since I was not allowed to have candy in my foster home, the weekly candy bar was a delicatessen for me. I savored that candy bar every week, so I read so much to make sure I was on top. To this day when I eat a Hershey's Bar with Almonds I think of this wonderful lady. She had other rewards like lunch with a friend or lunch with the teacher. I always chose the candy bar. If I could, I'd go back and chose lunch with the teacher at least once. I think I missed out on some wisdom.

I usually finished my work early. Our agreement was that if I finished my work earlier than the rest of the class, she would check it, and if it has no errors I could read my book until she addressed the class again. I worked quickly and with great accuracy on all of my assignments so I could read. One day she was teaching math. I already understood the concept and I felt she was belaboring its explanation. If these dummies don't understand by now, then would never get it was all I could think. I zoned her out and started reading my book. I was so engrossed in reading my book that I did not hear her call me name. Apparently she had called my name several times, but the book had my full attention. She stepped to my desk and slapped it with her ruler. My attention quickly shifted and fear rose in my heart. I thought she was about to hit me. My heart started beating quickly, I was searching for my exit route, and scoped the room for any potential weapon. That shit freaked me out. She held out her hand. I was confused. I focused finally on what she was saying. She was telling me to hand my book over. I froze. Had she lost her damn mind. I am not giving her my book. I had not finished reading it. She repeated her demand. The entire class was looking at me and I could feel my anxiety building. I practiced my breathing exercise the therapist taught me. I clutched my book and quietly told her no. Giving her that book was like giving up my only escape from the life I was living. I could not be free of its grasp until I had completed it. She grabbed the book from my hand and told me to pay attention. She slowly walked to her desk and put my book on it. I was so angry and hurt. She was one of them. All this time I believed this saintly woman had been cast from the heavens. She had ruined my allusion of her. I hated her, in that moment. She had threatened my world. I know it seems silly to be upset over something so simple, but when you have nothing, whatever I was reading gave me something. It gave me adventure, comic relief, normalcy. All that was now sitting on Mrs. Cottman's desk.

I did not know what possessed her to snatch my book out of my hand and then place it on her desk, in front of the whole class. It was not going to fly with me. I had this eternal rage of being fed the fuck up and was tired of people bullying me. I wanted, with all my might, to slam my fist into her face. The only thing that stopped me was the slight notion I had some measure of respect for her. I understood that this was a test of hers and the measure of my worth would be based on how I responded to her blatant disrespect. So, I bit my tongue, literally, and lowered my eyes. I swallowed my pride and I controlled my impulse to react. I had learned to control myself. I was proud of myself. I did not show my delight, but I felt it on the inside. I, with the help of the artful skill of Mrs. Cottman, had learned to tame my inner beast. I sat in my desk, paid attention to the lesson, and learned something new. At the end of class, Mrs. Cottman approached me and handed me my book. She did not say a word, nor did I. I took my book and quickly left. I read the rest of that book that night.

Such was my relationship with Mrs. Cottman. She was a hardcore teacher, that had a strong silent love for her students. At least I know I felt it. She respected the boundaries I had placed on our relationship, yet she would push my boundaries if I needed to learn a lesson. I grew as a person my sixth-grade year. One day, she gave the class and entire English period to read a book of our choice. I was elated. I had calculated that with an hour of time,

I could finish the current book I was reading and start a new one. I read with vigor and soaked in the story. I was reading <u>The Secret Garden</u> by Frances Hodgson Burnett. I had transformed into Mary Lennox and was engulfed in my adventures on the moor. I was startled by Mrs. Cottman walking next to my desk and putting a yellow Post-It note on it. It was folded in half. I stepped out of the novel and nervously opened the note. I was quickly thinking about what the note contained and if I had been doing something wrong. I unfolded the note and read: "Thank you for smiling." There was a smiley face in the bottom right corner. I was stressed out. I was analyzing a million things as to when, where, why I was smiling. I did not remember smiling. I had nothing to smile about. The only thing I could conclude was that when I was reading I smiled at something in the book. A whole other panic began. I tried to figure out why Mrs. Cottman was looking at me. What had I done that attracted her attention and of all the kids in this class, why did she look at me? Silly what emotional conflict that simple little note spiraled me into. I sat, contemplating the note. The bell rang for afternoon recess. I walked to my usual spot on the wall with my book. I was not in a mood to read, because I was still trying to figure out the note. Mrs. Cottman came up to me on the wall and leaned next to me. She did not look at me, that was one of our silent rules. She peered straight at the playground and the field and surveyed the other students. We remained like that for about five minutes. Neither of us talking, just looking straight with so many unspoken words floating in the air. She finally lowered her head and leaned closer to me. I surprisingly did not flinch or move away. I just maintained my gaze on the monkey bars; but I eagerly awaited whatever she was preparing to say. "Soul, you have the power to write your own ticket in this world. You are smart and you don't owe anyone but yourself. You have to let people help you.

You don't have to do this alone. Lose the attitude or else you will miss out on great things. Keep your head up; others have it worse. And please, above all learn to smile. You lit up my day today."

She walked away and that was and would be the longest conversation she and I ever had. Once the bell rang for recess to end, it was back to business as usual. I could not focus for the remainder of the day. I had so many emotions that I was holding in because this woman had given me something so many people tried to take away. With that moment in time, those gentle yet mighty words, she gave me my humanity. She saw me for me and I was no longer the invisible girl. I no longer wanted to be. She gave me choice and power over my own life. Mrs. Cottman gave me permission to be a sixth-grader; to allow myself to find happiness as often as possible. I was changing, starting to anyways. I warily wanted to believe that I could one day be greater that my circumstances.

In this life there have been times that I understood all that my sixth-grade teacher had given me and wished I could thank her. I visited her twice when I was in seventh-grade. I moved to another foster home. Years later when I moved back to the district, I went to see her. I was told she had committed suicide. I was crushed. I did not understand how a woman who had changed so many lives and who was so beloved could be at a point in life she did not want to try anymore. I thanked her, but not enough. Yeah, my sixth-grade year taught me to hate watermelon and to love life. That simple note has pushed me through some tough times, because it makes me realize that I am only human and how I approach this life is my choice. I choose to, as much as possible, to keep smiling.

I stayed in the same foster home, just buying time, for my seventh and eighth grade year. I had become numb to the verbal and spiritual abuse. I played my role as a sweet, quiet, super doper grateful "po lil foster child" that these god fearing sanctified Jesus freaks saved from the savages of the world. So, the only thing I remember about seventh-grade is Sr. Segura, my Spanish 1 teacher. He had the coolest accent and I would practice, in the basement, talking to myself in the mirror, like him. I entertained myself quite often trying to sound like Sr. Segura. He called me "Souyana" because he said the I could not have two first names in Spanish.

He made me like Spanish and I wanted to speak fluent as soon possible. I also remember Mrs.

Fristhe. She was my honors English teacher and she made us diagram sentences for punishment. I learned the English language from her, not how to speak, obviously, but the structure of the language. She broke down the dynamics and linguistic influences on the English language. We not only had vocabulary and spelling words, but we had parts of speech quizzes all the time. If she gave you a word you better know how to not only spell it, but know its part of speech and use it correctly in a sentence. She drilled words and structure into our minds. She would bleed crimson ink all over your finest work. Nothing was ever good enough. I strived to get an A in her class and she did not make it easy, but I persevered. She helped me to better understand what I read because I better understand the use of the words. I appreciate her for that.

My home life was getting worse. I had gone on a hunger strike and refused to eat anything. I was convinced my foster mother was going to poison me. She threatened daily to call my caseworker and have me removed. I so badly wanted to yell and tell her to do it then and shut the fuck up. Instead, I stood there biting my tongue and keeping a neutral face to hide my anger and disgust of her and the whole situation. I wanted to leave. But, if I spoke up she would be pissed and refuse to call and make my life even worse. She may lie, which was quite probable. Who knows where I would end up, at least I know this crazy. So, I stood there, listened to her ridicule and threats and waited to be dismissed so I could go to my room and say to the mirror what I really want to say to this self-righteous bitch. She could say what the fuck she wanted to say. She and I both knew she wasn't going to call anyone because I was her cash cow. She got over twelve hundred dollars a month for me to live there. She needed me there to make sure the mortgage was paid. I went through the motions, contemplating daily my escape. I was empowered now to be my own person and there was only so much I was willing to take from anyone. The tides of change were rolling in. When I doubted my resolve, I would read Mrs. Cottman's note.

I left my foster home the middle of my ninth-grade year. I had finally had my breaking point after being sat on by the hippopotamus of woman and punched repeatedly in my face until I was choking on my own blood. My blood splattered across the large aquarium in the living room and after she had exhausted herself tenderizing my face, she told me to clean my mess up. The hatred I felt towards her and everyone that lived in that house nearly consumed me. I had to leave this house and these people, with or without the help of CPS. Murder was on my mind, and if I stayed it was not going to be good. I know I sound like a broken record, but words cannot adequately describe how I felt. When no one stood up for me, helped me as this beast of a woman beat me for standing up for myself against her psycho son, I felt a rage, fueled by loneliness and rejection, that blackened my soul. I had to leave. The strength of my rage was such that I loathed myself for the thoughts that circulated in my mind. So, I made my plan to escape.

I washed all of my clothes one night. I was only allowed to use the washer and dryer on certain days, but I wanted to take as much of my clothes as I could fit in my trunk. I waited until I was confident everyone was asleep and I washed and dried my clothes. I was not allowed to use the dryer; all of my clothes were dried on a clothesline. I was told I was not worth the electricity needed to dry my clothes in the machine. So, needless to say, I was both elated and nervous using the dryer. I was elated because I was breaking on of her cardinal rules, yet nervous because I feared what would happen if she found out. Once my clothes were done, I sorted through them and packed what I liked and neatly folded or hung the remaining. I washed my bed clothing and cleaned my room as if I was trying erase my existence in this bitter place. I neatly packed all of my clothing, books, personal hygiene products, journals, drawings, and my Cabbage Patch doll. All I owned in this world fit into a small trunk; yet I knew I was still more blessed than some. I dressed and gently laid on the made bed, as not to rustle up any dust in my mausoleum. I barely slept; I smelt freedom and daylight could not come soon enough.

The morning routine went on as usual. Everyone acted like they did not notice the swelling and bruising on my face. I got the measuring cup so that I could measure my cereal. We had to use the recommended serving size—nothing more. Eating more than the label recommended was denial of cereal, thus breakfast, for at least a month. I prepared my foster brother's breakfast and we sat down at the breakfast table. My foster mother came down the stairs in her white scrubs.

She looked at me with disgust, I averted my eyes so I would not portray both my hatred and my plan to leave. She spoke to everyone and listed some chores for me to do. I thought the list was exhaustive and wondered how I was going to get all of that done before she came home from work—which was the expectation. As she was walking towards the garage door, she looked at me and said, "After you drop him off at school, you need to bring your ass back home. Call me when you get back. You are not going to school today. I already called the school." I simply laughed in my mind. This stupid bitch thought she had control over me. This state-paid abuser thought she was going to keep me from going to school to hide the evidence. I replied I understood. She left. Fuck her. I turned my attention to my foster brother. The look on my face indicated that if he gave me any shit about going to school, he was going to die. I appreciated that he cooperated, because I was not looking forward to a life in prison over his dumb ass. I silently and briskly walked him to school. I dropped him off at his classroom door. I came back to the house and called my foster mother. She reminded me of my chores and told me to put ice on my face. I replied I understood. After I got off the phone, I ran downstairs and retrieved my trunk. It was heavy, but not unbearable to carry. I locked the house, put the key under the front door mat and carried my trunk to school.

I was winded and sweaty by the time I got to school. If I estimated correctly, it was about three miles from where I lived. The journey was arduous, my muscles strained and throbbed, but I relished in the thought that I would never step foot in that house again. I dragged my trunk into the front office of the school. I was late, so I had to sign in. The look on the receptionist's face was kind and when she took a mental evaluation of my face, the trunk, my resolve, she did not ask any questions. Well, actually she did ask if I wanted to leave my trunk behind her desk until after school. I managed a feeble smile, grateful I did not have to do a lot of explaining, as I was eager to go to class. I dragged the trunk behind her desk, she gave me a pass and I went to Spanish class.

Senor Segura reminded me of Don Quixote. I enjoyed listening to his accent and how he pronounced my name. Upon entering class, with my pass, he looked my face, said, "Aye, pobrecita." He handed me the quiz the class was taking and I walked to me desk. I was glad for the normalcy. I knew at some point the counselor was going to call me down. I figured that as I was taking my quiz the receptionist has contacted her and she was in the process of contacting either my foster mother or my case worker. I prayed she had enough sense to just call my case worker, since I had brought all my belongings to school. A lot of the time what I thought made sense, the adults would do opposite. Actually, many adults were diseased with stupidity. I took my quiz and felt pretty good about how I did. Spanish was interesting to me and I liked the idea of one day being bilingual. The only problem I had is that I only spoke Spanish in Spanish class, so the road to being fluent was going to take a long, long time. The bell rung to dismiss the period. I turned the quiz in and Senor Segura asked me to wait until the class cleared. Here we go. Once the last student left, he asked me if I was OK.

I replied, "Sure, it's written all over my face."

He looked sad and I know he was trying to understand what had happened, so he could help.

I really just wanted to prolong the inevitable and I simply wanted to just focus, for a while longer, on learning. He shook my hand and told me to hurry to my next class.

On my way down the hallway to my next class, my counselor called out my name. I acted as if I did not hear her and kept walking. She quickened her pace to catch up with me. I wanted to start running, but I decided not to, after all she was just trying to do her job. She called my name again and I stopped. She caught up with me and feigned surprise when she was close enough to see my face. You would have sworn I was disfigured beyond recognition by her over exasperation upon seeing me. She asked me to walk with her to her office. We walked in silence. Once in her office, which was cozy and friendly, I sat down and drew my knees up to my chest. I might as well get comfortable. I knew this was going to take some time. She sat behind her desk and I guess decided that when talking to a girl who was just abused she should be more affectionate. She got up and came and sat next to me and placed her hand on my arm. Weird. I cringed and she quickly withdrew her hand and asked if I was comfortable. I shook my head no, but she did not move. She asked me what had happened and what was in the trunk. I told her.

She got up and jotted some notes down. She offered me a pop and I gladly accepted. Truthfully, I was famished, but I was trained well not to ask for anything. She left and returned with a Pepsi and peanut butter crackers. I gratefully accepted them. She told me she was going to have to call my caseworker. I nodded that I understood the protocol. She called CPS and as anticipated, my caseworker was not in the office. She spoke to someone else. Based on what I gathered from her side of the conversation, my caseworker would be paged and I needed to be seen by the school nurse to document my injuries. We went to the school nurse, she looked me over and took some pictures. She even took pictures of the trunk, which I thought was interesting, but I'm sure that was a part of the procedures. After the nurse examined me, I was sent back to class.

Around lunch time, I received a pass to go back to the counselor's office. My caseworker was there when I arrived. We talked, I repeated the story, and I told her I was not going back. If she made me, I was going to run away. She reassured me that I was not going to be taken back, but I had to go to an assessment center, then she would try and find a temporary foster home for me in the area so I could continue going to the same school. I thought that was a nice gesture.

She left, I went back to class. She told me would pick me up after school, so when the final bell of the day rang, I went to the front office to wait for her to pick me up. I waited for what seemed like forever, but I was not impatient. I knew that I was not the only kid on her caseload, she was not expecting to have to place that day, so she was probably scrambling to find something, even probably a bed at the assessment center. When she finally came, she looked tired. I felt guilty for putting stress on her, but I knew I could not go back. She took me to McDonald's on our way to the assessment center. I enjoyed my hamburger and fries. I had been to the assessment center before and the food sucked, so if I was going to have to stay there for a few days, I needed to really enjoy this last meal.

When we got to the assessment center, I went through the check-in process. I was taken to an examination room and seen by a nurse. She looked at my face, poked here and there, took my temperature and other vitals. She asked me what had happened, I repeated the story again. I was annoyed because I figured my caseworker would have filled her in. Telling and retelling a traumatic experience, at that age anyways, was exhausting. Adults versus stupidity: stupidity won this one. After my exam I was taken to a waiting room. I grabbed a book, and settled in. It was going to be a long night.

My caseworker finally reappeared and told me that I had to stay the night at the center. So I had to go through the check in procedures and I was taken to my bed. The room was like a large, open dormitory. The beds were aligned in two rows. My assigned bed was towards the back. I took inventory of the other kids that were in this CPS purgatory, waiting like puppies at a pet store for someone to take them home. There was a lot of anger, loneliness, rejection, and fear in that room. Kids in the foster care system in a situation like this are like prisoners. Strange alliances are formed, you have to scope out who will be a threat and eliminate it as soon as possible. Crying, regardless of how scared you are, is a sign of weakness. I put on my "don't fuck with me face" walked to my bed and sat down. A direct care worker came to me and welcomed me. I did not acknowledge the welcome, because I was sizing her up to. Sometimes these direct care workers are vicious and I needed to assess what level of threat she posed as well as if she had the allegiances of any other the clients. I got really bad vibes from her. I asked where my things were. She told me there were checked in and that I was only allowed to have the hygiene supplied provided in my care package and a change of clothes. I demanded to see my stuff. This annoyed her, I did not care. All I had in this world was in my trunk and I knew that theft ran high in places like this. She told me she was not going to take me so I got up and started walking to the door. She grabbed my arm and told me to sit back down until she gave me permission to move. In front of the other kids I told her to get her hands off me and if she ever touched me again I was going to rip her fucking face off. She radioed for assistance. Two big men came to the room. I stood my ground and demanded to see my caseworker or their supervisors. They told me to sit down, I told them I would after I saw my truck. I had mentally prepared myself for a restraint. I yelled that they did not have the right to touch me and if they did I would press charges. To be honest, I had become hysterical. All I wanted was to see my stuff. I could not, at that time, rationalize why that was so import-ant to me, but it was and I felt panicky because they were keeping my things from me. One of the men told me if I calmed down, he would take me, but I had to come back here and I could not bring it to the room. The woman was pissed, I rolled my eyes at here and calmly walked with the man to the storage room where everyone who had been admitted stuff resided. I saw my trunk in the middle of the floor with my name and identification number on it. I went to it, touched it, then opened it. I took inventory of the contents and found a picture of my brothers. I also took out my journal. I had a lot to write about and needed to write to keep myself calm. I was confident I made the right choice to leave the foster home, I anticipated having to stay at the center, I did not realize the emotional attachment I had to the things in this trunk until I was told I couldn't have it with me. Crazy the things that are important to us in this meager life during times of desperation. I closed the trunk, gathered the picture and my journal and walked compliantly back to the hall of beds.

I refused to eat dinner. I refused to watch TV in the common area. I refused to acknowledge the female direct care worker's existence. I refused to talk to any of the other kids there. I was not here to socialize, I was in this holding cell until my caseworker found a placement, or I figured how and to where I was going to run away. I laid on my bed, more like a cot, and tuned the world out as I stared at the picture of my brothers. I had to make it out of this place and make something of myself for them. I had to be better because they deserved better. Tears started trickling down the sides of my face and wetted my hair. I felt exhausted and lonely. I picked up my journal and started writing. The more I wrote, the more I cried, the more I stared at my brothers, frozen in time, looking forlorn and lost. I had to go to the bathroom, so I placed their picture in my journal as a book mark. I placed that under my pillow and went to the bathroom. I was gone for no more than five minutes.

When I came back into the room, the other kids were snickering, but avoided looking at me. I glanced at my bed and saw that my journal and the picture of my brothers was torn and strewn all over the bed. I looked around to identify the vandals, but could not discern who had violated my space and who was cruel enough to destroy my brothers' picture. I was furious and hurt. I gathered the now confetti journal and picture up and put them in a pile. I walked up and down the room looking at each girl. I am sure the look on my face announced my murderous intentions. I was going to kill the bitch that destroyed my stuff, especially the picture. A heavyset girl who looked like she'd been on the streets and had to fight a lot in her life started giggling as I passed her. I stopped, asked her if she was responsible for destroying my stuff, she said she was and what was I going to do about it. Now, I could have gone and told the staff and she may or may not have received a consequence. Based on my interaction with staff earlier, I would not be surprised if they told her to destroy my stuff. I decided to serve justice myself. I walked towards her. She stood up. She towered over me, she was a big girl. I did not feel any fear; she was going to pay for touching my things. She balled her fist up and without any hesitation I punched her in the throat. When she bent over in pain, I grabbed her short hair and drove my knee into her face. She tried to grab me and she did get a few punches in as she was swinging wildly. I had full control of her hair and repeatedly kneed her in the face. Right when I was about to slam her face into the bedpost, I was grabbed from behind. I held tight to the girl's hair, and pulled harder the more whoever was behind me struggled to detangle us. I swung my head, viciously backwards, and connected with their face. I heard a yelp. I was oblivious to the other girls in the room and to the cries for help. I was blinded by anger and believed, at that moment, I was in the right to stand up for myself and I was crazed to the point I wanted to draw blood, which I did. I was eventually wrestled away from the girl and restrained by several staff members. The knee on my neck was crushing, so I stopped resisting. I was put in an isolation room for the night, which I preferred. It took me fighting someone who had violated my space, a restraint, and a few threats of charges to be left alone. I was still anger about my stuff being shredded and

I evidently threw it in the trash. I had to see the center's counselor the next day. I refused to talk. He gave me another journal.

I waited about a week before I was placed with a temporary foster family. They were an elderly white couple who lived in a modest home, near my current school. When I left the center, I walked away without a single good-bye. Trust me, I had not made any friends during my short stay. My caseworker told me she did not know how long I would be there. I was just glad to not be in the center anymore and to get back into the routine of school. I felt I had become dumber being around all those dumb people. I actually found many of the other kids to be repulsive. My teachers indicated they were glad to have me back in school. I was given the weeks' worth of missing assignments. I went to the home, did homework, ate dinner with the family, did my chores, and stayed to myself. I knew I was buying time until the next placement. I stayed for a month and then my caseworker told me I was being transferred to a group home in Black Forest, Colorado. I had no clue where that was and I was not looking forward to living with a bunch of girls. I was 15 years old when I moved to The Landing, a group home for girls, in the boondocks of Black Forest, Colorado, also known as Skinhead Country.

I remember the drive to my new placement. I was not happy with my caseworker, so we traveled in silence. Being placed in a group home is a horrible placement for a kid who just wants to be left alone. The last time I was in a group home with girls, they tried to rape me.

Now, I was being taken to a remote place. I had no idea what to expect. On the drive to the northern side of Colorado Springs, near the Air Force Academy my caseworker told me that the home had live-in house parents and they had a daughter. There were ten girls in the home and the plan for most of them was to go back with family. I could have weekend visitations with friends, if the house parents approved. I would be attending Shady Grove High School, since 9th grade was in the high school on this side of town.

Going from the south side to the north side of Colorado Springs was like traveling to another state. The people were different, the houses looked different. It was considered the rich side of town. Colorado Springs is a military town.

The south side was mostly Army since Fort Carson was there and the north side was mainly Air Force. There is a big difference in the cultures of those two branches of military. I was more comfortable around the grunts of the army than the elitist officers of the Air Force. Shady Grove was not a very diverse school. There was diversity, do not get me wrong, but there were few of any minority group. I think in the whole school there were only maybe ten black students and that is being generous.

The Landing was nestled in the pines of Black Forest. The ride leading up to the house was not paved. One could not discern the neighbors, as all the house were on large lots of a few acres and hidden in the forest. The Landing looked like a log cabin. As we drove up the drive, I could see that there were stables behind the house and the smell of manure was thick in the air. There was a Subaru hatchback and a Suburban sitting in the driveway. The house looked like a split level. I was told the house parents and their daughter lived in the bottom half of the house. We climbed the wooden stairs and entered into an expansive living room. The main floor was surrounded on all sides by windows. There was a large fireplace in the center of the room. Stairs led up to a loft of bedrooms and a bathroom. In all the time I was at The Landing, I only went upstairs if I was ironing clothes for money. We were paid $.50 for every one of the house parents clothes we would starch and iron. I hated it, but it was a way to make some money.

I was welcomed by the house parents and the residents. I looked at them, but I was not overly excited to be there. This was a strange world and I was trying to discern who was going to be friend or foe. This was a temporary placement for many of the girls so getting close to them was out of the question. I had bad vibes about the house parents' daughter. I disliked her immediately and while I pretended on occasion to get along with her, I never trusted her and thought she was an ugly person, inside and out. The only thing I could stand to look at was her hair. She did have gorgeous hair. She was obsessed with Holstein-Friesian (black and white) cows. She had cow eyes and, well, she reminded me of a cow, especially when she ate since she chewed like she was chewing cud. Anyways, I met the group home crew and was shown my room.

My room was in the back of the house, attached to the laundry room. Being the only black girl in the group home, being made to sleep in servant quarters, and surrounded by livestock, I wanted to run away. The problem with me running away is that I promised myself for the sake of my brothers to be better so I could graduate and make enough money to care for them. I had a promise to keep so I swallowed my pride and settled in to my room. I shared a room with Monica, who eventually became like a sister to me. We had a love-hate relationship probably because we had similar personalities. She helped me adjust to group home living and really helped me to tame my temper…well, kind of. I also became very close to Elaine. She was like a younger sister to me. Besides those two, I was nice enough to everyone else and made a few friends at my new school. I joined track and got involved in DECA and FBLA. I enjoyed learning about business and I really enjoyed running. Running made me feel free. I only ran at school though, because I was afraid I would be killed in the forest by a skinhead. Being black in Black Forest, CO was not a positive. One day when I came home from track practice I was followed home, down the mile-long dirt road by a known skinhead at school, Jared. He got off the bus after me. He walked behind me for about a quarter of a mile. He then started yelling at me and calling me a monkey and a nigger. He picked up rocks and threw them at me and told me to go back to Africa. I was fuming, but I was not going to give him the satisfaction of a response. I walked faster, he walked faster. I could hear combat style boots crushing the dirt behind me. He yelled more hateful obscenities and I heard his pace quicken. I started running. He screamed for me to go back to Africa again so I stopped and turned to face him. He had a big stick in his hand.

I told him in the calmest voice I could muster, "If you want me to go back to a continent I've never been to, buy my fucking ticket you piece of shit!" I turned around and ran at full speed the rest of the way to the group home. I was furious. I came into house and went straight to my room. I slammed the door to the laundry room and went and punched my bed, wishing it was Jared's face. The house parent came in and asked what was wrong. I asked to be left alone. She didn't. I then shouted to leave me alone; I had just been harassed and followed home by Jared. She seemed to understand the depth of that statement and left the room. I stayed through dinner and group time (every night we had to sit in a circle and share our feelings). The last place I wanted to be was in a room full of white people telling me I will be OK and that I was overreacting. I might have punched them in the face. It is real easy for people to tell you how to think and feel when they are on the outside looking in on your situation. The house parent came into the room to check on me, again. I was still not in a mood to be bothered. She told me I needed to talk out my frustrations, I told her to leave me alone. I did not want to talk to a white woman about being harassed by a white boy. She told me I was being disrespectful. I told her to call my caseworker then and I'd be happy to leave. She walked away without further comment.

Such was my life at The Landing. I played nice for the most part, but I always looked for any opportunity to escape, this meant going on visitations for the weekends. All the girls, if they had family, could go home on the weekends. I was envious of this privilege because I did not have family to go home to. I had friends from my last foster home that I went to church with. Their mother liked me and offered to pick me up one weekend. I should have declined the offer.

I had a crush on my friend's brother. He knew it as I was, regretfully, transparent. I was very cautious about flirting and interacting with boys because of what I've experienced with my mother.

They picked me up for the weekend as I needed a break from the group home. I felt like a normal 15-year-old and enjoyed the movies and being around a "normal" household. School had recently started and I had entered my tenth-grade year. This was an extended weekend because of Labor Day. The weather was beautiful—crisp, sunny, and tranquil. It was the kind of weather that gives you energy and life. I felt happy. My friend's brother paid me a lot of attention. At times in the day I felt uncomfortable with how forward he was; but I did not protest. After all, I did like him, so I did not want to come off prudish. I was picked up on Friday and was going to be returned Monday afternoon so we had lots of plans.

Friday night was spent at the movies. We went to the $1.00 movie theater. As was practice, we went to the convenience store, stocked up on cheap candy and drinks and smuggled them into the theater in our hoodies. Everyone smuggled outside food in. The food at the concession stand in the theater were ridiculously expensive and the popcorn was either stale, too salty, not salty enough, or burnt. It only made sense to smuggle food in. The movie attendants knew, but they did not care. He sat next to me in the theater. I cannot remember the movie we watched, my stomach was all in knots because he was sitting next to me and he kept touching my leg. I tried to play it cool, but it was nerve wracking and confusing. On one hand I liked the attention and the light touches on my leg, on the other hand I was uncomfortable and felt vulnerable. Whatever energy I was putting out made him feel that the attention was wanted and he became bolder. I got up and went to the bathroom just to get myself under control. I wanted to go back to the group home, but I wanted to stay with my friend. Yes, I had a crush on her brother and he was showing me attention, yet I was uneasy and confused with my conflicting feelings. I took my time returning and I sat in another seat just to avoid him touching my leg. My mind was in turmoil because I did not know how to act towards him. I was running all kinds of scenarios in my head. I felt stupid for being so confused. I decided that I would play it cool towards him and be nice, but distanced myself so that I did not send mixed signals. I was so disappointed that I had gotten myself in this situation.

After the movie, he came up behind me and touched my shoulder. I felt a shockwave travel through me and I was both excited and fearful. He asked me why I had moved. I told I wanted to different view. He shrugged and grinned and told me he could not wait for the sleepover. He winked and I wanted to go home. The ride home was silent. The music was loud, the windows were rolled day. The evening was a warm and the breeze was cool. The smell of pines and leaves infused the air. It was a beautiful evening, but I sat in the car dreading the evening. I did not know how to act in this situation. I felt so lost and alone that I nearly started crying. I looked intensely at the moving scenery as we whisked by toward their house. I really wanted to hang out with my friend and escape the group home. I really liked her brother, but I felt uncomfortable around him. I felt it would be rude to ask their mother to take me back to The Landing. Black Forest was quite a way from where they lived. I would not recommend black people driving in the forest at night because of Jared and his kind. I decided to suck it up, enjoy spending time with my friend, and ignore her brother. It was just one night, I could do this. I would make up a lie, so they would have to take me back in the morning.

As soon as we got into the house my friend dragged me to her room. I was relieved. We sat in her room. She was extra cool because she had a phone in her room and she had her own number. Having more than one phone in the house was a big deal and as a teen you had arrived to adolescence if you had your own phone, let alone your own phone number. I shared a house phone with thirteen other people. I was a master at turn taking and saying what I needed to say quickly. Our phone calls at the group home were timed. That may be the reason I am so blunt today because I was trained to get-to-the-point during my stay in the group home. Anyways, she was took me into her room and we sat on her bed.

She wanted me to witness her talking to her boyfriend. She called her boyfriend, stretched out on the bed and talked—forever. She acted as if I did not exist. I sat there for forty minutes and watched her talk on the phone. She sent me on two errands: one for a pop and another for chips. Each time I ran her errands I would glimpse her brother sitting on the couch in the living room, watching television. He would look at me and smile. I would scurry back to her room with the requested item and continued sitting there as she talked to her boyfriend. I started to get real annoyed and really wished to go home. I mouthed to her that I wanted to go home. She rolled her eyes at me and said she would be off the phone in one minute. Fifteen minutes later, she was still on the phone. I got up and went to sit in the living room. I was so angry that she agreed to have me spend the night at her house and all she did was ignore me. I sat on the recliner. It was the seat furthest from her brother on the couch. He asked me what was wrong. I said nothing, but I wanted to go home. He asked me why, I told him that I did not come all the way here to sit and watch his sister on the phone. He got up and walked past me without saying anything. He went down the hallway. I could hear him say his mom's name a couple of times. I then heard him tell her I wanted to go home. I could not hear what she said, but I heard him say "OK." I then heard him open another door. He yelled at his sister to hang up the phone, that she was being rude to her guest. She yelled back she was sorry, but she needed to finish her conversation and then she would right out. He walked back into the living room. He stood over me and said that his mom said she's too tired to drive, but she'll take me back first thing in the morning. He suggested we start watching a movie on the VHS, until his sister could join us. I agreed. He invited me to sit on the couch, so I could stretch out. I do not know why, but I did. I was attracted to him, but I was not going to cross any boundaries. He gave me a light blanket. I took it and covered myself after I placed a couch pillow next to me. I know it sounds stupid, but at that moment that was all I could think of to be my defense against him. He made me uneasy, but I was trying to play it off. I felt trapped, so I wanted to make the best of it. We sat and watched the movie. I cannot remember the movie, but I remember it was funny. We laughed and he would occasionally touch my arm that was leaning on the pillow dividing us. He paused the movie and went to the kitchen to pop popcorn. They had the popcorn machine you plugged up—again the latest in technology. I took the opportunity to check in on my friend to see why she had not come into the living room yet. I slowly opened the door. She was laying on her bed asleep. I walked over to her and nudged her. She grunted something unintelligent and rolled over. She repositioned her body and was back to sleep. I was disappointed and angry. I did not understand why she wanted me to come here and then treat me as if I am not. I turned off her lamp, walked out the door gently closing the door behind me. Her brother was still in the kitchen. The popcorn had just begun to pop and the aroma was buttery and earthy. I knew that this would be the last time I talked to her. I wanted to leave, but I had no one to pick me up. I walked into the kitchen and got a Pepsi. He told me to cheer up and asked what was up with his sister. I told him that she was asleep. He responded, "Good!" and the hair on the back of my neck stood up.

He was being nice to me, I was attracted to him, yet he crept me out on a subliminal level. I walked back to the sofa and sat down. I watched him in the kitchen through the serving window. He was handsome and had an appeal that was magnetic; however, he was a bit sinister. He finished making the popcorn and brought the bowl of fluffy goodness and handed it to me. He walked away and went down the hallway. I could hear him open and closing doors. He called his mom and sister's names. I could not hear any responses. He walked back to the living room and sat next to me on the couch. He picked up the pillow I was using as a barrier and tossed it to the other side of the couch. He said he did not want us to get butter on it, I sensed that was not necessarily true. He sat next to me, I did not move. I was frozen with excitement and fear. I was still navigating puberty and though I am an avid reader, I did not read anything about how to act in a situation where your feelings are conflicting. The battle between lust and instinct had begun. He grabbed the bowl out of my hand and said he wanted to hold it. I sat, frozen, for reasons I did not understand. He had started the next movie and I blindly watched. Colors danced before my eyes and sounds funneled into my ears. I was occupied with my feelings. His sitting next to me sparked a tingle in my gut that started the butterfly effect throughout the rest of my body. I had not experienced this sensation before and it was exciting. I desired him, in what way I did not know, but I felt drawn. I also had a very loud voice in my head yelling to go to bed. I felt an urge to run away from him. I got up and excused myself. I went to the bathroom to get my composure. I needed to figure out a way to go home tonight. My intuition was frantically telling me that I needed to leave. I would leave as soon as the movie was over. I would call a cab and have it drive me to Black Forest, if they went that far. I walked out of the bathroom, comfortable with my plan. I opened the door of the bathroom and he was standing right there. I yelped and he put his hand over my mouth. I panicked. My brain was not computing and I heard him say he was sorry he did not mean to scare me. I calmed down and inched past him. He walked behind me and pulled me into the kitchen. He pushed me towards the corner in the kitchen, the one area that could not be seen from the living room or the hallway. He must have felt my muscles tense because he told me to relax. I could not think. He put his hands on my waist and told me he has been waiting all day to have me. My thoughts were a jumbled mess and I felt like cry-ing. He leaned over and kissed me on my cheek. I mini explosion occurred inside of my loins, my inner voice screamed "LEAVE!" I pulled away from him and asked him if I could use the phone to call a cab. He told me I could not leave; his mom would be upset if she woke up in the morning and I was gone. I was fine with that.

He told me he would drive me home. I told him I preferred to take a cab. He stepped closer to me, reached out and grabbed my waist.

"Why do you want to leave so bad? Why take a cab?" He asked.

"I just need to leave. I came here to hang with your sister, but she basically ditched me." "Well you can use the phone to call a cab, if you insist on leaving, if you let me kiss you on those pretty lips." He was standing too close to me, way too close. I figured a peck on the lips would not hurt, so I pursed my lips. He kissed me, but not a peck like I intended. He grabbed the back of my head and forced his tongue into my mouth. I actually thought he was an alien from the show "V" and was trying to shove his reptilian tongue down my throat to feed on me. I tried to pull away, he pulled me closer to him and harder. I did not want to make a ruckus because I did not know how to explain this to his mother or sister if we should disturb them. With his free hand he shoved it up my shirt and squeezed my breast. I was mortified into immobility. I was thinking too much and needed a plan. It was difficult to develop a plan with his forceful kissing and crab crawls pinching my breast. I managed to pull away from him, but he kept control of my arms. He asked me to loosen up, that I had been flirty all day with him and he knew I wanted him. He wanted me too. I said, in a ridiculously feeble voice, that I found him attractive, but I did not want him in that way. This seemed to anger him because he snarled that I knew I wanted to have sex with him. I told him that I was a virgin and did not want to have sex with him. He softened at the word virgin and loosened his grip on my arms, but he maintained a hold. He smiled and said, "Now I understand why you're acting stuck up. I'll loosen you up. Trust me." I didn't and wanted to yell, but I was also trying to be respectful and not wake up my former friend and their mother. He pushed me up against the wall and pressed his body against mine. I wanted to cry and fight, but I did neither. He pulled me to the floor and told me to lay down. I refused and repeated that I did not want to do this. He said I did and told me that I was just scared because it was my first time. He told me to pull my pants off, I sat on the floor and pulled my legs to my chest and wrapped my arms around them. He grabbed my hand and bent it backwards, forcing me to unfold my legs. He was stronger than me, both physically and mentally. Holding my wrists with one hand, he deftly used his free hand to undo my pants and pull them down. I tried to wiggle out from underneath him, the attempt only made him stronger. He forced another kiss and kissed my neck, then my cleavage, all the while he tightly held me arms above my head. A lone tear solemnly crept down my face. He was great at multi-tasking.

As he held my arms, kissed on me, he also pulled my bottoms down past my butt. He was trying to pull them down further, but I held my knees firmly together. He clamped down on my wrist with the intent on causing pain. I winced and he licked my face. He told he to stop struggling, this is how all virgins act, and relax. I told him I did not want to do this. He said I did and pinched my nipple again. I winced in pain long enough for him to move my pants down further. He continued hard kissing me, trying to force my mouth open. I clinched my eyes and moved my head side to side, moronically still trying to be quiet as to be respectful to his mom. At some point he pulled out his penis. It repulsed me, but I did not say anything. He climbed on top of me, and sat on my midsection. Still holding my wrists in his death grip, he held his penis and began rubbing it. The tears were flowing, but I never uttered a sound. He inched back down my still closed legs. He grabbed the insides of my thighs and moved his hand towards my vagina. I do know how many times I whispered no, I obviously did not say them loud enough for him to hear, because he proceeded in taking my pants off. Once half naked, I laid on the cold, linoleum floor, slightly sticky from old grease that had spattered out of frying pans. I took advantage of him not being on me and quickly scooted up and wrapped my arms around my bent legs. He pounced on me, grabbed and yanked my knees apart. My yell was muffled under his massive hands.

Wrestling, half naked, I had moved into a position, trying to get away from him, that gave him an opportunity to jam his penis into me. The pain took my breath away. I felt like I had been torn open. I started to cry and he repositioned himself on top of me. He reinserted himself into me, this time gentler, but still with venom. His hand over my mouth limited the air I could take in and I felt light headed. I felt him, but didn't. He started pumping fast then shuddered and went limp. I was numb and my womanhood throbbed. I felt nauseous and suffocated under his weight. I nudged to get him off of me. He pulled out of me. I quickly started gathering my clothes. He grabbed my nipple and pinched hard. He asked me if I wanted more, that he usually goes longer. I told him I going home. I got off the floor and picked up my clothes and hurriedly walked to the bathroom. I made it in enough time to vomit my dignity into the toilet. I felt disgusting. I went to pee and saw the blood. I did not, at that time, understand what had happened. I felt broken and like a failure. All the Christian guilt I could muster made me believe I was a shameful fornicating sinner who must have enjoyed what had just happen because I did not fight hard enough to make it not happen. I checked to make sure the door was locked and sat on the toilet for a while, hating myself. When I came out of the bathroom he was nowhere to be seen. The lamp next to the couch was on and a larger blanket and a bed pillow where placed on the coffee table. I took this to mean this is where I would sleep. It was two o'clock in the morning and I figured I may as well sleep and leave in the morning. The worst had already happened. So I thought.

The ride back to the group home was quiet. Their mother seemed annoyed that she had to take me all the way back. She had called the group home and asked if someone could meet her halfway. No one was able to, so this put her in a bad mood. My former friend sat in the front seat saying she was so sorry for falling asleep on me. She asked me how the movie with her brother was. I sat silently and declined to respond. Her mother started jawing about respect and I tuned her and the world out. She stopped lecturing and asked me for the directions. I gave them, we drove. I asked her to drop me at the bottom of the driveway. The driveway was long and winded around the trees. I wanted some thinking time. She pulled up to the driveway and I got out with my stuff. She started pulling off as I was still closing the door. I was so lifeless and uncaring that I did not have the energy to be upset. I stepped back and watched as the car disappeared down the dirt road that lead to the paved road. I would never talk to these people again and I was happy with that. I decided that I would pretend that last night did not happen, make up a story if asked how it was, and avoid the memory at all cost. Unfortunately, the memory came knocking three months later.

I did not tell anyone about what happened that weekend. As far as anyone knows, we went to the movies, skating, and kicked it at the park. I noticed that my periods were lighter and lighter. I figured that it must be a puberty thing and was grateful that my typical cramping, bloating, and headaches had subsided. I was tired all the time, but I figured it was due to my anemia. I did not have an appetite and was losing weight. I needed to have an annual physical and the house parent wanted to make sure I told the doctor how I felt. I gave urine and blood at the doctor's appointment. My house parent and I waited in the lobby as they ran the urine test. The blood test had to be sent off site. The nurse appeared and asked us to come back to the doctor's office. That is when I was told I was pregnant.

I hated myself. I was taken to get a sonogram to determine how far along I was. The first time I am penetrated I get pregnant. I was devastated. Devastated is an understatement. I was suicidal. I no longer wanted to exist on this earth. I had to explain the whole situation to the houseparent and the sonogram confirmed I was three months pregnant. We asked about abortion, but I was too far along. I was determined not to carry the pregnancy to term. I really think I went temporarily insane. Not only did have to endure the action, I also must have that asshole's child.

I did not want it. I wanted to forget the whole experience and a baby sure was not helping. I planned to throw myself down the stairs to force a miscarriage.

My caseworker was notified and then ensued the investigation. Basically, I was made out to be a whore, after all my mother was. I was called a liar and my foster child status made me an unbelievable character. I was told I was attention seeking. I was an emotional zombie, so I was forced by my caseworker to attend therapy. I was made to go to both group therapy for pregnant teens and individual therapy. I did not want to go to either and plotted to sit in my therapies and not talk. The only thing I wanted to focus on was how to terminate the pregnancy so I could save my future. I was initially detached from the fetus growing inside of me. I wish it would miscarry, then everything could go back to normal. No such luck. In group therapy, I was an outsider. All the other pregnant teens were looking forward to being moms, for some this was their second child. In individual therapy, my therapist Joan, had me do a pros and cons list about keeping the baby. The affirmative side, to keep the baby, was very short and I knew I was not emotionally ready to be a teen parent. After a few sessions with Joan, I decided to put the baby of for adoption. It was an emotional, but the absolute best decision for both of us. My caseworker helped to screen prospective families. I interviewed three sets of prospective parents and decided on a nice black couple. They were unable to have biological children and they felt I was the answer to their prayers. So, I resolved to grow the healthiest baby I could. I did not want to know too much about the baby at my prenatal appointment, including sex. The less I knew, the easier it would be for me to relinquish my rights as this child's parent. As the birth neared closer and the baby moved more, I started to feel maternal, or at least what I thought was maternal—I cared about the future of this child. I was nervous about the actual birth, after all, I was now sixteen.

No one in my world understood me. I could stay at the group home until the birth, but I felt even more like an outsider. The girls in the home kept their distance, which was fine with me. The girls at group therapy shunned me because I chose the adoption route. My few friends at school did not know whether to be supportive or to disown me. I did not fit the stereotype of a pregnant teen. I was in all honors classes, on the Speech and Debate team, involved in clubs and track.

Most people at school did not know I was pregnant, I did a good job hiding the baby bump. Thank goodness the style of the time was baggy jeans and oversized flannels. The pregnancy was something I had to go through, but not something I had or wanted to advertise. The sooner it was over, the sooner I could move on with my life and forget that horrid night on the kitchen floor.

On a sunny day in May, I gave birth to a healthy boy. His adoptive parents were in the room when I delivered. The nurses kept me from seeing him and gave him directly to his new mom. She was overjoyed with tears and gave me a very tender hug. I was a wreck. I struggled with whether I was making the right decision. In a few days, I was scheduled to appear in court to officially relinquish my parental rights, as a sixteen-year-old mother, so the baby could be adopted. Until the court date and my signature, I was still this child's mother and I was so confused. I did not understand love, but I understood that I wanted this child to have a better life than me. Joan, my therapist came to the hospital to visit me. We reviewed the pros and cons list and I knew, after consulting with her, that a mother's love is selfless. I was not prepared, either mentally or emotionally, to be a good mother to this child. The circumstances of his conception were engraved into my mind and I did not want to go a lifetime resenting this innocent child because of what had happened to me. He went home, as a foster child, with his prospective adoptive parents three days after he was born. I went home, as a foster child, back to The Landing. Five days after giving birth, I legally relinquished my rights as his parent in family court. I wrote the baby a letter explaining my decision and gave a picture of myself to his adoptive parents. She promised me should would keep both and share with the baby when the time was appropriate. I walked out of the courtroom with my head held high, but my heart heavy and spirits low. I knew I had made the right decision; I just prayed they were amazing parents to him and they lived up to the promises they gave me to love and care for him.

I left the group home the next month. The group home closed and all the girls had to be relocated. Many went to live with family. Some of the girls went to other group homes. The group home parents were moving to Canyon City, CO. They told me I could live with them, until I decided on something else. It was the summer before my junior year in high school. I had just had a baby, given him up, and now I was being asked to make another big decision. I did not want to live with strangers and I was researching ways to emancipate. I was tired of living with strangers, tired of moving, tired of everything, so I decided to move to Cañon City the summer before my junior year.

7

Cañon City is a small prison town. The Royal Gorge, one of the world's highest suspension bridges, is in Cañon City and besides the prisons, tourism helps keep the lights on in the town. In the actual town, the main attractions were Main Street, high school football, and the local Pizza Hut. About 15,000 people called this desolate, nostalgic, All-American town home. Cañon City was the epitome of the ideal of America. When people talk about the "good ole days" of America, they are thinking of places such as this. Men and women worked hard, most only had high school diplomas. It was the norm to get married right after high school graduation and have babies soon after. If your parents worked the land, you worked the land; if your parents were prison guards, doggonit you were going to be a prison guard. The local bar was full on Friday and Saturday nights; church was full on Sundays. Everyone knew almost everyone. Football was king and Friday night lights was the weekly social event, attendance was mandatory. Cruising down Main Street was what the cool kids did in their pickup trucks after a game. Everyone ate out one day of the weekend at either the Pizza Hut or the local steak restaurant. Nearly all Cañonites were Republican and many enjoyed the benefits of government assistance. Rugged jeans, flannels, and cowboy boots was the typical dress. Being fancy was for the rich folks and the city folks who came, promptly left. It was one of those towns that nearly everyone was employed by the prison system and the only minorities in the town were locked in one of the state prisons—and me. The day we arrived to the gently used ranch, was the day I decided that my stay in this place would be limited.

I was one of three black students that attended Cañon City High School. The other two lived there because one had a parent locked up and the other had a parent who was a prison guard. I lived there because I did not have a parent. I did not talk to either of them because I did not want to be known as the "Three Blackateers" as someone so rudely shouted in the hallway on my first day of school. The laughter that boomed through the hallway was enough to make all three of us avoid each other like our lives depended on it. I mean, this town was once the home to KKKland, a fun-filled traveling carnival for your typical bible beating, hooded White Protestant supremacists. The white-rob friendly attraction no longer hoisted excited patrons on a Ferris wheel, but the sentiment of dislike of anything non-white and non-Protestant still permeated the air. The stench of hatred tarnished the fresh mountain air and wilted the beautiful Columbine flowers. Consequently, true to my defiant nature, I braided my hair and wore a leather African medallion popular in the 90s. It was my way of telling these racist assholes to go fuck themselves. Of course, this caused some to feel the need to retaliate and I was honored for my ethnic pride by some inbred that put a skinned black cat in my locker with the endearing term, "nigger" painted on the pelt—so original. I took the pelt to the vice principal's office and gingerly laid it on his desk. He feigned disappointment in the cousin-brother-uncle that broke into my locker to leave this macabre gift, and he assured me that he would find the person responsible. I had no faith. I simply told him not to worry about the perpetrator, the whole school was under my suspicions. He frowned, but knew it was true. He sent me to class with a final feeble apology.

I was used to being the only minority in the honor's classes, I was not used to being hated because I was in the class. The teachers, except for my English teacher, who became my Speech and Debate coach, acted like they resented the fact that I was not only smart, but smarter than all the sweet, lily, rosy cheek white cherubs that graced their classrooms. Most of my teachers refused to even say my name. That was cool with me. I sat in the back of the class, did my work and more, and made straight A's. They would try to challenge me so that I would fail, not possible. My foster sister, Sandy was in my honor's United States History class so I knew that the standard for admittance in the honor's classes in this redneck town were low because she was dumb. The only thing she was good at was pretending to be good and riding horses. I was intellectually offended that I was in classes with people like her. Needless to say, I excelled beyond their capabilities to teach me. I would do group projects by myself: not only were my projects done prior to the deadline, they were done so well that my teachers would show my work to the students as the example. The best way to beat racist assholes is to simply be smarter than them and to show them how intellectually inferior they were to me.

My English teacher, Mrs. Carmuchi was intrigued by me. She was impressed with my writings and my contributions to class discussions. She was also nosey. One day after class she asked me to come see her after school. I had no idea what she wanted to discuss, I mean I had the highest grade in the class so it could not be about my academics. She must have read my suspicion on my face because she told me I was not in trouble, but she had a proposal for me. I agreed to stop by after school. My foster mother was a drug and alcohol counselor at the school, so I stopped by her office to let her know I would walk to the house. She did not believe me, I did not care. I was intrigued by the invitation and I was going to see what Mrs. Carmuchi wanted. Up to this point, I hated everything about this town and she was the only teacher attempted to connect with me. She deserved me at least going and hearing her out.

When I entered her classroom after school, other students were present. I do not know why, but I felt like this was some sort of intervention. Most of the students in the classroom were seniors and for a split-second I was afraid. I know my feeling was irrational, but when you've been called a nigger and lived in a white dominant racist town, one tends to think irrational thoughts in a room full of white strangers. Mrs. Carmuchi invited me to sit down so she could explain why she had requested my presence. Each student around the table introduced themselves. They were all members of the school's National Forensics League and asked me if I would be interested in joining. My teacher had shared with them how well I wrote and thought I would be a good fit on the team. She felt that I would do well in Lincoln-Douglas debating and Poetic Interpretation. She asked the members of the team to explain the event they participated in and to show me a sample of their performance and the structure of LD debating. It was interesting. They talked about the team being a family and how the skills learned would benefit me in life. I agreed to join. In this small, rural, white-washed, racist town, I found a sense of belonging with the Speech and Debate team. Mrs. Carmuchi, like Mrs. Cottman, had seen something in me and stepped out of her comfort zone and pushed past my defensive stance to pull greatness out of me. She had earned not only my respect, but my loyalty. I vowed to be the best Lincoln-Douglas debater and Poetic Interpretation performer I could be to make her proud. She and the team gave me a sense of belonging that I had so desperately needed.

I excelled. I made friends that I would not have normally made. I came out of my defensive shell and opened myself to being a team member and supporter of this small, but incredible group of people. Mrs. Carmuchi, as many teachers were, was very interested in my "story." She and my team members formed an alliance around me and defended me against the rest of the school, including my foster parents and their cow-looking daughter. My foster mother and her daughter went on a smear campaign to make me look like I was a troubled youth that they had rescued. They tried to paint me out to be ungrateful, angry, and savage. Mrs. Carmuchi taught me to channel my frustrations into my research for the debates and my performances. It was the best therapy. I loved researching and developing arguments for different social topics. I loved pouring my emotions into the characters of the poems I interpreted. I was good, which made others uncomfortable or jealous. I did not care. Besides running track and being smart, I had found my niche at Cañon City High School. Dammit, I was going to prove my haters wrong and make Mrs. Carmuchi, my teammates, and myself proud. I did just that. I was the only student in Cañon City High School history to make it to state level competition in both Lincoln-Douglas debate and Poetic Interpretation. I made it to the second round in both, but was then eliminated. The girl who beat me in the Lincoln-Douglas debate, in my opinion, should have been disqualified for making personal attacks during our debate, but the judges, though mentioning it in their notes, gave her the win. The girl who won the Poetic Interpretation won using a Dr. Seuss poem about fish. The word "cunt" was in my poem, which offended some the judges. What can I say? They were a bunch of cunts. Regardless, I was proud of myself and my coach and teammates cheered me on. I had made school history, but my name was never mentioned in the school announcements.

Besides excelling in oration skills at school, I worked at the local Pizza Hut. Pizza Hut was the local hangout spot for many of the town residents on Friday and Saturday nights. It was packed on Fridays after a football game and full of families on Saturdays. I did it all. I took phone orders, ran the cash register, made the pizzas and served customers. It was a full-service restaurant and I was one of three waitresses that tended to the demanding needs of the patrons.

The only thing I did not do was drive deliveries and that was because I did not have a car. Also, a black girl driving and delivering pizza in a rural racist town would surely end with me on the side of a milk carton. Really. I enjoyed working at the restaurant because it kept me away from the house and all the bullshit that existed there. Also, I made really good money in tips, even though the other waitresses made more. I did not care. I stacked my cash. I planned to buy a car and to save enough money to move to Colorado Springs and rent an apartment. Yes, I was only sixteen, but I knew that my time in foster care was coming to a swift end. I could no longer tolerate living in this town. I was suffocating under the pillow of racism and hatred. I was becoming more and more bitter. I hated not having control over my destiny and as long as I was in foster care; someone else had control. My goal was to save enough money to pay six months of rent and the deposit. I also had to petition the courts to be emancipated. I knew I could do it, but it was going to take some time. So, I tolerated having patrons snap their fingers at me, call me names, make disgusting messes just because they were assholes, and working six days a week. I had only one weekday off during the week and I worked after school until close. On the weekends, I worked all day. I put all of my tips in a bucket in my room and would deposit in the bank at the end of the month. My caseworker had to cosign for my bank account, but I trusted her. I saved enough money to pay for my driver's education classes. I searched the classified every weekend until I found a car I could afford. My first car was a 1976 Toyota Celica. It was gray and rust. It had a manual transmission and the guy I bought the car from gave me a crash course in how to drive it. I drove, rather stuttered-stopped-jerked-rolled, the new car to the ranch. My foster father was sure to let me now that I had made a stupid purchase. I did not care. For $900 I had purchased my freedom from this hell hole. All I needed to do was save more money, keep earing stellar grades, and figure out the day and time I was going to leave this country bumpkin ass town.

One of my coworkers at Pizza Hut had a friend who lived in Colorado Springs. He sent him information about apartments in the Springs and said he would help me find a place to stay. I talked to my caseworker about moving away from my current placement. She was supportive, but perplexed. There simply were not any open placements to send me to. I told her I was not planning on staying with another foster family. I also informed her that I was leaving Cañon City with or without her permission. I had been practicing how to drive my new car, because I did not want to stall on the highway heading to Colorado Springs. She expressed concern, but again, showed support. I did not have it all figured out, but I knew that the day was nearing that I needed to make my escape because my hatred of my current situation was starting to consume me. The only reason I stayed as long as I did was because of my Speech and Debate team and Pizza Hut.

My relationship with my foster family was becoming more and more intense. I did not belong here. I cared for and loved Elaine, my red-headed foster sister who came with me from The Landing, but I despised everyone else. I was saddened that I would have to leave her, yet I knew it was for the best. My day of reckoning came on a Saturday. I had gotten off work early and decided to buy a new professional outfit for my brother's upcoming court date in Denver. He had gotten into some trouble and I was asked to come to court to be a character witness for him. I wanted to look professional so I grabbed $500 from my tip bucket and walked to Main Street to shop. Main Street was Cañon City's downtown and retail area. There was a cute boutique that had a mannequin displayed in the window. The suit the mannequin was wearing drew my attention and I thought it was the perfect outfit to wear to court. It was youthful, yellow, and a pants suit. I did not wear dresses or skirts, so I thought it was just right for me. I entered the boutique and immediately the sales clerk was watching me. She did not greet me, just watched me. I asked where the suit displayed in the window was. She pointed. Maybe she was a mute, I did not know, but I felt uncomfortable and I could feel she was uncomfortable with me being in the store. I walked to the rack and found the object of my desire. I was relieved to see they had the suit in my size. The clerk came from behind the counter and approached me. I thought she was going to offer me some assistance, like showing me where the fitting room was at.

I was blind-sided when she said, "You cannot afford anything in here. Woolsworth is down the street."

What?!? What about me made her think I could not afford the suit? I had $500 cash on me and I was beyond offended. I turned to her and asked, "Excuse me? What makes you think I cannot afford anything in the store?" I genuinely wanted to know.

She was obviously nervous, yet resolved to get me out of the store. I looked at the price tag.

The suit cost $150.

"Woolsworth is down the street," she reiterated.

I took the canary yellow pants suit, in my size, off the rack, walked to the counter. She looked confused as she followed behind me. I took out $200 and placed it on the counter. I tore off the price tag, placed the cash on the counter, snatched the suit and turned to her. She was red with embarrassment or anger, I could not tell nor did I care. I said, "Here is the money for the suit and a little extra for you, so YOU can take your ignorant ass to Woolsworth!" I walked out the store with the suit I no longer wanted. I threw it in the trash when I was out of sight of the store. I was furious. It was time for me to go. I walked the five miles from the boutique to the ranch on the outskirts of town. No one was home, they were at a rodeo. I packed up my few possessions, put them in my car and left. I did not leave a note, I did not call anyone, I simply left.

I did not have a plan other than to leave. I drove to Pizza Hut and talked to my manager. We had been talking about my plan to leaving Cañon City and she has already arranged for me to transfer to a store in Colorado Springs. I appreciated her help. I did not have a place to stay, so I planned to stay at a cheap hotel near the Pizza Hut I was going to work at until I figured something else out. I had about $3000 to use, so I was not worried about sleeping on the streets. At that moment, by biggest fear was driving from Cañon City to Colorado Springs on the highway with a manual transmission. I was getting better with the stick shift, but I had not quite mastered the highway. Oh well, there was no going back now. I called and left my caseworker a message. I did not want anyone to report me missing, thus triggering a search or worry. My manager let me make a pizza before I left and she gave me a 2-liter of Pepsi. She teared up as I hugged her goodbye. I promised her I would call her when I made it to the Springs and I would go directly to the Pizza Hut she had arranged for me to work at. Her kindness was touching. I wrote a note to Mrs. Carmuchi and the Speech and Debate team; she told me she would drop it off Monday morning. I hugged her again, put the pizza on the passenger seat so I could easily reach it as I drove. I confidently and quietly drove to State Highway 50, then to CO-115 towards Colorado Springs. The journey was only about an hour, but I felt like I was driving to another world. As I got on the highway, I glanced at Cañon City in my rearview mirror. I sighed a breath of relief, fixated my eyes on the road again and I never looked back. I was good at leaving.

I did remarkably well driving on the highway. Once I got into fourth gear, it was smooth sailing. I jammed my mixed tape with songs like Whitney Houston's "I Will Always Love You," and Naughty by Nature's "Hip Hop Hooray." It was cool outside, but I had my window rolled down to enjoy the invigorating air and the sense of freedom I felt. I knew my decision to leave, unannounced, was going to piss some people off. I knew my leaving created more questions than answers, but I did not care. I needed to be free of the system one way or another and leaving Cañon City, CO was the start of my emancipation. As I drove on the open road to my destiny in the Springs, I mulled over my plan, which I must admit had a lot of uncertainties. I would figure it out. I was going to find a place to stay and I was going to enroll in school, graduate, then leave this state with a smile on my face.

I followed the directions to the Pizza Hut I was being transferred to. When I arrived, I was greeted with such enthusiasm that it was overwhelming. My new manager, Steve, ushered me into the restaurant and asked me if I was hungry. I told him I still had a half-eaten pizza in my car. He laughed the most infectious, boisterous, heart-warming laugh I had ever heard. I was going to like working here. He told me that they were seriously short staffed, so my transfer could not have come at a better time. I asked him if I could use his office phone to call my manager in Cañon City to let her know I had made it safely. He gave me access to his office and I called. She sounded happy and relieved. She could not talk long because it was rush hour and now that I was gone, they were short-staffed. My leaving was one person's solution and now her problem. I apologized, half-heartedly, and again thanked her for her help. She made me promise I would come visit her. I told her I would, she and I both knew it was a lie.

Steve asked me when I could start working. I told him I could start working immediately. He laughed and told me to go home, clean up, and unload my car. He told me that I would start and open the restaurant the next day which was Sunday. I did not have a home to go to, so Steve gave me some hotel names that were nearby. I went to every hotel in the surrounding area. I was underage, so they would not give me a room. I used a phone booth to call my caseworker to let her know I was in the Springs. I knew she would not get the message until Monday, so I made sure to leave the number of the Pizza Hut as I did not have any other way for her to contact me. I drove back to the Pizza Hut and Steve was, understandably, surprised to see me. I explained to him my situation. He told me he would help me out. I followed him to the nearby Super 8 motel. I gave him $500 cash to pay for the room, which cost $26 a night. It was enough money to put a roof over my head for almost a month, which would give me time to make a more permanent plan. He gave me the room key and told me to unpack, unwind, and rest up. I was grateful for his help and I went to my motel room.

I did not realize how mentally exhausted I was. After I brought my meager belongings into the room and put things away; I showered and fell asleep. I woke with a start around midnight, I thought I had slept through my shift. I set the alarm clock besides the bed. The only channels available on the television in the room were local channels. A rerun of Sanford and Son was showing. I watched it, but my mind could not focus. I had a lot to do on Monday, so I used the pad of paper and pen provided on the nightstand to write my to-do-list. The nap made it impossible for me to go back to sleep. After writing my list, I thumbed through the Holy Bible that was in the drawer of the nightstand. I pondered why there was a bible there, maybe the person who stayed before me left it. At that time, I did not know most hotels and motels had bibles in the rooms. I could not fathom the rationale behind this industry practice. Maybe most people came to motels to search their souls and decide on their destinies, so the bibles offered comfort and inspiration. Who knows. I wrote in the back of the bible on the last tissue-like page: Soul was here.

I went to work at nine o'clock in the morning. Steve did not give me a specific time to be at work, but if this store was anything like the one in Cañon City, prep work started early and the lunch crowd would be heavy after churches released their sanctified patrons. Pizza Hut was within walking distance of the motel, so I did not bother to drive. I enjoyed walking and the quarter or so mile to get there was barely enough to even be considered exercise. When I got there the doors were locked, so I knocked on delivery door. Steve answered and greeted me with a warm smile. He invited me in and told me to meet him in the dining room so he could go over my schedule and sign the transfer paperwork. He offered me a donut and coffee which I happily accepted. In the dining room, I went to the table that had paperwork on it. Steve sat across from me and handed me two uniforms, a name badge, my schedule (which was blank), and some paperwork. I signed what he told me to sign and then I excused myself to change in the bathroom. I returned and we sat back down in the booth to develop my schedule. He told me I could work as much as I wanted, but I could not exceed thirty hours a week because I was still in school. He and I both knew I was going to work more than that, but I guess he had to pretend to follow some employment rule. He told me that I would work the dining room as a waitress on the weekends, and help cook during the week. We also knew that was not true. They were short staffed, so I was sure I would be taking phone orders, prepping pizzas, stocking the buffet bar, serving patrons, and cashing them out. I did not mind, I liked working. He shared with me that the weekends and paydays drew a lot of GI's from the nearby base, Fort Carson. He warned me about flirting with the soldiers and he forewarned me not to expect tips from them. I smiled at him. If I could get racist jackwipes in Cañon City to tip, I could get young, broke soldiers to tip.

Steve introduced me to the doughboy, Matthew. Matthew was a thirty-something loner. He made all the various pizza and breadstick doughs for the day, hence the nickname Doughboy. He kind of looked like the Michelin man, just greasier, grimier, and hairier. He was very shy. He could barely look at me when Steve introduced us. Matthew had some sort of speech impairment, it was a combination of a lisp and stuttering. I imagined that he was bullied when he was in school. He nodded at me and said something that could only be deciphered as "Nice to meet you" though I really have no clue if that is really what he said. I could tell he was uncomfortable with having to talk to me, so I told him I was glad to meet him and if he needed any help with making the dough, I was trained and would assist if needed. He turned away from me and muttered, I think, "I do all the dough." Steve gently nudged me to follow him. He told me Matthew was the best doughboy in town and he was possessive about doing it. He also washed dishes. Pizza Hut was Matthew's life; he had worked there for five years.

He lived in an efficiency apartment, took care of his cats, and kept to himself. I know it sounds crazy, but I understood Matthew. In some ways, we were similar. We were both loners, I just hoped that my loneliness wore better on me than it had on him. He was nice, but gross, no wonder he was kept in the back. I would not eat here if he was the face of Pizza Hut.

I enjoyed working at this Pizza Hut. Based on my experience in Cañon City, I was more experience than the other employees and more versatile. The store had more volume than where I previously worked, but I liked it. I had to get used to serving a more diverse crowd. My first day, I worked ten hours, and when I left I was exhausted. When my shift ended I went to walk to the motel. Steve insisted on driving me. He told me that this was not the safest part of town and that I needed to start driving to work, so I could drive home at night. I used to live in a ghetto, so I did not see what the big deal was; I promised him I would drive from here on out. I was drained from being on my feet all day, so I really did not resist the offer. When he dropped me off at the motel, he told me he was glad I was here and that I had done a great job. I thanked him. I was asleep before my head hit the pillow.

Monday. I had a lot to do. I did not have to go to work until four that afternoon, so I needed to get in touch with my caseworker and enroll in school. On top off that I needed to find a more permanent living solution. The motel was fine, but I figured it was not sustainable. I needed an apartment, even if it was a small studio apartment. My age was the biggest roadblock to getting an apartment, so I had to get help from someone. I used the phone in the room to call my caseworker. Let's just say she was not happy with me. She told me she was going to send an officer to pick me up and bring me to Child Protective Services. I told her I would leave before that happened. I was not going back to any foster home, group home, temporary placement. I would disappear and she would never be able to find me. I had money, transportation, and a will that was unbendable. She asked me where I was at and I told her to meet me at the Pizza Hut.

We met up and I told her my intentions, again. She told me I could not just leave foster care, I had to be emancipated by a judge. I told her that is what I wanted to do, but I also needed to enroll in school. It was the second semester of my junior year, I left Cañon City High School with straight A's and I did not want to fall behind in school. She reluctantly agreed to help me and she asked for my number at the motel. She had to consult her supervisor and she admonished me for being so stubborn. I regretted, in a small sense, putting her in an awkward situation. Mary was the one caseworker that had stayed around and she had always been supportive of my brothers and me. She was a state employee and had rules to follow. I was making her job difficult. It was an inconvenience for her, but it was life or death for me—truly, or jail time because I was bound to lose all control and hurt someone. I just needed to be left alone to live my life and my dear caseworker posed a threat to my freedom. She told me she would get in touch with me on Tuesday, after she got some more information from her supervisor. I reminded her I was not going back under any circumstance. She confirmed she understood and got up to leave. She asked me if I needed anything, I told her no and she walked out of the restaurant. She looked so defeated, that I almost changed my mind…fuck that, she would figure it out, just as I had.

The next day Mary called the motel and told me that I needed to meet her at the CPS office near downtown. I was not sure what the meeting was about, but I drove to the same boring, drab, brown government building I used to visit my brothers many moons ago. Both of my brothers had been released from the children's home and lived in different foster homes. Lam's foster family wanted to adopt him. He did not want to be adopted. He had adopted the streets. Eddie was in a juvenile detention facility. I had failed them. Anyways, when I arrived, Mary met me at the reception desk. She took me to the third floor. The floor was littered with cubicles, stacks and stacks of papers, files, and caseworkers who looked like they slept there. The aroma of burnt coffee, lingering cigarette smoke, and cheap perfume assailed my nose. We entered a conference room that hosted a stained conference table and an arrangement of puke green office chairs.

There were several people already in the room, sitting and chatting animatedly. When we entered they stared at me like I was some alien. Mary motioned for me to sit next to her and introduced me to her supervisor, a hearing officer, a psychologist and a lawyer. The lawyer was some guardian ad litem, an attorney appointed by the courts to make decisions in my best interest. I had never met this person before, yet apparently, he had been appointed to my case for a while. I did not understand how he could make decisions that were in my best interest when he did not even know me beyond what he read in my file.

He was a tall, lanky man with dropping shoulders and a weary look. His hair was a white and gray bird's nest, that looked like the bird had just recently left. His glasses were hanging for dear life on the tip of his beak like nose. I decided in that moment that he looked like an ostrich in a suit—a cheap suit. His eyes were weary, but gentle. He was likeable, but I that did not make me warm up to him. I felt sorry for him. I am sure he when he dreamed of being a lawyer he dreamed of something more glamorous than dealing with the likes of me. He stood and offered me his hand, I shook it, then quickly dismissed him. I was informed that meeting was going to be a hearing to discuss my emancipation from Child Protective Services. I was incredulous. I thought such meetings happened in a court room with a judge. Mr. Birdman explained that the decisions made would be legally binding and this was similar to court, but with a more holistic approach. All I heard was I was about to be free.

Mr. Birdman started by saying, "Alma's mother failed her." All I could think was, "No shit, Sherlock." Thankfully, I kept that comment to myself. I mean, I was trying to appear grown and professional. In a monotone voice, he reviewed my case history. I guess he had to go over all of it for the hearing officer, but damn, it took forever and was uncomfortable to hear. It was as if he was talking about someone else. Surely, they could have discussed this before I came. The hearing officer asked me what I wanted to do. I shared I wanted to be independent of the system and the steps I had taken to do so. I articulated my desire to finish high school. I shared I was going to college and eventually would take care of my brothers, so they would not be a burden on the State. They listened. They asked questions of each other and me. I was becoming impatient. The more they talked and asked questions the more I wished I would have just ran away. Emancipation would have been easier than me sitting here listening to them talk about me like I was not there. To them this was a job; for me it was my life. I was appreciative of the oracle skills I had learned from Mrs. Carmuchi, because I used them to convince the system to allow me to have partial emancipation. I was still going to be a ward of the state, but I could live on my own. My caseworker would still do visits and they gave me certain stipulations that I had to meet or else they would put me back in a home. I would run away if that happened and I told them so. I was required to go to school and maintain good grades, work, go to therapy (therapy was the State's solution to everything), and I had a curfew. The stipend that had previously gone to my foster parents to care for me would now come to me to help pay rent. I would retain my health insurance, Medicaid, until I was eighteen years old. I was put on a wait list for subsidized housing, better known as Section 8, but I could not move in until the end of summer. I agreed with the terms and conditions of my modified placement and walked out of the meeting a partially free person.

It was close to Spring Break and I did not want to start another school that year. So, the remainder of my junior year, I did independent study. My school coordinated with the local library to have my work and tests sent there. I would complete my work and mail it at the end of each week to my teachers in Cañon City.

Before or after work, depending on my shift I would go to the library and study, though I did not need to study much, the work was insanely easy. I felt in control. I was weary of living at the hotel and bouncing from couch to couch. I never told my caseworker, but there were times I just slept in my car. There was a Bally's gym near my job, so would sneak in on those days and shower. I just needed to make it a few months, until my apartment was ready. Those were some long months.

8

I had made some friends. I use the term very loosely, but I met some girls who were nice enough to me and their parents felt sorry for me. Karlissa was one of these people. I met her at the library and she remembered me from seventh-grade, when I still lived at the Bane's. I did not remember her, but pretended I did. She invited me to a party and I reconnected with other kids who remembered me from sixth, seventh, and eighth grades. Again, I did not remember any of them, still, I acted like I did. I started hanging out with them and crashing on their couches, while I waited for my government housing to come available. Thus, for a few months I lived on their hospitality. I paid my way, of course, and that seemed to attract financially convenient sympathy from their parents.

Karlissa's mom was a single parent with three children and she was broke. She worked as a caretaker at a nursing home. She needed financial help, so I agreed, after getting the OK from Mary, to stay at her house and pay rent. If she went through the foster parent training and signed up to be my "foster parent" she would receive the financial benefits to care for me. This setup helped us both. I had a stable roof over my head, she had some extra money coming in to help pay bills. She was nice and really left me alone. I was rarely at the house because I worked a lot. Since I did not have to go to school, I worked two jobs: Pizza Hut and Ponderosa. I also had a part-time job at a strip club where I illegally waited on lonely men.

I wore a uniform—just in case you're wondering. When I wasn't working I was at the library or hanging out with friends. I was given my own room and I paid for my own phone line. She received not only a monthly stipend to have me live there, but she also received food stamps. The arrangement was great. I planned to enroll at Widefield High School at the beginning of my senior year and I thought, quite erroneously, that this set up would last until I graduated. Yes, I was waiting for my apartment, but it felt good to help out Karlissa's mom. She was kind to me and if I could avoid living in the projects again, I decided I did not mind staying with them. Besides, Karlissa's siblings loved me. I never asked for anything, but did anything that was asked of me. For a minute I was just a typical teenager. The summer before my senior year was running smoothly.

Karlissa started to change towards me. To be honest, I have no clue exactly why she started changing towards me, but she definitely had an attitude. There was a boy from her church that showed interest in me. I only attended their church twice out of respect for her mother. She asked me to go with her and it was difficult to say no. On both torturous occasions, Karlissa pointed him out to me and groveled over how good he looked. I knew she liked him, even though she said she did not. "He's like a brother," she would tell me. Whatever. I had brothers and I never talked about how big their hands were or commented on their smooth skin. I could have cared less about her feelings for him. He was a church boy, so I was absolutely not interested. I even told her she should go out with him. She just repeated that same bullshit.

She and I had gone to a mutual friend's house together just to hang out. The guy was there and was flirtatious towards me. I did not return the attention out of respect for Karlissa.

According to her, he asked her to hook us up. I told her and him I was not interested, because I wasn't. I was still working through my issues with boys. I had a mission to accomplish and a relationship, regardless of how juvenile and trivial it would have been, was not in the plan.

Karlissa appeared to hold a grudge against me after that party, even though she was there when I turned him down. Tensions between us intensified. She stopped talking to me and talking about me to our mutual friends. Karlissa started rumors about me calling me a hoe and a slut.

Alliances were formed, and I was booted out of the group. She turned against me because some skinny, ashy kneed, big-eyed, funky breath boy like me over her. Really? I was hurt and anger. She wanted me out of her house. I told her I was not leaving because I paid the fucking bills and plus I knew if I left, her mom could not afford the house. I cared about her mom and siblings and did not want to put them out. I tried to be a better person, but as I've said many times before in this manuscript, even I have a breaking point.

Karlissa had the entire basement to herself. My room was on the second floor of the house, next to her younger brother and sister. The laundry room was in the basement. I would do my laundry late in the evening when I got home from work, which meant I had to go into the basement. One day I came home from work and went to my room. On my bed was a handwritten note from Karlissa. Instead of using my name, the letter was addressed to "The girl nobody wants." I did not read the letter, instead I crumbled it and threw it in the trash. Fuck her! If it was not for me, she and her family would be living in a one room apartment eating beans and rice every day. I gathered my dirty laundry and headed towards the basement. It was about eleven o'clock in the evening. I had assumed Karlissa was not home because her raggedy car was not in the driveway. Her mom, whose room was also on the second floor was asleep as were her siblings. I tiptoed down the creaky stairs, as not to disturb them, towards the basement. When I got to the basement door it was closed. This was odd, because the door was always open, as a matter of fact, her mom insisted it stay open. In the basement, Karlissa had a living room, bathroom, a separate bedroom, and the laundry room. I tried the door knob and discovered that the door was locked. This, again, was confusing. It was late, so I decided to head back to my room and do my laundry the next day. As I turned away from the door, I heard sounds on the stairs behind the closed basement door. I paused, turned, and softly knocked on the door. It sounded like a latch was being detached and Karlissa opened to door. I know I looked both surprised and confused. Before I could say anything, she quietly, but forcibly growled something incomprehensible at me. I asked her what she had said. She venomously said that I was not allowed into the basement anymore. I asked why. She spat in my face and said something about the note I had thrown away. I was so taken aback by her reaction that I froze for what seemed like eternity. I was grappling with the fact this bitch just spit in my face, why and how to best resist my instincts to fuck her up. Remember, it was almost midnight and her family was soundly sleeping in the house I was technically paying for. I chose to fight this battle another day and I turned to walk away. I needed to walk away because I knew that if I stayed there, my fury would take over. As I turned, I took a deep breath and bent over to pick up my laundry basket. She stepped into the kitchen and lost her damn mind. Karlissa spat on me again, but on my back this time.

She said in a controlled whisper, "You better keep walking if you know what's best for you."

Internally, I lost it. I had to get away from this bitch because I did not know how much more control I had in me. I deliberately stood erect, turned and walked towards the kitchen sink. I grabbed a paper towel and wiped the spit off me. I felt her behind. I turned and smashed the paper towel with her spit on it into her face. She did not have time to react before I then grabbed her hair, yanked her ass to the basement door. With as much force as I could muster, I shoved her down the stairs. Had this been an Olympic gymnastics' event, she might have scored a ten for her tumbling. Karlissa looked like a Raggedy Ann doll and she went head over heels down the stairs. Amazingly, the spit dampened paper towel stuck to her face. Her flailing arms desperately sought a banister or wall to stop the downward momentum, but failed to connect. She landed at the bottom of the stairs in a heap of disgusting and ungrateful humanity. I was furious. I flew down the stairs and before she could recover and untangle herself, I grabbed her again by her brittle, but greasy nappy hair and yanked and pulled her back up the stairs. She was screaming at this point, so I punched her in the mouth to shut her up.

At the top of the stairs, I lifted her by her hair and forced her to look me in the face. I spat an epic loogy in her face; it landed on her right cheek. She grabbed my hair, so with my free hand I punched her in the throat and I pushed her back down the stairs. I closed the basement door behind me this time and locked the door. I was surprised her mother did not wake up with her screaming. I flew down the stairs, kicked her in the side, and pulled her by her shirt towards the living room area. She was bleeding from her mouth, which unfortunately for her, fueled my fury. She had underestimated me. She thought because I was the girl nobody wanted, she could disrespect me, spit on me, and I would simply walk away. This night she learned differently. She tried to swing and hit me, I was quicker and very precise with my punches. I held her head by her hair and punched until I became aware of my hand hurting. The blood from her busted lip combined with the blood from her busted nose that combined with the blood from the cut above her eye. I could have whooped her ass all night, but I was tired and I felt I had made my point.

Amazingly, all the ruckus we made did not wake up her family. If it did, no one came to her rescue. I let go and stood over her. She did not attempt to fight back, rather she scurried to her room and locked herself in. Through her sobs I heard her vow to kill me.

"Try bitch!"

"I hate you!" She hissed through the door.

"Get in line bitch! You started this, not me. If I hear you telling people you beat my ass, I'll whoop your ass in the middle of the fucking street for everyone to see. The next time you think you might want to spit on me, I'm going to cut your fucking tongue out." Damn, I felt good.

I walked to the top of the basement stairs into the kitchen. I gathered my laundry and a knife. I was going to do my laundry like I had originally planned to do. I brought the knife just in case she had a weapon on the other side of the door and was planning on surprising me. I loaded the washing machine, whistled and waited. I knew she could hear me in the laundry room. The sobbing slowly ceased. She came out once and hurried to the bathroom. I assumed she was assessing the damage. If you ask me, I did her a favor in rearranging her ugly face. She had no one to be mad at but herself. She created the situation. Hopefully, she learned a valuable lesson—know your opponent. I sat on the couch while my clothes soaked, washed, rinsed and spun. I had two loads, so I stayed in the basement, sitting quietly and pensively in the dimly lit room until both loads were washed, dried, and folded. I could hear snoring, even though the light peeked through the bottom of the door. It was now about two o'clock in the morning. I took my clean laundry to my room. I was exhausted, but I knew still had things to do.

I opened the bedroom window to allow the serenity of the early morning to creep in. The sky was clear and the stars twinkled brightly. The air was cleansing and it cooled my lungs as it traveled through my body. My mind was made up. I went to the bathroom and removed all my toiletries. I had not showered since coming home from work, but I decided to shower later, after I finished doing what I needed to do. I cleaned the bathroom. I cleaned my bedroom, wiping even the walls down with bleach water. I changed the linens on my bed, took the old linens and bedspread to the basement and washed them. I returned to the room, disconnected the phone, packed all my belonging into my trusty trunk. I went back to the basement and folded the now washed bedclothes. When I returned to the room, I closed the window and fished the letter from Karlissa out of the trash. I chose not to read it, it no longer mattered, but I placed it on the pillow. I pulled a spiral notebook out of my backpack and wrote a letter to Karlissa's mom and siblings. At the crack of dawn, around four o'clock in the morning, I placed my housekey on the side table next to the sofa in the living room. I quietly closed the door behind me and I left.

I drove to the Motel 8 I had stayed in when I first drove to Colorado Springs. Since the clerk was familiar with me, she rented me a room. I paid to stay at the motel for a week. When I went to the room, it felt like déjà vu. I brought my truck into the room, shut the world out, and showered. After I showered, I fell into the abyss of darkness. That night I did not dream. I did not fear. I did not care. I knew I would have to face my caseworker about what had happened; I knew the Karlissa's story would be only partially true. Sleep enveloped me and I was comforted in knowing that whatever the day was going to bring, I would face it with a righteous indignation and an unwavering confidence. I may be the girl nobody wants, but I was damned if I was going to be treated like trash. It was me against the world and I was going to win—by any means necessary.

I did not have to be to work until the evening shift the next day. It gave me time to deal with the bullshit from the previous night. I called my caseworker and left a message for her to call me at the motel. I treated myself to a sit-down breakfast at Denny's. My car needed an oil change, so I went to the nearest auto parts store to get oil; I changed it myself. When you have a raggedy 1976 hunk of junk, it was important to know how to do simple maintenance on it—there was always something to fix. I loved my rusted-hole in the floor-no heater or AC-sometimes needed to be jumped started car. I learned how to change the alternator, the starter, the oil, and how to rig the muffler so it would not bang on the under carriage. Anyways, I changed the oil and decided to go to The Garden of the Gods. I needed some divine inspiration and I found solace in nature. Nature is uncomplicated, pure, honest.

I drove to the Garden of the Gods and basked in the glory of the amazing rock formations.

The drive up the winding road to the hiker's trail reminded of my ride in the mountains so many years ago, when my mother left me. The familiar feeling of loneliness tapped me on the shoulders and I had to fight the urge to feel sorry for myself. The majestic views of the mountains in the backdrop to the Garden of the Gods shook their elegant finger at me through the pine trees and whispered to me through the wind that I was going to be alright. I walked the trail and basked in the resiliency of White and Red Lyons sandstone and the Fountain conglomerate. These rock formations had undergone uplifting, faulting, and erosion. They stood tall and proud and reminded me that greatness is a long, carefully designed process. I understood why Rufus Cable said this place was fit for the gods to assemble, because the beauty of the spires was heavenly. I climbed to the top of the Red Rocks Amphitheater and sat, looking at everything, but seeing nothing. My mind was clear and I felt a calmness wrap around me. I was sitting on a stone that had taken millions of years to become what it was this day. It had survived erosion, being nothing more than a heap of sediment. It survived climate change, sand dunes, and being amongst a sand sea. It survived mountains forming, plates colliding, dinosaurs dying and now it stood strong and beautiful. The events of the previous night no longer burdened me. I would survive; I would move past this moment in life and stand strong and majestic as these formations. I took a deep breath, trying to breath in the wisdom of the ages as it swirled in the brisk breeze. I reflected on how small I was in comparison to the garden. I looked at the park and the town beyond and while I felt but a speck of dust, in that moment I understood that the speck that I was in the universe was divinely designed and my purpose was being molded by my experiences. I did not want to leave the Garden of the Gods. I felt at home; I knew I was drawn to this place for a reason. While I did not understand the celestial pressure I was undergoing; while I did not understand the why behind the tribulations I had experienced; while I did not understand Karlissa's behavior the night before; I understood that this too shall pass I was going to be better because of it. Reluctantly, I climbed down from my perch and walked the winding trail back to my car. If I could stay here forever, I would. It was regal and spoke to my soul. I was going to be alright, this I knew. I drove back to The Springs and to the Department of Child and Protective Services. I hoped my caseworker would be there so I could be the first to tell her about last night. When I got there I saw Karlissa's mom's car in the parking lot. I was too late. Damn. The tranquil feeling I had from the Garden of the Gods was squandered and I braced myself for whatever I was about to encounter. I just prayed that Karlissa was not with her, I was in too good of a mood for a confrontation.

No such luck; Karlissa and her mother were waiting in the waiting room when I arrived. I almost turned around and left, but there was no way in hell I was going to give Karlissa the satisfaction of seeing me retreat. I walked, head held high (probably too high, I'm sure I looked like I was counting ceiling tiles) and signed in at the front desk. The receptionist recognized me and told me to follow her, she had been instructed that if I showed up to escort me directly to the conference room on the second floor. I did not look at the mother-daughter pair piercing me with their stares. I did glimpse bruising on Karlissa's face, but I walked past her without making any eye contact and dutifully followed the receptionist to the elevator. I hated this place. It smelled of poverty, despair, and rejection.

I was taken to the conference room where we had made the arrangements for my independence. I read frustration on Mary's face. I hated that I had put her in this situation. She really was a kind woman and she really, really wanted to help me. I was not an easy case, for sure. I told myself that by dealing with me, she was getting better at her job, so in a way I was helping her. Yeah, I know, that is a stretch, but I did not want to feel guilty, so this was how I rationalized the situation at the time. She pointed to a stained, grimy orangish cloth office chair. It looked like someone had peed on it, but I did not protest and sat on the edge of the chair. We sat in silence for a few minutes and then she asked me to explain what had happened. I did. She told me that Karlissa wanted to press assault charges on me, I told her to tell her to go ahead, she spat on me twice and in the eyes of the law spitting was assault with bodily fluid. Mary managed a very weak, but still charming smile and asked me what my plan. I told her I was going to stay with another friend until the apartment was available. Luckily, I would be able to move in in a couple of weeks. She asked that I try to resolve the conflict with Karlissa. I ignored her request and asked if I could leave. I did not give her a chance to reply, I simply got up and left. As I was leaving, Karlissa and her mother were still dutifully sitting in the waiting room. She said something, I did not register her words. She no longer existed in my world. I had to get to work and figure out the rest of my life.

9

As my independent studies for the remainder of my junior wrapped up, I received two major honors. I was one of three kids to receive The Colorado Youth of Year Award and I was selected, though I am not sure how, to represent Colorado at the annual National Young Leaders Conference in Washington, DC. Only two students per state were selected, and I was one of the two from my state. Mary was excited for me to join her in Breckenridge to receive my award and I am sure she was instrumental in me going to DC. These two events propelled me into my senior year and confirmed for me that I was erasing the stain of my mother's sins.

First, the award. Mary called me excited. It was a sunny day, with butterflies fluttering about and the smell of spring was in the air. Her mood matched the weather. I was drawn into her joy. She told me that I had been selected, from all the children in foster care in the state of Colorado as a recipient of the Colorado Youth of the Year Award. I was, understandably, confused. She must have been the person that nominated me, though she never admitted to it. I was to attend the annual Department of Family Services conference in Breckenridge, CO to accept my award. Mary was going to drive me to the conference and we were going to stay, with other caseworkers at the mountain resort. Mary told me to write an acceptance speech. We were going to leave on a Friday morning. I had about two weeks to prepare.

Mary picked me up from a friend's house. In the car, with her was another caseworker, one of my former caseworkers, who now lived in a different part of the state. She, Kathy, was excited to see me. I remembered her and was happy that she was joining us. The ride to Breckenridge was full of the ladies chatting away about all their adventures as protectors of children. I sat in the backseat and half listened. I was still in shock that I was receiving an award. Surely, someone had made a mistake. I had never heard of a such an award and I had been in CPS custody most of my life. Mary reminded me a few times to write an acceptance speech. It was to be no more than five minutes. I had no clue what to write, so I ignored her requests and thought to myself that I would simply say thank you and walk off. Mary told me it was a state- wide conference and that once we checked in, we would get ready for dinner. The award was to be given at the end of the dinner. Prior to our trip, she told me to pack a nice, professional looking outfit. I did not have such an outfit and I did not want to spend money on one, so I went to Goodwill and found a long, flowing multi-colored dress, that was probably more suited for a grandmother, but hey, it only costed me five dollars. I wore a pair of white sandals; which did not match my colorful outfit, but they were the only "nice" shoes I had. To me, the outfit was nice enough; to others I looked a damn mess.

When we arrived at the resort, I was in awe. The entrance was massive, with polished wood beams and a grand stone fireplace in the lobby. I thought only rich people could be in places like that; the grandeur was overwhelming. Mary checked in and we went to the room—more like an apartment. Kathy explained to me that many people have timeshares here, though I had no idea what that meant and I was too embarrassed to ask. I wanted to look and act as sophisticated as the resort, so I dared not ask stupid questions. I would read about timeshares some other day. Our room was breathtaking. It was a rustic look that was full rich hues of reds and oranges. There was a two-way fireplace in the living room, with a deer head mounted above. On the other side was a dining room that lead to a full kitchen that was stocked with white china and polished silverware. There were three rooms, so we did not have to share. What was most impressive to me was the entire living room wall was windows. The view from the windows perfectly framed the mountains. We were in the mountains, but the view from the living room made the mountains look surreal, almost like a gigantic painting. There was a door in the windows that lead to a magnificent balcony. I could see deer roaming through the trees below. It was simply the most beautiful place I had ever been.

Mary called my name and told me I needed to start getting ready for dinner. I put on my thrift store dress and was instantly ashamed of my choice when I saw how nicely the two caseworkers were. I should have asked what to wear, but my pride let me to make the foolish selection I was now donning. Even though Mary told me I looked nice, I knew better, but it was too late to do anything about it. She reminded me to grab my acceptance speech that I lied and said I had wrote. I grabbed a blank piece of paper from the nightstand, folded it so she could not see that it was blank, and placed it my bra. I did not have a purse; so, my bra would have to do.

When we walked down to the lobby, it was full of people, dressed similar to Mary and Kathy. They all looked so professional and again I looked like a stole some grandmother's outfit. Mary introduced me to some people; I shook hands and introduced myself back with a frozen, insincere smile. I was hungry and ready to get this show on the road. A light, but audible bell dinged and the crowd in the lobby started heading towards a colossal banquet room. Mary was right, there were hundreds of people there. There was a mixture of caseworkers, lawyers, politicians, advocates, and other professionals that had some title in the foster care system. Mary pulled out a card from her purse and showed the attendant at the door. I was a guest of honor, so we were escorted to the front of the hall—right in front of the stage and podium. On the table was a simple sign that read "Reserved for Alma Gonzalez and family." The table was large enough to sit ten people; there were only the three of us. My heart ached in that moment. I looked at the other reserved tables in the front of the room and they were filled. The other two recipients had their entire tables full of supporters. Seeing them beaming and smiling with their families made me sad. The only people who were there to support me was my caseworker, who by the way, was paid to look after me. I know I should not have been so upset, but I was. I felt lonely in that room of a hundred strangers.

The dinner was a typical banquet meal: grilled chicken, grilled vegetables, rice, a basket of different breads, gravy, tea and either cheesecake or chocolate cake. I could barely eat my food. I was feeling sorry for myself, looking at my empty table. I kept up with the conversation of my two compadres, but I was not present mentally. Here I was about to receive an award I did not think I deserved, I did not have one family member, not even my brothers there to cheer me on, and I looked poor. Self pity has a way of turning a great situation into a grave one. As I finished eating the barely palatable, unseasoned chicken the director of the agency made his way to the podium. He gave a speech about something; my self loathing deafened me to his words. He introduced the first recipient, a handsome Hispanic boy. His family erupted into cheers and applause as he made his way to the podium to receive and accept his award. I did not hear anything he said; nor did I hear the words of the other recipient, a meek girl with pretty blonde curls, who followed him. Both recipients read their prepared acceptance speeches and in both I did hear them thank their families. Damn. I should have written my speech like Mary told me too. The director returned to the podium and introduced me. I slowly, very slowly, got out of my seat and was encouraged to walk to the podium by a light, respectful applause. I hated myself in that moment. I did not know what to say and I was so full of feeling sorry for myself because I did not have any family there that I was at a loss for words.

"Alma, get your notes out," Mary gently chided as I walked the slow march to the podium. I did not want to disappoint her. She was a good person and I knew she wanted the best for me.

Thankfully, I had some experience in oration from my speech and debate team, so I decided to speak from my heart. The director gave me a firm handshake and I stood with trembling knees in front of a room of strangers who where eagerly awaiting what I had to say. Well, maybe they were not eagerly awaiting my acceptance speech, but they were staring at me nonetheless.

Disappointed in myself, but determined to make Mary proud, I accepted the award.

"Good evening ladies and gentlemen. My caseworker told me to write my speech down, but as she knows, I'm hard headed, so I didn't and now I wish I had." There was a soft collective chuckle in the room. "I have to admit when I first came into this hall and was escorted to my table, I wanted to run out. On my table there is a sign, as you can see, that says 'Reserved for Alma Gonzalez and family.' I was upset because when I looked to my left and my right, the other two recipients had the same sign and their tables are full. I felt sorry for myself because you see, the only people who are at my table are my caseworkers: past and present." The mood in the room changed.. I could see some people trying to look to see who Mary and Kathy were. "I felt sorry for myself. I don't have any family at my table. I don't have a mom or dad, grandparents, aunts, uncles, cousins or even my brothers here to see me get this amazing award. I felt sorry for myself because I was embarrassed to sit at a table meant for ten people who care and love me. I don't have any of that." I could hear mumbling in the audience, but I continued. "Here I am receiving an award, that I probably do not deserve because I know I'm not an easy kid to deal with, just ask my caseworker." There was more chuckling as Mary vigorously nodded her head. "See, she agrees," I said jokingly as muted laughter circulated the room. "So, here I was feeling sorry for myself because my blood is not here. My blood gave up on me. My blood hurt me, left me, forgot me. So yes, my blood family is not here. Then I realized something. My table is not big enough to fit my family." The room was silent in anticipation and confusion. "You see, ladies and gentlemen, my table is not empty. My family is here." I watched people look around, perplexed. "You are my family. I am a child of the great state of Colorado. You raised me. I have been in foster care for most of my life and the fact that I am able to stand here today is testament of the dedication each of you have given to children, the unwanted children, like me." I could hear sniffling, but dared not search for the source. I was trying to not cry. "You, each of you, have chosen a profession that helps the families of Colorado. You have chosen to hug the motherless and fatherless, find homes for the homeless, advocate for the voiceless, guide the lost, educate the ignorant, and above all show compassion the hopeless. You, each of you, have given up hours of sleep, accept subpar pay, have case loads that are unmanageable, deal with the worst society has to offer, see the pain of children every day, talk to parents who need guidance, and at times forsake your own families so that a hard-headed girl who has an empty table can have a chance in this world." I could see people wiping their eyes. "I want to thank you, each of you, for choosing to mend families. Thank you for choosing to be heroes in an unforgiving and cruel world. Thank you for this award. I will use this opportunity as a step in my ladder to success and I promise to make you, my family, proud. Thank you again." I quickly turned from the podium and walked off the stage. The room erupted in applause. The applause seemed to last forever and as I made my way back to my seat I realized everyone was standing. Mary and Kathy both greeted me at the table with the biggest hugs. I was overcome with emotion, but I had learned not to cry, so I sat down and pretended the whole thing did not happen.

A few weeks after receiving the Youth of the Year award, I received an invitation to attend the National Young Leaders Conference in Washington, DC. My speech at the conference must have inspired someone, because the cost of attending the Young Leaders Conference and my airfare were donated. Actually, United Airlines donated my ticket in response to someone's request and I still do not know who paid the cost for me to attend, but I am grateful.

Mary drove me to the airport and helped me check in. She was reassuring and patient because I was a wreck. I was scared to fly. I had never been in an airport, let alone on an airplane. I cried, almost to the point of hyperventilating when I got on the airplane to fly to Washington, DC. The ignorance of my small, ill-informed world was displayed with my hysterical crying because I could not reconcile in my mind the wonders of flying. The air stewardess, too, was very calm, polite, and reassuring. She sat me down in first class next to a window and gave me some very sage advice: "Keep your eyes closed during lift off and landing. However, once the plane is in the air, look out the window and marvel at your place in the world. The sky and its clouds have a funny way of making you feel either significant or insignificant in the grand scheme of life. I think you are significant." She then handed me a barf bag and scurried off to make the other first-class passengers comfortable. An elderly woman sat next to me. I mean, I call her elderly, but that is really because she had a head full of white hair. She seemed elderly, especially since she was hell bent on calming me down with an endless supply of peppermints and butterscotch hard candies. Maybe her trick was to put me in a sugary stupor so I would calm down. She wanted to talk, and she was nice enough, but once we were leveled in the air, I really just wanted to watch the sky as had been suggested. The peppermint lady was intent on engaging me, so I obliged her for a while. We talked about her experiences as a young White House intern and now her role as a political analyst. She crooned about the galas she's attended and the powerful people she's met. In between her breathes and her thoughts, I would glance at the window and imagine myself dressed like a movie star going to galas with rich, powerful people. Then, there would be turbulence to shake me back to reality and I would clutch the barf bag harder and return my attentions to my seat neighbor's stories. Her stories helped pass the time away. She told me she needed to take a little nap, but to wake her if I needed her. I thought her generosity was refreshing. Before she settled down to slumber, she gave me a book from her purse. She encouraged me to read it and told me that I could keep the book, it was one of her solid traveling companions and felt I would benefit from it. <u>Walden</u> by Henry David Thoreau kept me company during my flight neighbor's nap. It was an odd book to give a high school junior, but it became one of my most cherished possessions. A book from a peppermint giving, chatty stranger who was intent on helping me get through my first airplane ride inspired me. It worked and I understood what the flight attendant had told me about the clouds and sky. In the book a line stood out to me, and honestly it has guided me ever since I first read it: "Every man is tasked to make his life, even in its details, worthy of the contemplation of his most elevated and critical hour." That was my goal.

The conference was amazing. I flew into Maryland and met up with the conference's welcoming committee. I was in awe of all the students from around the country that were already there, waiting. Apparently, I was the last student to arrive, so we got our luggage and boarded the charter bus that took us to our lodgings. We were staying at the University of Maryland. We stayed in a dormitory, four students to a room. Per our agenda, we also had a few sessions at the university. I was so excited to be on a college campus and I was looking forward to learning all I could about being a leader. I felt honored to have been chosen to attend as a representative of my state. I was also excited to meet the other delegates. When you never leave your state and your surroundings and the things you do are very limited, everything and everyone you meet outside of your little world seems exotic. I don't know why meeting students from different states was so exciting, it was like I was meeting people from different countries. My preconceived notions about people from different states were shattered. For example, one of the delegates from Alaska was black. I had no clue that black people lived in Alaska. Mind blown! I was shocked that people had the same reaction towards me being from Colorado. The other Colorado delegate was also a black girl, now that tripped me out. My walls of ignorance were quickly being demolished and I embraced every experience during my week-long stay at the conference. We had lunch with United Nations dignitaries and delegates. I sat next to the Ambassador from Ghana, I had gone to school with his daughter at Liberty High School. He did not remember me, but I remembered him. What a small world. The entire experience was amazing and inspired me to become a lawyer. I found being around powerful people in fancy suits to be empowering and I wanted to be one of them. I wanted to travel the world, influence public policy, make a difference, and more importantly I wanted to have a job in which I could afford to dress in one of those suits and wear expensive, designer shoes. I know for some, this seems extremely juvenile and trivial, but when you grow up and your only model for financial success is the neighborhood dope dealer, then modeling my dreams after successful politicians doesn't seem like a bad choice. I now know better.

I went back to Colorado with a renewed sense of purpose. I was ready to start summer and prepare for my senior year. My name came up on the waiting list for the subsidized apartment. The rent was $300 per month. The building looked like a big, brown box with windows and it was full of shady characters, drugs, teen moms, gangbanging baby daddies, and income limited elderly. None of that mattered to me; I was happy to be on my own. I stopped working at the Pizza Hut because my manager moved and I did not like the new manager. I also stopped waiting tables at the strip club. Now that I had my apartment, I wanted to keep it and if my caseworker found out, she might pull the plug on my independence. I focused on working exclusively at Ponderosa Steakhouse. It was a restaurant where people could order bad steaks and load up on pasta salad and pudding at the buffet. I was head waitress and was responsible for the other wait staff on my shift. I made good money in tips, worked hard, and got a long with everyone. I also met a lot of people that became my regular customers. There was something very gratifying about having people come to my place of work and request my service because they felt like I treated them like family. My managers were good people and looked out for me. If a table ever left without tipping me, my managers would always compensate me.

I moved into my apartment two weeks before the commencement of my final year in high school. I had two goals in mind, to graduate and then leave the state. I was overwhelmed with the fear that if I did not leave Colorado when I graduated I would be suck and doomed to a life of mediocracy. I could not, would not let that happen. I needed to show my brothers that there was more to the world than this godforsaken town. I had promised my "family" I would make them proud. I had to leave when I graduated. I did not consider any other option.

10

Before I moved in to my apartment, I spent most of the summer staying here and there and everywhere. I relied on the mercy of acquaintances and I slept on a few couches or inflatable mattresses. I stayed in storage rooms in people's houses, climbing over Christmas decorations and boxes of winter clothes. I worked so much, that I had little time for sleep, so I was not around enough to be an imposition to my hosts. I would go to work early, nap in the break room, work until close and then head off to my job at the strip joint. I would get off work from there around five o'clock in the morning, go to where ever I was staying, shower, nap, and get up and leave to go to the library. I spent many hours looking through catalogues to help decide which colleges or universities I would apply to. I also found a list of all the books I would be required to read as a senior in my honors English class and decided to read them in the summer. It was a productive summer to say the least. I saved enough money to pay for my college applications, the SAT and ACT tests, my rent and my car (which always needed maintenance). I even had enough money to buy new clothes and shoes.

My apartment was small. It was not considered an efficiency apartment because the bedroom was enclosed. When I moved in there was a waterbed in the bedroom. It took up the entire room, literally. I had to enough room to stand between the bed and the closet, but besides that, I had to dress outside the bedroom. I did not complain, because it was a free bed. I simply cleaned the plastic down with bleach, added more water to it (rigged a hose from the bathroom sink to the nozzle on bed). A waitress at work donated a wicker couch and end tables. I picked up a black and white TV at a pawn shop. I only had the four public channels, but I did not mind, I had my own apartment and I did not have to worry about where I was going to sleep. The kitchen and living room were one. I had a two-burner electric stove top. It did not come with an oven, so I had to buy a toaster over, which took up an entire counter. The refrigerator was small, with one door and the freezer on top. There was not any room for a kitchen table, but one of the managers at Ponderosa sold me a two-top wicker table, that I placed behind the couch. It served as a coffee table and a dining table. I learned how to maximize small spaces way before IKEA created do-it- yourself boxed furniture.

My apartment was on the second floor. It was the type of apartment building that the doors to the apartments were on the inside. There was an entrance on either end of the building and there was always a gang banger slinging drugs at the entrance. He was like a hood rat doorman who kept an eye on who was coming and going from the building. I was known as "Choir girl" which meant I was a good girl and not to approach me about buying dope. Only poor people lived in the building, all was on Section 8 housing. I was too, though, to be honest. There was only one laundromat in the building. You had to sit with your laundry, otherwise, if you walked away, you would come back to empty machines. Three days later you may see a neighbor sporting your favorite shirt that is two sizes too small for her, but one would not dare accuse her of stealing. In this building, I learned quickly to mind my business. My neighbors were elderly. One had a warn-ing sign on his door that smoking was prohibited because he was on oxygen. I really did not know how that worked because quit often when I would open my living room window, he would be hanging out the window smoking weed. I guess the weed was not included in the "no smoking" warning. My neighbor to the left of my apartment was an older woman who always kept her door open. I thought it weird, but it was not my business. She would yell a greeting at me when I came home and gave me bags of collard and mustard greens that her sister would bring from her garden. Her apartment smelled of Bengay, bacon grease, greens, and moth balls. She was a Jesus freak, so I always tried to quickly open my apartment door to avoid her need to share the daily scripture with me and warn me about Revelations. According to her, the world was about to end and I needed Jesus to save me. Across the hall from me was a retired pimp and his wife. He labeled himself that. He found Jesus (probably because of my other neighbor) and decided to put his pimp cane down and pick up a bible. I was not sure how far he put the pimp cane down, because I would see his wife giving blowjobs in the parking lot on the nights I came home super late. The doorman seemed to be on the lookout, but hey, it was not my business.

The top floor of the apartment building had apartments that were reserved for teen parents. They were apart of some program through the state. I picked up an extra hustle because I would babysit some of the babies and toddlers when their moms went to their parenting classes. I would read to them and let them color. There was not a park, per se, outside to take them. There was a broken-down basketball court with no hoops, a swing set, metal slide, and playground roundabout all in a section of the parking lot that was haphazardly fenced off to protect the children. Part of the fence was missing because I am sure some crackhead discovered that he could take it to the recycle lot and get money. Regardless, I did not find it to be a safe place for the kids I watched to play. Abandoned used hypodermic needles were not favorable playground equipment and exposing toddlers to used condoms was not my idea of being a good babysitter.

The teen moms would sometimes take advantage of my generosity and be gone longer than the agreed upon time. I was paid to babysit through the agency that helped them get the apartments, so I would take the children, if their parent was too late to the front office and leave them. The agency then asked me if I would mentor some of the moms, since I was responsible. I agreed, they paid, and hopefully I made a difference, though I was more focused on getting out of high school than inspiring a teen dropout. My babysitting and mentoring ended shortly after school began, which was fine by me. I volunteered occasionally with the group, only because I needed volunteer hours for my transcript. It was a win-win situation, if you ask me.

The night before my last first day in high school, I had trouble sleeping. Sure, there were all kinds of street noises around me: dogs barking, cars rolling on the pavement, a drunken argument, police or ambulance sirens (it was hard to tell sometimes), and whistles. There were all kind of whistles in the night. Every whistle call had a particular pitch and pattern and meant something of significance to the person or persons listening for it. Sometimes the whistles meant a drug dealer had a certain type of drug. That could be a high-pitched swoop swoop call. It could be a pimp calling all his hoes in for a company meeting. The whistle meant everything. Too bad I sucked at whistling. The only kind of response I could get from my whistle was a lamed, one- eyed stray that was looking for a place to lay down and die. My whistle beaconed him to his final resting place. I was used to those sounds and they usually lullabied me to sleep. I had trouble sleeping because I was about to start my senior year. I had made it and here I was about to graduate. I felt such a sense of accomplishment and a sense of intense responsibility at the same time. Yes, I had made it this far, but the race was not over. I had to graduate by any means necessary and not only that, I had to be the best. Game on. Tossing and turning on the waves of my water mattress, I set my goals for the upcoming year. I was going to graduate top of my class and I would get accepted to a college that would take me far from here. Nothing nor no one was going to deter me from my goal.

The next morning, with only two solid hours of sleep, I deliberately dressed and groomed myself. I felt determined, but my old sense of insecurity had crept in during the night. I did not feel I was pretty, I was quite drab looking. I had on new clothes, but they looked homely. I grabbed my new satchel, that I bought because it made me feel grown up. I got in my Celica and drove to Widefield High School. I parked in student parking. I did notice that my car was the worse looking car in the lot, but then I looked at the kids who were getting of the school bus and flicked all of them off in my mind. As I was walking towards the entrance, I saw Karlissa with some friends out of the corner of my eye. I had not spoken to her since the day I whooped her ass in her basement. Amongst the group of friends was Veronica. They were standing together with a group of other girls and a few boys. I felt their eyes on me as I walked swiftly past them. I believe I heard laughter, but I cannot testify to that because the pounding of my heart was too defying for me to distinguish any other sounds. I felt that a pact had just been made and I was the target. I had been acquaintances with both. I had lived with both and left both houses under difficult circumstances.

Veronica was a half black half German military brat. She was one of the friends I had met at the party Karlissa and I met at when I first moved to The Springs. We got along well enough for her to let me crash at her house for two weeks in the summer. She pretended to be pro-black and she was disgustingly disrespectful towards her German mother. Her mother was nice to me and would sit and talk with her, without Veronica present, when I had a chance. She let me sleep in the spare bedroom, that also served as their storage room. There was an army cot in between the piles and piles of boxes. I had to climb over boxes to get to the cot, but I was appreciative.

Veronica did not like my friendliness towards her mom, so she accused me of trying to take her place. Ridiculous. One day, while I was living there, I stopped by momentarily to pick up something on my way to work. I had a coworker from Ponderosa in the car. I invited her in, while I ran to the closet to get what I needed. Veronica's mom was home, so I introduced her to my coworker. My coworker then saw the cookie jar and helped herself to a cookie. She thanked Veronica's mom for the cookie and we left. Veronica felt that I had disrespected her mother and her house by inviting a stranger in, who she called hood trash because she got a cookie before asking. I stood up for my coworker and myself. We got into an argument in which she slapped me, so I slapped her back. She kicked me out.

Now I was walking past her and my other arch enemy whose ass I whooped, entering a school we all had to share. I begged the universe that I did not have any classes with either of them. My personal hell would be if I had both in a class and any of their minions. If that happened, I would transfer schools. Dealing with these heifers was going to end me in jail and they were not worth ruining me dream. I needed to avoid them at all cost. That was not going to be easy. They both had a vendetta against me and they knew everyone at the school, I was the new kid—again, and I am sure any secrets I may have shared with them about my life the whole school now knew. I kept me head held high as I walked past them into the school. I located the table that my schedule was at. Since I was new, I was asked to sit in the front office to meet my counselor then get a tour of the school. I did as I was told. I felt nauseas because of my brief encounter with The Bitches and I was trying to calm my heart down enough so I could hear my thoughts. As I got control, I looked down and studied my schedule. I had all honors and Advanced Placement classes and gym. I also had early release because I was a working student. I surveyed the front office and admired all the gladiator paraphernalia. Widefield, home of the Gladiators, made the school seem fierce and strong. Most of the students who went here were military brats. The school had a warrior mentality and winning was a school tradition. I looked through the yearbooks on the end table and vowed to make sure I took a photo for the yearbook. I wanted to leave a piece of history. The bell rang and a man approached me. He was my counselor and of course he said my name wrong. He seemed more annoyed than gracious about my newness to the school. He awkwardly escorted me to his office and asked me to sit. He had a folder on his desk, it was quite thick. I glimpse my name on the tab. All I could think at that moment was "why was my folder so damn thick?" I refocused as I watched this uncomfortable man fumble through the big ass folder. "What the hell was he looking for?" I shouted in my mind. I was getting irritated and just wanted this encounter to be over, so I could go to class. I'd rather take my chances dealing with The Bitches than to spend another disturbing minute in his office. He asked me how I was doing and if I needed anything. I just stared at him. Maybe he would think I was a mute and send me to class saving both of us from interacting with each other. He really creeped me out. I think he was baffled by me. I was not adding up to the image of me he had created after reading my file. He was expecting a delinquent. He was expecting a future welfare check recipient who mooches off the system. He was expecting someone who spoke more Ebonics than standard English and who replaced "d" for "th" in all words. He was not expecting me, that is for sure. It was written all over his confused, ugly face. He looked at my schedule, looked at me, and looked at his bookshelf.

"Can I go to class?" I asked him.

He looked confused, "Uh, sure, uh Alma. Uh let me show you around. Uh, welcome to Widefield."

"I don't need you to walk me around. Just tell me the general layout and I'll figure it out. You look busy," I said. I wanted to tell him he looked stupid, but I figured it would be best to keep that to myself.

"Uh…sure." He abruptly turned and walked to his office. He returned a few seconds later with a map of the school. Before he could explain it to me, I grabbed it and nearly sprinted to class. The start of my first day of my senior year was way more intense than I had anticipated. Hopefully, the rest of the day would get better once I was in class.

My first class was AP English. Since I was late, no thanks to my weirdo counselor, all eyes were on me when I entered. I felt so uncomfortable that I wanted to run out the door and register at another school. I did not want to deal with the judgement of all these people. It was a suffocating feeling, standing there, watching a room full of strangers watch me, watch them, watch me. The teacher walked over to me and asked to see my schedule. I could hear the "you're in the wrong class" tone in her voice as I handed her my schedule. She looked at me, at my schedule, and back at me. She showed me my desk that was in the front row, next to the far wall. It looked like a death trap, but I walked briskly to my seat. I could feel everyone's eyes on my every move as I walked the mile across the room. As I approached my desk, I was aware of a book on it. I sat down and examined the book more in depth. <u>The Scarlett Letter</u> by Nathaniel Hawthorne taunted me as it glared at me from its position on my desk. I felt that the whole class new my life history and that this book was specifically chosen to out me. I felt like I had a Scarlett Letter. I had already read this book, so I knew was it was about. It was on the summer reading list, so it was one of the ones I had read over the summer. What a coincidence that this book was the first book we would read. I felt like the universe was plotting against me. First, I had to deal with The Bitches, then the creepy counselor who could not mask his amazement that I was smart, then the English teacher who had the same reaction, now this damn book. I was enraged on the inside. On the outside, I was tense and stoic wanting nothing more than for someone to pull the fire alarm so I could go home.

The rest of the day was a blur. I made it to all my classes. I had at least one of The Bitches in a class, but neither were in the same class. In Physics I had to ask the teacher, at the end of class, to move my seat away from Veronica. I had Karlissa in Athletics, actually, she was in PE, but we dressed out in the same locker room. She was not smart enough to be in my academic classes. It was easy to ignore her in gym because I gravitated to the guys. Guys were easier to deal with than girls and I enjoyed talking to them—no drama. I was glad when dismissal bell rang to end my first day of my last year in high school. I had homework that I needed to do before work, so I hurried to my car. My car would not start. I simply put it into neutral, pushed and steered it out of the parking space. I turned it on the downslope of the parking lot. I hopped in and popped the clutch. The car started and I puttered out of the student parking lot. People were watching, but no one offered to help. That was fine with me. What I did not know my independence had somehow made an impression with the guys at the school; but, I also made more enemies with the females. The ringleaders of my haters club were The Bitches.

I made it, without serious incident, through my first week of my senior year. I got into a grove of work, homework, and school. My classes were not that challenging, and since I learned quickly my schoolwork was not too tedious. I worked shorter evening shifts during school days and double shifts on the weekend. I managed to stay clear of Karlissa and Veronica. I did not have to talk to my coun-selor and my English teacher was already assigning independent work since I had read everything. I enjoyed my gym class because the gym teacher was the wrestling and weightlifting coach. He would let me workout with the boys and encouraged me to channel my negative energy into molding my body. I stayed oblivious to most of the peo-ple and things around me. I was hyper focused on school and work and did not get into the whole high school mentality. The things the kids around me worried about, I thought was stupid. I did not care about the latest hip hop album that dropped. I did not care who dated who. I did not care about any drama, and since I did not have any friends at the school, I was never involved in gossip. I stayed to myself and went home. Everything was good enough after the first week of school. I felt hopeful.

During the second week of school, I worked out a plan with my gym teacher that since I got out of school early, I would come to the gym during that period and work out. He told me it was the Athletic period and if I wanted to work out with athletes, I needed to be one. I told him I would join the track team, he also coached track, and he allowed me to workout with the guys. I enjoyed working out with motivated people who could banter and cuss each other out one minute, then sing the school's fight song in camaraderie. Boys did not take things too seriously and I enjoyed being around the friendly competition. Well, it was friendly for me. Some of the guys were offended about working out with a girl, mainly because I was stronger than them.

Coach would tell them they could quit if they were intimidated by a girl. This always seemed to piss them off, which made them feel they need to prove they weren't intimated by me: they were. The girls in the school did not like the fact that I was working out with the male athletes. Rumors started to circulate that I was a whore and I that I had AIDS. Someone saw my stretch marks on my stomach while I was changing in the locker room and wrote on the bathroom mirrors: "Alma is a slut." I ignored most of it. I was secure in myself enough not to be lured in to ignorance by some jealousy driven rumors. I stayed to myself, ignored the rumors and sneers, turned a blind eye to the hateful notes and locker graffiti. I refused to stop working out. The camaraderie of that I had with the guys made my senior year bearable. If people did not like it, fuck them—I did not care.

When people noticed that I was not fazed by the rumors, they stopped. The nasty attitudes and social isolation did not, but the rumors did. I was determined to make straight A's and I wanted to go to state in track. I wanted to also join the speech and debate team. I needed to figure out how to balance it all. Word had gotten out that I had my own apartment. A few kids approached me about having a party there. I would simply look at them until they became uncomfortable and walked away. My locker mate (we all used our lockers and had to share) even approached me about having a "get-together" at my apartment. She said it could be called a rent party and people would have to pay a door fee that I could keep. I told her no. My popularity was not going up. I was not going to do anything that would jeopardize my ability to live on my own. I did not owe any of these assholes at Widefield High School anything, and they were not worth me putting my independence in a craps game. I stayed focused.

One day, I was in the school library reading one of the encyclopedia's, one of my favorite things to do. I was so engrossed in the passage I was reading that I did not notice a big looming shadow above me. I was startled by a heavy touch on my shoulder. I looked up and was temporarily blinded by the fluorescent light looming above. A dark shape emerged from the shadow and I recognized it as one of the players that workout in the gym with me. Big D smiled an immense smile that was both honest and shady. He was FINE. Big D was a 6'5, 350-pound chocolate milkshake. His skin was smooth and his face was framed by a tailored beard and goatee. He looked like Gerald Lavert and I caught myself blushing. He asked me something, my mind was in such a fog of awe, I did not comprehend his words. He sat down next to me and asked me was it okay for him to sit next to me. I simply offered a lopsided, weak and feeble half- grin. He flashed his ginormous, perfect smile at me. I was mesmerized; I developed a crush on him in that moment. Big D touched my hand causing me to involuntarily jumped. He asked me was everything alright. I blushed and asked what he wanted.

Big D wanted me to tutor him in math. He was on the verge of failing and if he failed he could not play football and that would be devastating for Widefield's football program. The school was on a winning streak and he had several offers to play at some colleges. He rambled on about asking the math teachers who they thought would make a good tutor and I was suggested several times. He said he admired how hard I push myself in the gym and I really needed to watch my technique, or I would hurt my back. He told me that he would pay me to help him. I told him I was extremely busy; I would not be able to help him. He grabbed my hand and I changed my mind. I was smitten by the most popular, finest, most desired football player in the school. He wanted me to tutor him and I wanted him to like me. Stupid high school brain.

Being around all of these morons had contaminated me. I did not know how to flirt. I just sat there for a minute with a stupid half-grin, nodding like an imbecile. We decided on Wednesdays and Thursdays. We would study first, then go work out.

He was very charismatic—very, very charismatic. I was a loner and awkward. I was the least liked girl in the school and he was the most popular. I knew he was simply hanging with me because he needed to pass his class. Trust me, I had to tell this to myself often to keep my head out of the clouds. I did enjoy hanging out with him. He was nice to me and he was funny. I looked forward to our tutoring sessions. I would get excited when he understood something. We'd high five in the library like a pair of nerds. I almost felt normal. The girls in the groupie group hated me. I was sure The Groupies and The Bitches were behind all the nasty writings about me on the bathroom stalls. I worked hard, really hard at ignoring their shenanigans and being the bigger person. The more they hated on me the higher I held my head. If people had issues with me, that was simply their fucking issue. I had such a stank funk attitude and rumors has spread that I had brothers who were big time gangbangers, thus the girls would gossip, but none directly approached me. Rumors had also spread that I had been kicked out of my old school because I had beaten a kid to within inches of death. The only person's ass I beat was Karlissa and she was not about to advertise that. My attitude, though, projected that I had all kinds of whoop ass in stock. Above all, I had Big D's approval, so no one bothered me directly.

I continued tutoring Big D, even after he was passing the class. We enjoyed hanging in the library and then one day he asked to hang out with me after school. He suggested we go to the park and walk. That sounded silly to me, but I was excited to hang out with him I agreed. I even called my job to tell them I was going to be late for my shift. I drove us in my raggedy car. He looked funny squeezing in to the passenger seat. Since my car was a stick shift, I kept rubbing his massive leg each time I shifted. He made no effort to move it. The park was nice. We had a great conversation that was a good mix of heart, laughter, nonsense, and silence. It was a moment out of some romance novel. It was perfect. We walked and talked for nearly two hours. Big D asked me a few times about my apartment. Out of character, I was a freaking blabbermouth. I felt like I had not talk to someone in depth in such a long time, I just could not get myself to shut up. He was patient, kind and extremely accommodating. He listened and asked clarifying questions. I talked and purged my soul to this fine ass man-child. It felt good.

As we were about to leave the park he said, "Hey Alma, you know I really dig you, right?" "Uh, you do?" I sounded dumb.

"Yeah. You're cool people and I was want to thank you again for helping me out." "Uh, yeah, no problem. Glad you are passing your class." I was so inept in teenager conversations.

"I'm not good at these things," he said as he rubbed his goatee. "You have gotten so much better at math!"

"Nah, I'm not talking about math. Yeah, I'm better thanks to you, but I'm not good with this romantic shit," he said.

I was confused, "What?"

"Look, do you want to be my girlfriend?" he hurriedly asked as he jammed his hands into his pockets. He looked like a shy little boy.

"What? Me? Girlfriend?" I was frozen. I looked around to see if there was some hidden camera somewhere. I panicked and thought he was playing a mean joke on me. How in the world, why in the world would the most popular guy at school ask me… ME…to be his girlfriend?!? I was excited and cautious.

"Is this some kind of joke?" I asked. He smiled his movie star smile, hugged me and in the kindest, most velvety voice assured me that he was serious. He said he enjoyed being around me. I made him laugh, he could be himself, blah, blah, blah. He gently pushed me back and held me at arm's length and asked me, again, to be his girlfriend. My inner voice told me to say no.

Something did not feel right. The giddy, foolish, star-struck high school girl in me said yes—out loud. Big D swooped me up in his arms and hugged me as if I was merely a Raggedy Ann doll. He then pressed his mouth firmly against mine and kissed me fervently. I was swooning. I was Big D's girlfriend! I was excited, yet I was unsettled. I told my inner voice to shut the fuck up.

The news of our going together spread like wild fire through the school. He insisted I wear his letterman jacket, which was ridiculously big on me, but it was a status thing. I thought it was stupid, but kept my opinions to myself. Big D liked walking down the hallway holding hands, again, something that made me uncomfortable because it drew unwarranted attention. He proudly walked me to my classes, which was dumb, because he would be late to his. He was Big D, star football player, so he was allowed to be late. People were nicer towards me, but I knew it was only because of Big D. The Bitches and The Groupies tried to incinerate me every time they saw me with their glares. Little did they know my superpower was blocking trifling haters. Big D and I spent a lot of time together. His parents liked me. His siblings like me. Everyone at school hated me. It was an equal balance.

Big D was not who everyone thought he was. He presented himself as this meathead jock, that dates the smartest girl in school because he was a nice guy. He was really a high-ranking lieutenant in a street gang that originated in Chicago. Big D was a big-time crack dealer and had several soldiers beneath him. He was also an arms dealer. He once hid two large suitcases of guns, including grenades, in my coat closet. Of course, I did not know at first, but when I found out and asked him to move them he told me no. I did not want to be mixed up with any of his side shit. I did not want to lose my independence and him doing illegal shit in my apartment could jeopardize that. He did not care, he told me he would move them when he was ready and I needed to learn to mind my business. I should have listened to my gut and not gotten into this relationship. In dealing with my mother, the tone in his voice reminded me of how her pimps talked to her before she stepped too far out of line and had to be dealt with. I felt trapped. I was going to be his girlfriend until he decided I was not his girlfriend anymore. The Big D that people saw at school was the fake. The real Big D was a big man with the potential of extreme violence. He was a businessman that was running a successful, though illegal, enterprises and business was booming. I finally realized that the whole charade of dating me was so he could have access to my apartment and I was pretty enough. I soon learned that I was meant to be seen and not heard, unless spoken to. My responses were to be short and to the point. I learned how I was to act in the presence of Big D by watching how his soldiers' women acted around them.

They were a bunch of scared and lost women. The way those women allowed his crew to treat them angered me, but I dared not say anything—I was good at minding my own business.

Christmas break was approaching. Since I had started dating Big D, he forbade be to workout in the gym with the other guys, so I picked up extra shifts at work, just to be away from him. One evening, he was dropped off at my job and waited until I got off. He wanted me to drive him to pick up a batch of crack. I had recently bought a new car because I had totaled the Celica after skidding on black ice. I jumped a curb and slammed, head on, into a big oak tree in someone's yard. The cost to repair my first car was more than it was worth. The money from the insurance claim allowed me to buy a new Geo Metro. Big D liked my car because it was reliable transportation and had enough room to hold his homies. So, I found myself being his chauffeur. I drove him to do a lot of his pick up and drops.

This particular day, he said he wanted to drive because I looked tired. I was tired, tired of him, but I dared not say that.

I simply gave him the keys and got into the passenger's seat. He needed to pick up some product. We drove to the shittiest apartment complex in The Springs. It was worst than my apartment complex, so that meant it was only one step above a rat trap. The air around the complex felt dirty. I literally held my breath because I did not want to catch the disease of ignorance that permeated the air. When we arrived, I told him I would sit in the car and wait for him. Instead of honoring my request, Big D got out and came to the passenger side and opened the door for me, as was his custom. He could be such a gentleman. I was not in the mood to plead with him to allow me to stay in the car, so I got out and followed him. He grabbed my hand, a little hard, and lead me to a staircase. It did not look reliable, but if it could hold him, I was good climbing it. We got to the second floor and the smell of burning crack sucked the breath out of me. I was getting paranoid that I would get a crack contact high and then I'd be an addict.

"Big D, babe, how long are we going to be here?" I sweetly asked.

"I hate this fucking hell hole, so not long. Hey, when we get in here, be sure to sit on the edge of any mutha fuckin' seat. I mean it. Sit on the edge." He advised.

"Why?"

He smiled at me, "You'll see."

Big D pounded some beat on the door. This all seemed ridiculous. We were surrounded by crack heads, poor and desolate people and they felt they needed a secret door knock to fool everyone. I wanted to leave, but dared not say anything else. The door opened slightly, and I followed Big D into the apartment. It was dimly lit and smelled like sweaty bodies, stale grease, burnt hair, and bug spray. There were several men and a few women in the room. I saw a stroller in the corner, but no kids. Big D and one of the men, who was wearing all black, including a black bandana tied around his head, did a minute-long handshake. It looked like they were doing the itsy-bitsy spider gestures, but I knew damn well not to say that. It was their code. I looked around the room for a chair.

The only chair available had a box sitting on it. Big D pointed at the box and another man in the room sprang up to remove it. Big D motioned for me to sit down on the now vacant seat. He smiled and pointed his index finger to his temple and mouthed, "Remember, sit on edge." I walked to the chair and sat on the edge as instructed. Big D went to a back room in the apartment and left me in the living room. As my eyes slowly adjusted to the dismal light, I heard a slight hissing sound. I looked around the room and then I nearly bolted. The room was infested with roaches. I'm not talking there were some roaches here and there. I'm talking the walls moved because there were so many roaches. They were all over. I looked at the chair I was sitting on and saw some roaches galivanting across the back. I understood why Big D told me to sit on the edge. How in the world were these people sitting here and acting like they didn't see all these damn roaches?!? These nasty, cracked out filthy, gang-banging dropouts were sitting in filth as if they were lounging in the Astoria Hotel. I felt itchy and dirty and wanted to leave, but I knew not to disturb Big D's business. I swore a roach had crawled on my back, so I jumped up and decided to stand near the chair until we left. He needed to hurry the hell up. I was sure I would need some kind a vaccination after being here. How in the hell did I get myself into this situation?

A woman stomped from one of the rooms in the back. She was a thick, ebony, dirty crack whore. There may have been a time in her life when she was attractive; that time was long gone. She had had her share of ass whoopings from men and life and it looked like a tooth or two had been knocked out. She walked over to me and in a voice, that did not match her face, asked me if I wanted something to drink. I kindly declined. There was no way in hell I was eating or drinking anything in that apartment. She asked me if I was sure, I assured her, and she turned and walked away. I was concentrating on the whereabouts of the roaches in my vicinity, I did not hear nor see what occurred prior to me hearing a slam and a yell. The woman who had just offered me a drink was heaped on the floor holding the side of her face. I was confused. A man I had not yet seen before, grabbed her by her hair, pulled her off the floor and then punched her face. I was in shock. I saw Big D standing in the doorway of the room he had gone to. I pleaded with my eyes at him to stop this. He simply shrugged his shoulders and went back in the room. The man dragged the woman by her hair towards the back of the apartment. She managed to get away and was scrambling to get to a room, when he grabbed her by her ankle. He yanked her towards him and then he kicked her. The people around me did not flinch, truth be told, she barely made a sound. I considered intervening, but then remembered I needed to mind my business. I headed to the door and I asked someone to tell Big D I would be waiting for him in the car. I was not going to sit here and watch her get beat up. As I made my way towards the front door, I heard Big D yell for me to wait. I turned at the exact moment the man put a gun against the woman's forehead. Big D read the horror in my eyes. I looked at him, not knowing the ramifications for defying him and walked out. As I crossed the threshold, I heard a gun cock. Big D called my name. I turned to look at him, he was holding the cocked gun at the guy that was beating the woman. The woman stood up and looked at me with such anger that I was confused—then I understood. In her eyes I could see she blamed me for her current situation. Not only did I not accept her hospitality, now my bougie ass was leaving, causing her man to be embarrassed in front of his boss. She would pay for his embarrassment.

Big D walked me, holding firmly to my hand, to the car. He had a bookbag he did not have when we got there. He told me he was going to drive and after he finished some business we would go out to eat. He apologized for how nasty the apartment was and said he should have never brought me to a crack house.

"You shouldn't feel sorry for that crack bitch. Crackheads don't feel pain." He chuckled.

"That bitch is where she wants to be, doing what she wants to be doing; otherwise, she would do something different." He took the keys and drove to his next stop. I stayed in the car at the second stop. He had his guards watch out for me in the car. He was a gang member after all and he had enemies. I believe he believed he was equivalent to Scarface. He wasn't, but self- perception is a powerful thing. He was king of the jungle and he was ruling it with an iron fist.

Star athlete in the day, vicious drug lord at night. I was stressed being with him. I had not yet figured out how to get out of the relationship, but I knew I needed to find a way—soon. I did a good job maintaining the persona that everything was good. My grades were good, my job was good, everything was good except my star football player boyfriend was really a criminal gang banger who sold crack and guns on the side. Oh, and he condoned women getting their asses beat.

One our way back to my apartment, Big D said he was going to drop me off, but he still needed my car. He did not have a license and I did not want my car involved in any more of his illegal activities. He parked the car in the parking lot of my apartments. He took my apartment key off the key ring and told me he would be back in a few hours. I sat silently in my seat, head slightly hung.

"No." I had mustered up the courage to tell him.

He was confused, "What the fuck did you just say?"

"No, you cannot use my car anymore tonight," I whispered. "You don't have a license and my insurance won't cover you if something should happen." I felt the wind of the slap before I felt the sting. He slapped me so hard that my tears dislodged from my ducts.

"Say no again!" He yelled at me. I was terrified and stunned. I had just witnessed a woman get beat and he could seriously hurt me.

"I'm sorry. I'm sorry for pissing you off. You can use the car." I said through broken sobs. I opened the passenger door. He hit me in the back of the head hard enough to make me head hit the car window. I hurried out of the car and ran towards the apartment entrance. The "doorman" looked at me and said, without moving his lips, "Let me know if you want me to handle that." I did not respond. I walked briskly up the stairs, then to my apartment. I could barely put the key in the lock, I was shaking so badly. How in the hell did I get myself into a relationship with a man who hits me? I was so disappointed in myself. I laid on my waterbed and floated on the waves. The tears of shame and disappointment flowed uncontrollably from my eyes. I was afraid to look at myself in the mirror. I was sure I had already started to bruise. I survived a crack house today, but I must go to school with a bruise on my face. Big D will be pissed to have to answer why I had a bruise on my face. I'm sure he'll make up a story and I'll just go along with it—to keep the peace. I needed this distraction out of my life.

Big D came to my apartment about three hours later. I still had not looked at myself in the mirror. Apparently, he made a copy of the key to my apartment, without my consent. He opened my apartment door as if he was the renter. I felt unsafe. He had flowers and a small gift bag with him. He sat on the edge of the bed and turned on the light. I was trying to pretend to be asleep. He stroked my hair and told me to sit up. I obeyed. He handed me the flowers and told he was sorry he lost his temper and hit me earlier. He said he felt horrible and then he started crying. Really, asshole? You hit me, but now you've somehow turned this around and I am supposed to comfort you? Really? I sat, looking at him with contempt. When he looked at me, I changed my countenance to one of sad concern. I reached out and gave him a hug. He embraced me tightly and sobbed like a big baby. As he held me, I rolled my eyes and plotted how to get out of this relationship. He kissed me then gave me the gift bag. I acted touched and surprised. He bought me a necklace that was the Star of David. The Star of David was used as a symbol of the gang he was in. He wanted me to wear it to show I belonged to him and was down with his crew. I did not want to belong, but I knew I could not say anything about it. His apology will be short lived if I did. I accepted the necklace with as much enthusiasm as I could conjure up. I told him that I could only wear the necklace when I was with him. I could not wear it around my brothers—they were in opposing gangs and it would be a sign of deep disrespect towards them. Big D nodded his head and grabbed me by the back of my neck and pulled me in to him to hug me. He put the necklace on me and told me as he kissed my ear.

"Look, I said I was sorry for hitting you. You better never take my necklace off though. Now come on. Get yourself together so I can take you to dinner." He acted like nothing had happened.

I moved slowly, but quickly enough as not to anger him. My head hurt where he had hit me. I went to the small bathroom and examined my face. The bruising was not as pronounced as I thought it would be. I was able to easily conceal it with some foundation. I begged the universe that I not run into my brothers or anyone who knew them. I doubt we would because my brothers hung out on a different side of town. If by some crazy circumstance, we were to run into them and they saw the necklace, they might shoot me for disrespecting them. This was all way too much stress and was distracting me from my goals. I needed to end this relationship, while maintaining my life, soon.

Big D slapped me two more times afterwards. One time he was around his homeboys who were chilling at my apartment. He told me to get them all a drink, which I had just done. I told him that I had. I guess he felt like I disrespected him in front of his friends because asked me to go to the bedroom. I guess I did not move fast enough because he sprung up from the couch and slapped me with so much force that my feet left the ground. One of his homeboys called him out for it. He told him not to hit me. Big D took his concern as translation that he was sleeping with me. Big D grabbed his gun and yanked me by the hair. He took his gun and held it to my temple. He demanded I tell him the truth of whether I was sleeping around on him or not. I told him I was faithful to him and I would never cheat on him. He pushed me away and then hit my shoulder with the butt of the gun. I cried in pain and grabbed my car keys and left. Big D's best friend Robbie came after me. He apologized to me on Big D's behalf. I told him this would be the last time he hits me. I had vowed to myself to never allow someone to hurt me and I would be damned that I was going to become some battered woman while I was still in high school.

Absolutely not. The allure of dating the star football player evaporated and my reality was that I was in a dangerous relationship with a narcissistic gang banging drug dealer and if I did not get out soon, I would probably get my ass beat so bad that I would forget my name. I decided to tell my younger brother, who was well connected in his gang, my woes and let him help me figure out how to end the relationship. I never got a chance to talk to him before the next incident.

I did not need by brother's help after all. It was early February. I came home from school early. I was not feeling well. I was tired from all the stress and wanted to go home and sleep. I had even taken the day off from work. Big D told me that he was hanging with his homeboys that night and would not be over. He told me to page him when I got home and if I decided to leave. I got home and took a long, hot shower. I knew I was going to piss my neighbors off, because their showers for the next thirty minutes or so would be cold. I did not care. I needed to relax and think of a plan of escape from Big D and Colorado. The first semester was almost over and I had not yet received any acceptance letters from the four colleges I had applied. I needed to refocus and to do that, Big D needed to be out of my life. I finished my shower and decided to make myself a homecooked meal. I settled on making fried chicken, cornbread, mashed potatoes and corn. It was a comfort meal and I would treat myself to ice cream afterwards. As I was prepping the kitchen to cook, I noticed that the heat vent above the sink seemed loose. I was confused as to why it would be loose, unless maintenance had done a check and did not screw the vent back properly. It was not a big deal, just puzzling. I grabbed my screwdriver from under the sink. I stood on my dining/living room chair, subsequently I could reach the vent. As I was aligning the vent cover up to the holes to make a tight seal, I noticed something was stuffed in the vent. I removed the vent completely and peered into the dark hole. I reached in and grabbed the package that was blocking the air flow. I placed the package in the sink and deliberately opened it. The packaged contained two cellophaned wrapped crack bricks. Each brick weighed about two pounds. I did not know the street value, but I knew who was responsible for putting it on the streets. In an act of pure stupidity and defiance, I decided to flush both bricks in the toilet. If my caseworker found out these were here, she would strip me of my independence. I would act like I did not know anything and blame it on maintenance. That was my plan. As soon I flushed the drugs down the toilet, I immediately regretted my decision. Big D, whose drugs I'm sure it was, was going to kill me. I had just flushed his money down the toilet. He most likely owed someone money; as he would say, all money has an owner. I was freaking out and considered call Lam for help. I abstained from calling him because I did not want to get him involved in any bullshit. I also did not want him to be disappointed in me. He had enough problems of his own. I did not know how to get in touch with Eddie, he had become somewhat of gang banging rolling stone of late. Big D had told me that he was not coming over tonight, so I had at least a night to figure out what to do. I relaxed a bit and went back to cooking my meal. I put on the radio, opened the windows and seasoned my cast iron skillet so I could start frying the chicken. I was going to make enough to have dinner for a few days.

I started baking the cornbread in my toaster oven. The potatoes were peeled, cubed, and boiling. The chicken was seasoned, as was the battering flour. I had just tenderly laid a pieced of floured chicken into the hot and bubbling grease, when I heard my front door open. My heart dropped. Big D came around corner. He was wearing his signature smile and seemed in a good mood.

"Hey babe, what are you cooking? It smells good."

"Fried chicken, mashed potatoes, and cornbread." I replied trying to sound normal. "I thought you weren't coming over tonight."

"Why does it matter that I did? Are you expecting someone?" His mood changed, darkened.

Trying to lighten the energy in the room I said, quite feebly, "My caseworker may stop by that's all."

"Oh, cool. I won't stay long. I just need to get something." He then reached under the sink and got the screwdriver I had recently used. He was tall enough, so he did not need the chair to reach the vent. I focused all my attention on the browning chicken, trying to look as normal and unassuming as possible. He reached into the vent and then stood on his tiptoes to get a better view. He looked baffled. He turned to me. I did not make eye contact, I was intently frying chicken.

"Where's my shit?" He asked in an alarmingly calm voice.

"What package? No one has delivered anything since I've been here," I said innoncently. "Where. Is. My. Shit. Alma?" He repeated himself, slowly and with rising anger.

"I don't know what you're talking about. Why are you looking in the vent anyways? I had a note from maintenance that they came in earlier today to do their monthly pest control." I was rambling. Big D stood there staring at me. My heart stopped beating, I stopped breathing, my mind stopped thinking. All I could do was focus on browning the chicken. I knew I was in trouble, so I planned my route to the phone so I could call the police. Yelling for help in this apartment complex does not warrant attention. Everyone in this apartment practices the art of mind your own business. I turned the chicken in the grease and then grabbed to colander to drain the water off the potatoes. Big D loomed by.

"Where in the fuck is my ssshhhiiitttt?!? He hissed through gritted teeth. It was now or never, so I pointed to the bathroom.

He stomped towards the bathroom and then he realized what I had done. He came back into the kitchen. "What the fuck did you do?"

"Flushed it down the toilet. I couldn't have that in my apartment if my caseworker came." I said defiantly. I put a spat of butter on the potatoes. Without making any eye contact, I took the chicken in the skillet out and placed on the newspaper to drain. I put three more pieces of chicken in to boiling grease when I blacked out. Big D had punched me in the face. He then grabbed my head and slammed it into the wall. I heard, rather than felt the slam into the wall. Actually, I initially did not feel any pain. My legs buckled under me. I felt Big D's vicious kick in my side. I knew he was hitting and kicking me, but I was so dazed that I did not feel it to the extent that it was happening. I heard him shout he was going to kill me if I did not figure out how to get him his money. A flashback of the night I bit Carla's leg zoomed across my mind's eye. I had to get up or he would have stomped me to death. I struggled to get back on my feet. The phone was not that far away, but he was blocking my way. He had stormed out of the apartment and I used all the strength I had to stand up. I was unbalanced and I realized that I was bleeding from somewhere, though I had no clue where. I managed to stand up and reached to turn the hot grease off. I could smell the chicken starting to burn. Big D returned and called me a stupid bitch and again threatened to kill me. I stood as tall as I could and told him that he would never hit or hurt me again. He stepped towards me and balled up his fist. Without thinking, I grabbed the handle of the hot cast iron skillet. I swung it, contents and all, and made sound contact with the left side of his face. I swung that skillet like I was trying to use his head to hit a home run. I heard a crack, him screamed then fell to the ground, screaming and withering in pain. The grease had burned the left side of his face and had gotten into his eye. By the looks of his mouth, it appeared he jaw was broken. He was yelling, screaming, crying something unintelligent. As he was holding his battered and burned face, I stood over him and said,

"I told your ass you would never hit me again…I meant it." As he laid shrilling in pain on the floor, I stepped around him and called the police. The arrived quicker than expected. One of my nosy neighbors must have called them before I did. When they arrived, their reaction validated my act of self-defense. My face had swollen to twice its normal size and the bruising was already a kaleidoscope of blues, greens, and purples. There was deep bruising on my side where he had kicked me. My nose was bleeding and his hit had busted a blood vessel in my eye. I looked a hot mess. I admitted to flushing the drugs and hitting him with the skillet. Big D was taken away handcuffed to a gurney. He had third degree grease burns on his face and neck. He lost the use of his left eye and his jaw was broken. The star football player-gangbanger-drug and arms dealer had fallen. From that day forward, when he looked at himself in the mirror, he would remember me. That was the last I saw or spoke to him. The officers took pictures of me and asked if I needed medical assistance. An EMT checked me out and offered to take me to the hospital. I declined, but assured them I would go to the doctor. The officers needed my medical report to substantiate the battery charges Big D received. When they left the only thing I wanted, needed was to eat my dinner and go to sleep. That was the end of that detrimental relationship.

The news of Big D's "assault" circulated through the school quickly. Many people came to me asking me what had happened. The swelling and bruising on my face took a while to fad, as did the ringing in my ears. The blood I had noticed when I picked myself off the floor was actually from my nose and my left ear. The impact of his punch had ruptured my eardrum.

Anyways, the story I told everyone was that Big D and I both were attacked in an armed robbery. I even made him the hero. I told everyone that he tried to protect me. I figured that word would get back to him of what I was saying, so making it someone else's fault and painting him as heroic would grant me some grace with his crew. I avoided most people, so I did not have to tell the lie over and over. Christmas break was upon us and I planned to distance myself from all the drama. Thank goodness high schoolers have short and fickle memories. When we returned from the break, I was left alone. I was no longer the girlfriend of a star athlete—I was back to being a nobody, which suited me just fine.

10

The final semester of my senior year had arrived. With Big D behind me, I focused all my attention on getting into college and figuring a way out of Colorado. I just knew that if I did not leave, I would be sucked into the pits of despair and trapped in the state. I needed to leave, no matter what, for my sanity and survival. My brothers were doing their own thing and in order for me to give them hope and options, I had to lead by example. The desire to leave became an obsession. Luckily, I had only three classes my second semester. I was given early release and I was a teacher's aid for one period. I quit the track team so I could work more. I still had not received an acceptance letter from any school and I also had not heard about any of the thirty or so scholarship applications I had submitted to my counselor prior to the break. I stopped by his office at least once a week to check on the application statuses and to inquire what else I was supposed to be doing. I was feeling desperate. I did not have a backup plan—I had to get out Colorado and I had to go to college. It was my only guarantee that I would survive the madness of my life. So, I waited patiently to get some news of what the next step in my journey of life would be. I say I waited patiently, but honestly, I was really stressed that I had not heard anything from the colleges or about the scholarships.

In early March, I asked my Calculus teacher, Mr. Visser, if I could leave class to see my counselor. I had a sinking feeling in my stomach because my peers were getting acceptance letters and I knew I was smarter than them. With my GPA and class rank, I was a contender for valedictorian. Jason, a preppy athlete whose grandfather was on the school board was also in the running for valedictorian. While I did not really care about the title, I felt if I deserved it, I should get it, but I also knew that there was no way in hell Jason would lose the coveted title to a poor weirdo who only rose to popularity because of Big D. I was sitting in class when I overheard him bragging about getting into Colorado University and was offered a full-ride academic scholarship. Internally, I was fuming. I was smarter than him and in more need of a scholarship. Why had I not heard anything!

When I arrived to the administration offices, the secretary asked me what I needed. I asked to speak to my counselor. She, quite curtly, told me I could not leave class to see my counselor. I showed her the pass that Mr. Visser had written giving me permission. She rolled her eyes and told me I needed to make an appointment. I told her I was not going to make an appointment, I needed to speak to him now. If he was busy, then I wanted to see another counselor and if they were busy I was going to walk into the principal's office. The choice of who I was going to see was hers, but I was not leaving until I spoke to someone about my scholarships and college acceptance letters. She rolled her eyes again and barked for me to sit in the waiting area. She picked up the phone and called into my counselor's office. I overheard her telling him that I refused to leave without speaking to him.

I waited for an entire period, and would have waited all day. In my gut, I knew something was wrong. There was no way that Jason Smith was getting accepted to schools and I was not. My counselor finally came out of his office. He looked my direction and pretended to review notes that were on a clipboard by the secretary's desk. I stood up and walked towards him.

"Soul, I am so sorry you had to wait. You really should make an appointment to see me.

You are not my only priority."

"I was never a priority of yours," I cuttingly said. He looked hurt, but quickly recovered and tilted his head to the side. There were other students in the office and a parent. He had to save face in front of them.

"I am sorry you feel that way. I am here to help you. Please come in," he surveyed the other office occupants for their approval. I followed him into his office.

He motioned for me to sit down, but I was frozen at the entrance of his office. The moment I walked in, I noticed a thick purple folder on the bookshelf behind his desk. It was lying on top of a stack of books and it had a small stack of papers on top. My heart stopped and my mind began racing. That folder looked like the folder I gave him, which I was told I had to do, that contained all of my scholarship and college application requirements. My counselor followed my eyes to the folder, and I could see the resignation in him. He motioned me to sit down again. Instead, I walked past him and went behind his desk to the bookshelf. He was saying something but I didn't hear a word. I was thinking about how I was going to react when I confirmed that he did not do his part in getting the scholarship and college applications out on time. Most of the things I had placed in the folder required the counselor's signature, a copy of transcripts, SAT and ACT scores. I grabbed the folder, ignoring the papers that were on top, which in my haste fell to the floor. My counselor was behind me telling me that I had no right to touch things in his office. I did not respond to him as I opened the folder. Sure enough, it was my stuff. No wonder I had not heard anything - that asshole never sent my applications out! All this time he had me doubting myself and second-guessing my own abilities. He had me going to the mailbox every day, with the hope that my future would be in a letter.

Instead, that fucker put my life, my hopes and dreams and my way out of my living Hell, on a fucking shelf!

I dropped the folder onto his desk. He picked it up and again told me to sit down. I assumed he was going to try and explain himself, but I had no interest in hearing him out. His lack of action in sending out my college paperwork told me exactly what he thought of me. I wanted to rip his face off. His smug, uncaring, you-won't-amount-to-anything, pasty face made me have visions of pouring hot grease on it. I hated this man and I hated myself, in that moment, for trusting him and not being more persistent in following up with him.

"You asshole! You did not send my stuff out?! I've missed most of the deadlines! How could you do this to me!!!" I screamed at him.

"Soul, please calm…" he started to plea.

"Do not tell me to calm down," I interrupted. "You sabotaged me! I am going to the principal right now!!"

I snatched the folder off his desk and headed to the door. He stepped in front of me and the murderous look in my eyes were enough to make him move. I stormed out of the office, slammed his door, and stomped to the principal's office. My counselor followed me, but at a safe distance. When I got to the head honcho's office, I opened it without knocking. He was sitting at a conference table with some other people. I obviously startled him and his guests as they all jumped in their seats as my deranged looking ass barged in. My counselor started apologizing for the interruptions, but I cut him off.

"How about you apologize for sabotaging me!" I yelled. The principal and his guests stood up and he indicated to them to leave and he would get back to them as soon as he dealt with me. Once they left the room, he asked me and my asshole counselor to sit down. I complied and after he said a few words to his secretary about getting the vice principal and the school resource officer a heads up, he came in and sat down.

I put the folder in front of him and explained what had happened and why I was so upset. I also told him that I was going to report this to the Department of Child Protective Services, who were my conservators, even though I was technically emancipated. He listened, looked over the paperwork in the folder in silence, and then asked me to leave the room for a minute so he could talk to my counselor who sat there studying the lines on his folded hands. I was reluctant to leave, but I did. The guests who were in the office when I interrupted looked at me with curiosity and fear. I was so heated, I stared back and asked them what they were looking at.

They all started studying the lines on their hands too. After what seemed like an eternity, the principal came out of his office and asked me to rejoin him in his office. His countenance was softer, almost compassionate. My counselor was sitting in the same stoic posture and twiddling his thumbs. His face was beet red and he appeared to have been crying. I did not cry. If there was not an amicable resolution for his incompetence, I was going to make sure he lost his job. I did not know how, but I would destroy him. I sat at the foot of the table, while the principal took the head. The contents of the purple folder were neatly stacked in various piles on the conference table.

The principal started the conversation. "Miss Gonzalez, first let me apologize for Mr. David's oversights. We value each of our students and I understand why you are upset. We will discuss your approach later. Mr. David and I have reviewed the contents of your folder and I will personally make sure the applications for the scholarships and colleges go out today, for those whose deadlines have not past. There is hope, so I am asking for just a little more patience from you. I understand you've done what you were told to do and Mr. David understands that he should have done a better job helping and guiding you in the college and scholarship progress.

You are an excellent student and we will make this right. Will you trust me?"

"No. I will not trust you. You hired this man, who ruined my chances of getting funding for school. Are you going to pay for my college?" I was still angry and did not want to put the dagger down, not yet.

"I understand you are angry, justifiably so. I guess the only way to earn your trust is to show you I will do what I say I will do. Is that fair?" I could hear the compassion in his voice. I also noted tension, which I attributed to him being angry that his counselor put him in this predicament.

Mr. David never looked up from his hands. He was a coward. The principal was saying something to him and he slowly looked at him, then at me.

"Miss Gonzalez, I apologize for overlooking your paperwork. I will personally make calls on your behalf to hopefully put in favor in the consideration of some of the scholarships. Again, I will make it right."

"You will not do anything else with my stuff. He (pointing at the principal) will take care of it. I want nothing from you, except for you to be fired." The acrimony in my voice could have easily killed him if I knew how to focus it for such purposes. I looked at the principal and he nodded a reassuring nod that he understood my position and he verbally reassured me that before he left work that day, everything would be taken care of.

I turned to my counselor and asked, "Why did you not do your job when it came to me?" "I simply forgot. Besides, I thought it would be a good idea if you started at Pike's Peak Community college and looked into a secretarial pro…"

"Mr. David, you are excused," the principal hissed through clench teeth. He was doing damage control and wanted to stop him from digging his hole deeper. Mr. David, the deadbeat counselor, quickly got up and left. I sat for a while longer, trying to absorb the events of the last few hours. I did not feel resolved and would not until I got an acceptance letter and a scholarship. I left the principal's office with his reassurance again that everything would be taken care of. I rolled my eyes and left. I decided to leave, so I walked out of the school, got into my jalopy, and went home. Before I left though, I looked on the principal's wall calendar and noted the date of the next school board meeting. I was going.

The board meeting was on a Tuesday evening, so I called and told my supervisor that I was going to be late to work. Since Tuesdays were slow days, my manager did not mind. I had never been to a board meeting, but I had asked Mr. Visser about it and gave me a little insight. He shared that there would be an opportunity for the public to speak on matters of concern to them. I decided to use this forum to inform the board members and the public on what had happened with my counselor. Mr. Visser told me that they limit the amount of time each person could speak. I worked on my speech for a week, because I wanted to sound intelligent and articulate. I used my training as a Lincoln-Douglass debater to prepare. The day of the board meeting came, and I decided to dress professional.

There were very few people at the meeting. The board members sat in a panel and followed Robert's Rules of Order in conducting the meeting. I was happy about that, because I understood the process. So, after calling the meeting to order, reviewing the previous meeting notes, going over the current agenda, they opened the floor to address questions or concerns. I did not pay attention to what the three people ahead of me asked or commented on. I was reviewing my three-minute speech in my head. I approached the microphone, which I thought was silly, since there were not a lot of people in the room, but whatever. I told them that I was disappointed in the school district's hiring of my counselor and I quickly, but thoroughly explained what had happened. I ended with my request to have his continued employment with the district reviewed and I stated (even though I had no idea how to start) that I planned to sue the district for the full cost of my post-secondary education. They listened and took notes. A person approached me after I spoke and asked if I would stay after the board meeting ended to review my claims further. I agreed. Once the board concluded their meeting, I met with them alone. I went into more detail into what my counselor had done. Jason Smith's grandfather was a board member and he asked me a lot of questions. He and the other board members thanked me for the information and told me they would follow up with my principal.

They did as they said, because the next day I was called into the principal's office. He questioned why I went to the board and he seemed genuinely hurt that I did not trust him to do as he had promised. I told him that I felt I needed to utilize all the resources I knew of and got up and walked out.

I continued to work hard on my last three classes. Since I worked so quickly and often ahead of the class, my teachers had me run errands, mainly food runs for them. I kept to myself and minded my business. It was a lonely existence, but I liked it. Besides waiting for an acceptance letter, my world had calmed down. I took my senior portraits, bought my cap and gown, and ordered invitations. My brothers and caseworker were the only ones I was going to invite.

On the first day of March, I came home as usual from work and checked the mail. There were bills and advertisements from several colleges to apply to their school. There was a letter from the University of Texas at Austin, one of the four schools I had applied. I hesitated to open the letter, so I showered, made dinner for myself and stood in the kitchen. I held the letter in my hand and looked at my trembling hands. I did not want to open it, because I did not want to find out they did not accept me. I sat on the floor in the middle of my small kitchen and slowly, very slowly opened the envelope and unfolded the letter. I had to read it about twenty times. Not only had they accepted my application and were admitting me to their school, they also were offering an academic scholarship in the amount of $30,000! I was overwhelmed, overjoyed, and relived. I sat there, on the floor, holding my future. I cried uncontrollably. I cried because of my past and cried for my future. I was going to go to college, leave Colorado and this miserable life behind. I read the letter again and for the first time in a long time I allowed my self to hope. I called my brothers, neither answered. My whole life was about to change, and I was celebrating alone. Regardless, I was smiling. My time had come.

In the following weeks, I received acceptance letters from Stanford, Knox College, and Grambling State University. I had already committed to The University of Texas at Austin. Honestly, I would probably have gone to Stanford, but I didn't know that I could change my commitment. Oh, well, I ended up where I was supposed to be.

The rest of the semester was a blur. My senioritis was real and I could not wait to graduate. I was wasting time, and was ready to start my adventure in Texas. I did not go to prom. I was not asked to go, nor did I want to. While my classmates were going with their mothers to look for dresses, I worked. As graduation day approached, I prepared for my exodus from Colorado. I spent time with my brothers and I was honored at work with a party my coworkers put on for me. I did not even care about being the valedictorian. In the grand scheme of my life, it did not matter.

Graduation day was surprisingly calm. Our graduation ceremony was in the gym of our high school. There was a lot of excitable energy as everyone made their way to their seats so the ceremony could commence. I chose not to give the traditional valedictorian speech, rather, I conceded and let Jason do it. We apparently tied for the position. He cared about it; I did not.

As I sat in my seat, I surveyed the crowd to see if any one had come to support me. My heart was momentarily saddened when I did not see anyone. Then I heard my name being yelled out from the top of the risers. My brothers, Lam and Lil D, my caseworker Mary and a former caseworker, Judy were there. My family had come and as I walked across the stage to receive my high school diploma with honors, I felt blessed. Tucked into my bra was the post-it note given to me six years earlier. I was ready to conquer my destiny with a smile.